Family Secrets

Rather than outright lying, Evangeline proposed a prank.

They saw other people they knew at the drive-in theater, as well as Cousin Carolyn, and when someone they knew came by for a better look, they tried kissing. It wasn't long before Carolyn showed up. They were watching and saw her coming. They got real cozy and Carolyn rapped on the side of the truck to get their attention. Her greeting was an inelegant demand of, "What are you two doing?"

Jimmy grinned at her. "I think it's called kissing."

"Does Aunt Wanda know?" Carolyn demanded.

"Yes," Evangeline said.

Carolyn said, "I can't believe it," and wondered off looking bewildered.

Evangeline buried her face in Jimmy's shoulder and laughed so hard she was gasping for breath. She finally said, "That was so much fun. Harry was right. This is a hoot."

Jimmy was also laughing. He whispered in Evangeline's ear, "And this kissing business is fun, too."

A Points to Ponder Book

Ozark Heritage Points to Ponder books are non-traditional stories reflecting Christian values but raising thought provoking ethical questions.

Other Books by Mary Cambron-Collard
Survivor's Guilt
An Odd Soul
Incident at Indian Cave
Sanctuary
McDugal's Kirk: Book 1 of the Bigfoot Tales
Redemption: Book 2 of the Bigfoot Tales
Feud: Book 3 of the Bigfoot Tales
Searching: Book 4 of the Bigfoot Tales

Coming Soon:
Betrayal: Book 5 of the Bigfoot Tales

E-mail: cambroncollard@gmail.com

OHP
OZARK HERITAGE PUBLISHING
723 North Ninth Street
Poplar Bluff, Missouri
ozarkheritagepublishing@gmail.com

Dear Readers,

This tale comes with a heads up.

All families have a few secrets - an alcoholic uncle, a baby with an inconvenient birth date, a brief marriage long hidden - but some families have more than others.

This story raises some slippery ethical questions. Is justice always following the letter of the law? Is doing something illegal ever justified? Is it ever acceptable for a Christian to lie? Is concealing the truth out of kindness ever the best choice?

It also includes a really hideous villain.

This story is not suitable for children.

Sincerely,
Mary Cambron-Collard

Blessings!
Mary Cambron Collard

My ardent thanks to my sister who loves a good story and encouraged me to share this one.

DEDICATION

For
WA, J, M, S, B, A, A, and A
Every child needs grandparents.

Family Secrets

Mary Cambron-Collard

OHP
OZARK HERITAGE PUBLISHING

A Points to Ponder Book

This is a work of fiction. Any resemblance to actual persons, living or dead, is completely coincidental.

Copyright © 2016 Mary Cambron-Collard
All rights reserved.

Cover: "Midnight Spider"
by Robert Thiemann via Upsplash

ISBN-10: 1518858678
ISBN-13: 978-1518858673

Printed by CreateSpace, An Amazon.com Company

Family Secrets

*Behold, I send you forth as sheep
in the midst of wolves;
be ye therefore wise as serpents,
and harmless as doves.*

Matthew 10:16 (KJ)

❀ ❀ ❀

Prologue

Wanda Wilkerson heard the angry voices as she turned the corner of the convenience store and she stopped in her tracks. The tall red-headed woman she had just seen telling her small son to stay in the car was being confronted by a man with a gun. He was even taller than the woman and his hair and full beard were also redder than hers. His fierce brown eyes glared at the woman and his voice boomed out, "Where is he, you bitch? Where's Jimmy Joe? He's my son! Where is he?"

The woman said, "I'm not telling you. He's my son too and the court gave me full custody!"

A shot rang out. It hit the woman in the chest and she spun around and collapsed face down. As Wanda Wilkerson watched in horror, the man leaned down, put the gun to the back of the woman's head, and fired again.

Wanda Wilkerson was a 43-year-old school teacher and a grandmother. Her first thought was protecting the child. She had noticed his mother leaving him alone in her car saying, "You stay right here and don't get out. I'll be back in a minute."

When she walked by the car, she had glanced in the window and stopped. The boy was about the age of her missing grandson and he had red hair, like her grandson. Her heart had lurched and she stared but he wasn't her grandson. His hair was redder and curled. It bothered her that the woman had left the child alone in the car but he had a small toy and seemed content to play with it. The doors of the car were locked. He was safe unless he opened the door from the inside. As she watched, he continued to play with his toy, never looking up.

Now she darted back to the car and saw little Jimmy Joe looking in the direction of the shots. She pecked on the window and said urgently, "Open the window."

When the boy just stared at her, she took a deep breath and said more patiently, "Jimmy, open the window." The child just continued to stare.

Then, with hope and a prayer, she said, "Jimmy Joe, open the window for Grandma."

Instead, the boy opened the door. She said, "Jimmy, come with Grandma. We have to hide. Come on."

She unfastened his seat belt and took his hand. He was still clutching the small toy in his other hand and she saw a small backpack next to his booster seat with toys in it. She grabbed it and said again, "Jimmy, we have to hide."

❀ ❀ ❀
Chapter 1: Who Are You?

Wanda Wilkerson was 62 and had just retired after teaching school for thirty years. She had a pension and her dad was 89. She wasn't sure he should be left alone all day anymore. The house had needed painting last summer and after he had a dizzy spell and fell, she quit letting him get up a ladder or on the scaffolding, even though it meant not getting the house completely painted. This spring he had been very little help in putting in a garden so she hadn't planted much. He still spent time in the woods but he was no longer bringing home rabbits and squirrels. Last fall Jimmy had come during deer season and they had gone hunting once. Jimmy got a deer but he told his grandmother sadly, "I think Grandpa is past it. He can't seem to hit anything anymore."

Wanda thought of Jimmy and smiled. She was proud of him. Now he was 24. He had been an excellent student in school, valedictorian of his class, and had gone to college, mostly on scholarships. He was now a ranger with the National Park Service and had just been transferred to Sequoia National Park, a coveted assignment. Maybe she could take her father to see it.

Wanda was hoeing in the garden when she saw the truck headed for their house. They lived way out off a gravel road with a long dirt track driveway. She stood watching the vehicle drive up to their house and stop. It was Sheriff Barnett.

She moved to greet him with no real unease. He had been sheriff for years and she had taught all five of his kids in first grade. She smiled at him and said, "Afternoon, Roger. I got iced tea."

When they were seated in the living room and her dad had turned off the TV, she finally asked, "Roger, you just visiting or are you here on business?" Something in his manner had made her think he had come on business. She had tried to think what but could only come up with maybe someone complaining about her dad being too old to drive.

"Yeah," he said. "It's business." He shifted around, looking uncomfortable. She wondered if her dad had had an accident and not told her. But he went on, "A while back I got an odd phone call. The police in Bakersfield, California called and said you had filed a report with them 19 years ago saying your grandson was missing and you were worried about the boy. I told them you must have found the kid because he had grown up here and went to college and everything." The sheriff stopped again and she saw his eyes go to a portrait on the wall that she had painted. It was Jimmy at age 3. The sheriff looked back at her. Her heart was beating furiously but she sat quietly, waiting for the rest of the shattering news. "Yesterday, I got a call again from the Bakersfield police. They're saying they have the remains of a child, dead maybe 19 years. They said when you filed your report, you gave them a copy of a DNA test. They said that the DNA definitely matches what you gave them."

Wanda sat quietly while her heart thumped and tears formed in her eyes. She had always known that this day might come. She knew what she was going to say but she needed to collect her wits before starting. She looked down, running through it in her mind, and then sighed. "I'm not surprised," she told the sheriff. "I told the police then that he was in danger and I privately thought he might already be dead."

She stopped and Sheriff Barnett asked, "Well, what about Jimmy?"

"I adopted him," she said. "I never told anyone here because it was easier on him if no one knew. But he knows all about it. He had already turned 5 when I got him and he remembers."

"Huh," the sheriff said, exhaling audibly. He looked back at the portrait on the wall, then at another one hanging nearby of her daughter, holding a baby about 6 months old. "He sure looked a lot like your grandson, didn't he?"

"Yes," she lied calmly, "I think maybe that's why they let me have him."

The sheriff was silent, studying the portraits. Wanda waited, knowing how often she had known a child was lying by their nervous chatter.

The sheriff finally said, "I'm sorry. I guess you were right about your grandson being dead. I'll give you the phone number so you can make arrangements."

Wanda sat quietly thinking about the her dead grandson. Her tears overflowed and spilled silently down her cheeks. She reached for a tissue and then said, "I knew all the way back then that he was probably dead." She shook her head. "I knew too that the police didn't think so. They thought Jimmy Snyder had just moved so that I couldn't find them and get my month with the boy that the judge had said I could have."

The sheriff said again, "Ms. Wilkerson, I really am sorry. If you need help with anything, let me know."

When he was gone, Wanda's father said, "Do you think it'll come out? Maybe you should have just told Roger what happened."

Wanda shook her head. "Not yet. No one may ever question Jimmy's adoption. If they do, well he's grown now. He knows all about it so he's not going to be upset by it. He's not 5 years old anymore and needing protection. He's old enough to look after himself."

Wanda's mind ran back to what happened 19 years ago. She had never planned to steal the child, only hide him so that his murderous father couldn't find him. Back at the motel, the boy had said, "Grandma, I'm hungry." So was she and she decided a trip to McDonald's before she talked to the police wouldn't hurt. She had fed him and let him play in the Play Place, dreading dealing with the police. In the car, on the way back to the motel room, the boy fell asleep. She tucked him in bed and turned on the TV to catch the news.

It was the big story of the day. Wanda wrote down all the details as she listened. She learned that the child was Jimmy Joe Jones. His father was called Bo John Jones and he was from somewhere in Tennessee called Big Creek. Little Jimmy's mother alleged that Bo John had hit her frequently and when he broke little Jimmy's arm, she had taken the boy and run to a friend in Bakersfield, California. There she had been granted a divorce and full custody of her son. Bo John had come after her, been arrested, released on bail, and had promptly hunted her down and killed her. Wanda still remembered what he had looked like – tall, strong looking, fierce dark eyes, fiery red hair that curled and a thick red beard. Her Jimmy had grown up looking very much like his father but had never grown a beard nor shown any signs of unreasonable temper.

Later that night, Wanda had listened as a female reporter told the story again, adding that the boy's mother seemed to have no other relatives but did have the school friend with whom she and her son had been living. That friend had checked with everyone she thought the mother might have left the child with but no one could find the boy.

When he woke up very early the next morning, Wanda asked little Jimmy Joe about relatives. It took a while for her to sort it out but apparently she resembled his mother's mother with whom he had stayed while his mother went to school or worked. She and his grandpa and uncle had all died in a car wreck. His father had a father but no mother. When she asked the boy if he wanted to go live with his father's father, he said no and started crying. She asked why and he told her about his father and the broken arm. He was afraid of his father and wanted to hide from him.

Sitting there in the motel room, Wanda made a decision. She decided that God had put her in the right place at the right time to rescue the boy. She packed the car and she and little Jimmy left Bakersfield for Missouri, meeting the rising sun as they crossed the Tehachapi Mountains. At Walmart in Flagstaff, Arizona she bought him some clothes.

On the way to Missouri, Wanda discovered that little Jimmy was a well-behaved child and bright. He knew that his birthday was April 7th and he was 5 years old. That made him about 5 months younger than her missing grandson. He would start kindergarten that fall. By the time they reached Ellsinore, Missouri little Jimmy had known that his mother had gone to heaven, which was a wonderful place, but once you went there, you couldn't come back.

At home, Wanda checked and found that the search for the boy was in full cry. The boy's mother had no close relatives. Her parents and brother were dead. She had one living grandmother in a nursing home. Wanda located the grandmother, hoping to make arrangements for Jimmy, but the staff at the nursing home said the grandmother had suffered a stroke, was bed-fast and unable to even talk. They knew of no living relatives. Wanda said she had been a friend of her daughter's and started calling once a week to ask about her but she died less than a year later without any improvement. Wanda had sent flowers for her funeral.

Wanda's father had known, of course, that Jimmy wasn't Wanda's grandson but as they discussed it, he also arrived at the same conclusion. They had the resources to care for the boy and could give him the love and security he needed. When Wanda's daughter died out in California, supposedly in an accident, Wanda had suspected that her son-in-law had killed her. By the time she got out there, the body had been cremated. Her daughter had been phoning her and planning to leave her husband for about the tenth time. Wanda had tried to get custody of her grandson but had only been given the right to a month each summer. She and her father did not trust the legal system to do what was best for little Jimmy.

Wanda talked to Jimmy. She told him he could live here with her and her father if he wanted. They would adopt him but he couldn't tell anyone. They would have to keep it a secret. Otherwise his father's family might find him. The boy had looked at her solemnly and said, "I'll stay here with you. I'll get adopted and Daddy will never find me."

Wanda's grandson had been named James Edward Snyder, Junior, but since his father had been called 'Jimmy,' the boy had been called 'Junior.' The switch to calling him 'Jimmy' went unremarked upon and that fall Wanda used her grandson's papers to enroll little Jimmy in Kindergarten. Once it was explained to him, Jimmy had no trouble changing his birthday to November 14th. In true small town fashion, the school had called him Jimmy Wilkerson. Who wanted to remind the kid of a no-good father by calling him Junior Snyder? No one had ever questioned his identity as Wanda Wilkerson's grandson.

Wanda Wilkerson taught school for a living but she was an artist. The summer she got Jimmy, she was very busy painting. When her grandson was six months old, she had done a portrait of her daughter holding the baby. She painted another copy just like it except the baby's hair was slightly redder and his eyes darker. She had painted another portrait of her grandson at age 3. That summer she made another one but in this one again, the boy's hair was redder and his hazel eyes became brown.

As little Jimmy grew up, Wanda did sometimes check that he had not forgotten his mother. His memory was quite good. He remembered his father breaking his arm and beating his mother. He remembered the bus trip to Bakersfield. He remembered being taken to Disneyland after they moved to Bakersfield. Wanda took a picture of Jimmy's mother from a newspaper and framed it for him to keep. But it was all a secret. He couldn't tell anyone.

The prosecution of Bo John Jones for the murder of his wife, Amanda, dragged on for several years. He was even out on bail during most of that time which had increased Wanda's distrust of the court system. Bail had been a huge amount but his family raised it. His lawyer had used all sorts of tactics to get the trial delayed. Bo John claimed his wife had a gun. Of the eleven people who initially gave statements about the argument that caught their attention and watching Bo John murder his wife, only three stuck it out and testified at his trial. All three had complained about receiving threatening phone calls that couldn't be traced. Bo John was convicted and sentenced to prison for murder.

When Jimmy graduated from high school, he was eighteen. He was excited about working that summer in a program with the National Park Service. Before he left, Wanda and her father sat down with him and talked to him about his 'adoption.' Wanda told him, "I saw your father kill your mother. When I found out your mother had no family to claim you, I was afraid that your father's family would get you."

Jimmy saw the tears in her eyes and he hugged her and said, "I remember you asking me if I wanted to be adopted and telling me we had to keep it a secret."

He asked, "Did no one ever find out what happened to your grandson?"

"No," she said. "I think he's dead. I had the awfullest feeling of doom before I ever went out there looking for him. And in all the years since, I've kept trying to find him or his father but found nothing."

Wanda had asked Jimmy, "Do you want to know about your real family?"

He was silent and then asked, "I remember enough to know I don't want to look them up. Is there any reason I need to know?"

Wanda had smiled. "Well, you wouldn't want to accidentally marry your sister. And then, I thought some of your family might be worth getting to know. Just because your father was a terrible man, doesn't prove the rest of the family are all bad. Only, because your adoption was not done legally, there could be trouble."

Jimmy shrugged. "I wouldn't want to get you in trouble and as far as my real family is concerned, that's you and Grandpa. You all raised me and you love me and you'll always be my family regardless."

So Wanda had given him the information she had gleaned from the newspapers and then the internet. He had looked through it all and remembered that his name had been Jimmy Joe Jones. He had no urge to look these people up and had left the packet of papers in his room when he took off for his summer job. He had gone to college and then joined the National Park Service when he graduated. He had looked through the papers a couple of times over the years but they were not important to him. Somewhere along the way, someone had made a fuss about his birth certificate saying Snyder when he went by Wilkerson so he filed the papers necessary to officially change his name. If he wanted to use his mother's family name instead of his father's, he could do that.

After Sheriff Barnett was gone that day, Wanda and her father discussed what to do. Wanda phoned the police in Bakersfield, California and made arrangements to go after her grandson's remains. Like all small towns, the word spread and Wanda got phone calls from friends and relatives. One of her cousins said, "Wanda, that was naughty not telling any of us that you adopted that boy but he's turned out real good and I guess it was probably better not to tell anyone."

Jimmy came for the funeral. His supervisor had been incredulous when he asked for time off. He said, "You mean you were adopted by a woman whose grandson disappeared 19 years ago and now they've found the grandson's body? That's terrible!"

Jimmy met Wanda in Bakersfield and they went first to the police. She introduced Jimmy as another grandson and the police didn't question that. She was given a copy of the coroner's report. The coroner had noted a skull fracture that could have been postmortem but given where the body was found, was probably the cause of death since there was also a fractured cheek bone. He had also noted several older fractures and some partially healed cracked ribs. He was of the opinion that the child had died of abuse.

When they left the police station, neither Wanda nor Jimmy noticed a woman taking photos. Later, at the morgue while they waited for the remains, a woman had appeared whom they assumed worked in the morgue. She had chatted with them about the sadness of the boy's death and given her condolences. The wait was long and when the woman asked, Jimmy had no reservations about telling the woman that he had been adopted by Wanda Wilkerson after her grandson disappeared.

When they arrived home, the whole family gathered at the Wilkerson's house. It was the old Wilkerson homestead and Will Wilkerson had four sons besides his daughter, Wanda. She had been the youngest and when she had come home from college pregnant, her brothers had wanted to go after the guy but she would never tell them his name. When her daughter was born, she had given no name for the father. Rumor had eventually gone around saying that the father had been a professor at the college but Wanda had consistently remained silent. She never married and eventually had finished her degree and started teaching first grade at the school in Ellsinore.

Wanda's daughter may have had no siblings but she had had fifteen first cousins. Little Jimmy had no first cousins but he had an ocean of second cousins who were now producing children of their own. It was a close family and they continued to gather regularly at the old home place. Now they gathered and, in general, laughed about Wanda's deception, saying, "I guess if we'd have known, we would've treated you different so maybe it's just as well." They also shook their heads over the grandson's death and said, "Turns out she was right about her grandson. I expect she's right too about that bastard killing the child and her daughter, too." Jimmy knew that if Jimmy Snyder ever surfaced, it wasn't just the law he needed to worry about.

Jimmy's best friend had always been his second cousin Harrison Wilkerson. Harry had been a grade ahead of him in school and from the time he started kindergarten had acted as his big brother. Harry's sister, Evangeline, had started school the year after him and they had both looked out for her. Now Jimmy greeted them both with reserve but relaxed when both of them assured him he was still their best friend and as far as they were concerned, still family.

One thing his grandmother and great-grandfather discussed with him before he returned to his job was their Wills. He and all the family knew that they had both made Wills leaving the old home place to him. Now they told him they were making new Wills still leaving the place to him but clarifying that they knew he was not their grandson. Jimmy said, "Why don't you leave it to one of the others? I'm not blood family and some of them will resent it going to me."

But Grandpa had shook his head and said, "All my boys got places of their own now. None of them want to live out here. If you own it, they can still come hunt and that's all they really want it for."

They had a memorial service and buried the child's remains with the rest of the family in the old cemetery beside the small country church. Only as they were leaving, did Jimmy notice the woman taking photos. He stared at her in surprise. It was the woman from the morgue in Bakersfield. When he pointed her out to his grandmother, she was shocked. It was Jimmy who thought to ask Sheriff Barnett for help and he moved quickly to question the woman while everyone else left.

Later, she turned up at the Wilkerson place but by the time she found it, Sheriff Barnett had called and warned them she was a reporter. Wanda refused to let her in the house.

She passed Wanda a card with her name and was not unpleasant. She said, "It's just that it was such a tragic incident. You thought the child was in danger but the police didn't believe you. I wanted to do a story on it hoping it would help the police to take these sorts of incidents more seriously and investigate more carefully."

So they sat in rockers on the front porch and talked for a short time. The reporter asked about Jimmy's adoption but Wanda just said that adoptions were private and left it at that. The woman was pleasant, extended her condolences again, and left.

Jimmy returned to work and it was several weeks before it was in the news again.

❀ ❀ ❀
Chapter 2: Who Is This Man?

It was almost a month later when Jimmy checked into the park office as he was going on duty. Rita, who worked in the office, called out to him as she saw him leaving, "Hey, Jimmy. Did they tell you you're in the news."

Jimmy stopped reluctantly. Rita had flirted from the first day he arrived and he tried to tactfully avoid her. When he had asked another ranger about her, he had said, "She goes after every new unmarried arrival. Her main goal in life right now is a husband. She seems like a good woman. If you're looking for a wife, check her out." Jimmy was always polite to Rita but she was not someone he sought out.

Now Jimmy looked at Rita across the room and joked, "What'd I do? Rob a bank?"

"No," she said. "Concealed your true identity. Your photo is on the internet news and it says 'Who is this man?' Come look."

Reluctantly, he went over and there on the computer screen was his photo. He sat down and began reading the piece. The story of Wanda Wilkerson's grandson was recapped and then the reporter told about trying to find information on his adoption. She had learned on what date Wanda Wilkerson left Bakersfield and that she had arrived back in Ellsinore, Missouri shortly thereafter with a child that she had passed off as her missing grandson. The reporter could find no time or place for a possible adoption.

What she did find was that the evening before Wanda Wilkerson left Bakersfield, a man named Bo John Jones had killed his ex-wife. There had been an extensive hunt for his 5-year-old son, Jimmy Joe Jones, but the boy had disappeared. The shooting of the ex-wife had happened near Wanda Wilkerson's motel on Golden State Avenue. Jimmy looked at the photo of Bo John Jones taken at the time and knew he was looking at himself with a beard.

His first thought was, *Oh, no. Grandma's going to be in trouble.*

Rita interrupted his thoughts with, "So Jimmy, you been hiding your true identity?" Her voice was flirtatious and he resorted again to joking.

"Well," he said, looking up at her with a smile, "wouldn't you rather be named James Wilkerson than Jimmy Joe Jones."

"So you are this Jimmy Joe Jones!" Rita crowed triumphantly.

Jimmy shrugged. "Of course," he said casually. "I've always known that. I was already 5 years old when Grandma adopted me. I remember it."

"But this reporter says you just disappeared. She couldn't find any adoption," Rita exclaimed.

Jimmy remembered what Grandma had told that reporter. Now he looked up at Rita and said, "Adoption records are sealed. That reporter can't look one up. My father shot and killed my mother over custody of me. Everyone was making sure that he could never find me."

Jimmy had a sudden thought. His father had gone to prison for murder but it had dragged on for several years with him out on bail for most of it which was an added reason for Wanda Wilkerson to keep quiet about little Jimmy. His father had finally been convicted because three witnesses had stuck it out and appeared in court to testify. His sentence was supposed to be for 35 years but Jimmy had heard that people often got out on parole long before their sentence was finished. He had better check if his father was still in prison. As he turned back to the computer, he realized that Rita had been talking but he had not heard her. He looked up and said, "Sorry, it just occurred me that I should find out if Bo John Jones is still in jail."

Rita said, "He's not. He got out several months ago. That reporter says so."

Jimmy read the remainder of the article and told Rita, "If that Bo

John Jones calls here looking for me, tell him I was transferred to Alaska."

He left the office to go on duty but down the road he pulled over and used his cell phone to call Grandma. She and Grandpa needed to be warned.

What he said to Rita had been intended as a joke but two days later someone else in the office gave him a message. It was just a "return this call" note and he was unprepared when a voice said, "Jimmy Joe, this is your dad."

He was so shocked, he was dead silent and then he just pushed the *end call* button. The call had come in on the office phone and it started ringing again. Someone else answered it and then yelled, "Jimmy, it's for you."

He jumped up and said, "Tell him I'm not here," and ran out the door.

Outside, he called Grandma. Wanda said, "Jimmy, that man is dangerous. I actually saw him kill your mother. Making him mad is dangerous."

Jimmy said, "I remember him breaking my arm. He was beating my mother and I tried to stop him. I remember."

Jimmy went through the rest of his shift with his mind mostly on Bo John Jones. He reflected on the fact that he was not a child anymore and Bo John would have a hard time breaking his arm now. The thought made him smile. He was 6 foot 4 and strong. He remembered that Grandma had said that maybe the rest of the family were good people. Maybe he should get to know them, assess the situation, see if his father was the violent tempered man he used to be.

He didn't call his father back. Instead, he got on the internet and looked up the family. He found that the current sheriff of Grand County, Tennessee was Bo John's father, John "Johnny" Beauregard Jones. Perhaps that explained how Bo John got out of prison so soon. Jimmy considered the situation. Bo John was probably not going to give up. Could they file kidnapping charges this many years later?

Then, the reporter who did the "Who is this man?" piece showed up at Sequoia National Park looking for Jimmy. It was the woman he and his grandmother had first met in the morgue in Bakersfield. He looked at her and said, "Ma'am, have you got some kind of special license for making trouble for people?"

The reporter said, "I'm sorry. I talked to Bo John Jones and he says he's filing kidnapping charges. I wanted to hear your reaction to that."

"How can he file kidnapping charges? I wasn't kidnapped," Jimmy said. He was glad that he'd had some time to think this whole thing over.

The woman looked at him and nodded. "So what did happen?" she asked.

"My father murdered my mother and I hid. Some very kind people helped me hide," Jimmy told her.

"Do you remember it?" she asked.

"Of course," Jimmy said. "I was already 5 years old. It's not the kind of thing you forget, even if you're only 5."

"Did you see your father kill your mother?" the woman asked.

"No, I was around the corner in the car. I heard the shots."

"How did you know what happened?" she asked.

"Someone told me and they helped me hide," Jimmy said.

"If you didn't see your mother shot, why did you believe that your father had killed her?" the reporter asked.

"Because he had said he was going to kill her. I had seen him beat her several times. One day when he started beating her, I jumped in the middle of it and he broke my arm. When he came to our house there in Bakersfield, Mom called the police. The police took him away but he said he was going to come back and kill her."

"Why didn't you go to the police?" the reporter asked.

"My mother went to the police. They didn't stop him from killing her. So why would I go to the police?" he said.

"This is all very interesting," the reporter said. "So you maintain you were not kidnapped but simply ran away."

"Yes," Jimmy said. "I hid and I stayed hidden. I was scared of my father and I hid."

The reporter happily printed it all.

Jimmy thought it over. He did not want Bo John Jones filing kidnapping charges against Grandma. So the next morning about 10, he called Sheriff Johnny Jones. He had to go through a secretary who wanted to know what his call was about. He had said it was personal and she had balked, so he said it was the kind of personal that would get her in trouble if she didn't transfer his call. As he waited, it occurred to him that the woman might listen in or record the call so he should be careful what he said.

The sheriff finally came on, saying, "Yeah, who is this?"

Jimmy was ready. "Jimmy Wilkerson," he said, 'but up until I was 5 years old, I was Jimmy Joe Jones."

"Heck, boy," the sheriff said, "your pa has been trying to call you. They keep saying you're not there."

"I know," Jimmy said. "I'm not too eager to talk to him. I'll talk to you but I don't want to meet my father."

"Boy, you don't know nothing about it. You's just a little squirt when you's kidnapped. You don't know what really happened."

Jimmy said calmly, "I was 5 years old. I remember all about it. I wasn't kidnapped. I wanted to go with the people who took me away. They were good people and I'm glad they took me with them. But it was all a long time ago. I'm grown now. Like I said, I don't want to meet my father but I don't mind meeting the rest of the family."

Jimmy called his cousin Harry and they discussed the situation. Harry said, "Go visit. Beat Bo John Jones senseless and break the skunk's arm for him and see how he likes it!'

Harry's sister, Evangeline called him and they talked about it all. She said, "Jimmy, I'll keep praying for you." He hung up and prayed himself, remembering to thank God for friends like Harry and Evangeline.

The phone calls kept coming and so did the threats to file kidnapping charges. So a few weeks later, Jimmy managed five days off and he flew to Nashville, Tennessee and rented a car. He insisted on staying at a motel which almost offended his grandfather, the sheriff. He met the family with smiles and handshakes, unease and distrust carefully hidden.

His grandfather was physically an older version of himself, above 6 feet with the remains of a strong physic still visible under the extra pounds. His position was an elected one and he had the jolly back-slapping social manner of a politician. He was a widower. "Lost your grandmother years ago. We was out on the boat fishing and she fell in and drown." He shook his head. "Never met another woman like her so I never remarried." By the end of Jimmy's visit, he had figured out that the sheriff liked playing the field.

Jimmy was introduced to assorted relatives and saw his own fiery red hair, brown eyes, height, and skin that tanned instead of freckling repeated over and over. He slowly realized that the Jones family was extensively intermarried. Even first cousin marriages are legal in Tennessee. There was a lot of family and most of them lived out in the county, not in Big Creek. His grandfather had a place in town but also had another one out of town. An uncle called Bobby Ray Jones had a large produce farm, mostly growing tomatoes, and a small fleet of trucks that delivered the produce to its destinations. Jimmy saw what looked like acres of green houses growing the tomatoes. Most of the tending to the produce seemed to be done by a small army of black haired workers that looked Mexican. The trucks were driven by family members.

Jimmy realized that the sheriff probably had told the family to try to make a good impression. The men seemed to have plenty of time to discuss hunting. They had farms with some corn and soy beans but there was a lot barley, which he had not seen grown in Missouri. He saw cattle, horses, and quite a few chickens but he didn't see much else going on other than the huge tomato operation. All of the family seemed to smoke and several times he noticed the lingering odor of marijuana. The women were mostly quiet and sloppy looking but one young female cousin was flirtatious. She wanted him to take her dancing but he made excuses. He asked the sheriff about her and found out she was only 15, although she had looked grown. "If you like her, she'd probably marry you. Our women mostly marry young." The sheriff told him, "Marrying cousins works just fine, son. The woman knows what's expected of her if she's one of ours. We've never produced any idiots yet and good genes ought to be repeated. Your father ought to have married his cousin, Jennifer. Her family was all for it."

Jimmy had found himself biting his tongue over what he wanted to say about that.

The young cousin turned up at his motel driving a pickup truck and he asked if she had a driver's license. She had laughed and said that with her uncle being sheriff, it didn't matter. He had been on his way out to eat so he took her along. She wanted to go to a roadhouse but he already had a favorite cafe – where they didn't serve alcohol. She sulked and said she wanted a beer. He had shrugged and said he could get in trouble supplying alcohol to a minor. She said not with her uncle being the sheriff.

Later, she told him she could get him some pot, some good stuff, homegrown. She said she might could even find him some meth if he was into it. By then, Jimmy had long since decided she was trouble looking for a place to happen. When he said he was going to bed, he had to rather firmly refuse to let her into his room. He told her he was going to church in the morning and would pick her up if she liked. Her response was, "You look just like our cousin, Robby Lee, that's off on a run right now but you're nothing like him at all. He's fun but you're a wet firecracker." Jimmy had laughed and closed his door. He had learned very quickly that everyone kept mistaking him for this cousin, Robby Lee, who was a truck driver and had a beard.

Jimmy had asked his grandfather about churches and got an

invitation to his where he had again been mistaken for Robby Lee and greeted with politeness, hiding astonishment. When he explained that he wasn't Robby Lee, their re-action had been a warmer welcome and what he finally diagnosed as relief. He had no idea why, but he knew these people were happy he wasn't Robby Lee.

Jimmy sat near the back and was joined after the service was underway by his grandfather who wore his gun into church. The service was short, about an hour. It started with a couple of hymns followed by announcements and then a traditional scripture reading. The sermon didn't take much longer than the announcements. It came from the story of the Good Samaritan and was a vague little homily on love-your-neighbor that definitely lacked the punch Jesus had given it. The greetings from others at the end of the service had him thinking that the sheriff was more the Easter Lily, Christmas Poinsettia type attender than the regular pew warmer.

The sheriff surprised Jimmy by offering him a job as a deputy sheriff. Jimmy told him that he liked working for the National Park Service and wasn't interested but the sheriff was persistent. Jimmy finally told him that he'd think about it.

Then the sheriff started in on how much Bo John wanted to see Jimmy, Jimmy said no. But the sheriff talked about Bo John having health problems, being ill, possibly even dying, and he very much wanted to see his son. With great reluctance, Jimmy finally agreed to meet him, but not out at the ranch. They met at a gazebo on the grounds of the court house.

Bo John was waiting when Jimmy arrived. He was Jimmy's height and Jimmy was struck again by the strong resemblance. But Bo John's once strong physic now seemed slack, making an odd contrast to his intensely fierce eyes. He greeted Jimmy by saying, "You're *my* son!"

Jimmy felt a wave of antipathy rip through him like a jolt of electricity. He found himself saying, "So?" and then was shocked by his own tone. He normally was never insolent.

"I want you back!" Bo John said.

Jimmy shrugged and said, "I'm a grown man."

Bo John said again, *"You're my son!"*

By then, Jimmy's brain had gone back into gear and he said, "Anybody can tell that by looking at us."

The sheriff moved in to pour oil on roiling waters and said that he had offered Jimmy a job as a deputy sheriff and Jimmy was considering it. Jimmy got the idea that maybe the sheriff was afraid, not of Bo John himself, but of what he might do.

At the end of his visit, Jimmy turned in his rental car at the airport and slept all the way to California. He picked up his truck from long-term parking and arrived back at Sequoia National Park on time for work.

Everyone asked, "How was your visit?" and he replied with, "Interesting."

In the following days he was pestered with phone calls from his father and grandfather. He told them to quit calling the park office so they called his cell phone. After a few pointless conversations with his father, he told him to quit calling every day, he was busy. His father took to calling and ranting and raving and cussing. Jimmy quit answering his calls. His grandfather was more reasonable and Jimmy answered his calls when he could but kept the conversations short. Then, his father called from his grandfather's phone. Jimmy hung up and the next morning he called his grandfather.

Jimmy had settled on calling Sheriff Johnny Jones *Gramps*. *Grandpa* was Wanda Wilkerson's father, William Wilkerson.

When Jimmy got the sheriff on the phone, he said, "Gramps, would you mind explaining something to your son?"

"What d'ya mean?" he asked.

"I'm talking about Bo John Jones. He keeps on calling and now he's calling and cussing me out. He can't seem to understand that I'm a grown man with a job."

"Well, son, he just wants back what was stole from him." the sheriff said.

"I was not stolen from him. He took my mother away from me when I was 5 years old and still needed her. By rights, he ought to still be in jail. If you can't make him stop harassing me, I'll have to take steps. You know the law. Explain it to him." And then Jimmy hung up the phone and didn't answer when Johnny Jones called back.

Harry and his sister Evangeline were calling him periodically, just checking on him. He found their calls reassuring. He had no doubts about Grandma and Grandpa loving him but he had wondered if the rest of the family might not feel the same now that they knew he wasn't blood kin and that his biological father was a murderer. Harry and Evangeline both actually seemed even more determined to stand with him than before.

Summer was arriving and Jimmy was busy, too busy to make a trip to Missouri. He talked to Grandma and Grandpa at least once a week, often more. He settled into a routine of talking to Sheriff Johnny Jones, *Gramps,* every Tuesday morning. Every Tuesday, Sheriff Jones offered him a job and every Tuesday, he said he would think about it. Privately, to himself, he knew his thought would always be no. But he found himself telling Gramps that come winter, when things were slower, he would come visit again.

Harry and Evangeline started calling him often. They kept him posted on an ongoing discussion in the family. Aunt Audrey who was Uncle Harold Wilkerson's wife, was saying the old Wilkerson home place should not go to Jimmy. He wasn't blood kin. Of course, Aunt Audrey thought it should go to her husband as the oldest son and then, to their son, Billy, who was named for his grandfather, William Wilkerson. Nobody was really agreeing that it should go to Harold, not even Harold, but several members of the family thought it ought to be sold and the money divided between the kids. Harry and Evangeline both said they thought it was interesting that it was not old William Wilkerson's sons who were saying this but mainly Aunt Audrey plus some of the grandchildren.

Jimmy told Harry and Evangeline that Grandma and Grandpa had talked to him about it while he was home for the funeral. He said, "I told them they should probably leave it to someone else but they said no one else wanted to live out there, only use it for hunting, and if I owned it, they could still do that."

Jimmy worried about the possibility of kidnapping charges being filed and then wondered why it hadn't already been done. Was there a statute of limitations? Evangeline talked to somebody and was told no, kidnapping had no statute of limitations, but if charges were filed, it could go to federal court which the Jones family could not control. She thought that was why they had not filed charges.

Jimmy began to wish he had never made contact with Gramps and the Jones family. However, he also thought maybe his persistent statement that he had not been kidnapped had influenced the Jones family not to file charges. But he was getting fed up with their phone calls and refusal to take no for an answer on moving to Grand County, Tennessee.

❊ ❊ ❊
Chapter 3: Being Drafted

Jimmy, as one of the new young rangers, normally worked evenings or nights, leaving days to older rangers with more seniority, although they were beginning to use him occasionally for guided hikes and campfire programs. He was a good communicator. So when he got a call asking him to report in at 10 am, he did not expect anything unusual. However, when he was conducted back to the private office of the top park administrator, he knew something different was going on.

When he entered the office, Clarke stood and introduced a middle-aged man in a suit as Arthur Pendegrass. Clarke got straight to the point. "Pendegrass here is federal drug enforcement. He wants to talk to you." And to Jimmy's surprise, Clarke left his office.

Pendegrass motioned to a chair and they both sat down. Pendegrass opened with another surprise. "I hear that you actually are one of the Jones family out of Grand County, Tennessee. That right?"

Jimmy's heart did a nosedive. He figured whatever was coming, he wasn't going to like it.

He didn't.

Drug enforcement thought that a lot of marijuana and meth were coming out of Grand County. They also thought that the Jones family were the source. Pendegrass said, "That family were always moonshiners but now-a-days, moonshine doesn't make that much money. The big moneymakers are drugs and they haven't changed their spots, just their wares."

Pendegrass wanted Jimmy to go undercover, to take that job Sheriff Johnny Jones was offering him, and help drug enforcement break up the operation. Jimmy's first reaction was, "No way!"

Pendegrass kept talking. The National Park Service was willing to hold his position open, even give him a promotion if he took the job.

Pendegrass said, "That family has always been clannish and they never let anyone in that isn't family. The last undercover agent we sent in there hooked up with one of their women and we thought he was in until he turned up dead in a car accident. We couldn't even prove it wasn't an accident! That was almost five years ago and we've been afraid to send in anyone else."

Jimmy looked Pendegrass straight in the eye and said, "My father killed my mother. If he ever suspected I was crossing him, he'd kill me, too."

Pendegrass said, "One thing our agent did tell us was that Sheriff Jones tries his best to keep family members from using what they sell. He says that Bo John was using when he killed your mother and Sheriff Jones blames that for what Bo John did."

Jimmy grinned. "It's like making whiskey in a dry county; make it and sell it, but don't drink it."

Pendegrass didn't seem to see the humor in it. He said, "If I had my way, the whole country would be dry." Maybe the man had seen too many tragedies, Jimmy thought.

In the end, Jimmy did what he'd done with Gramps, and promised to think about it. He left the office but later asked Clarke, "Do you know what Pendegrass wanted to see me about?"

"Yes," Clarke said. "I'll see if I can get another ranger in here while you're gone but I'll hold your position open for you."

"You're assuming I'm going," Jimmy said.

"Pendegrass explained the situation," Clarke said. "It's just real providential that you're a Jones. I told him your grandfather had been hounding you to come back so it'll be easy."

"Well, I'm not sure I want to do it," Jimmy said.

Clarke looked at him in surprise. "Why not?" he said. "They can't get an outsider in there but here you are, the long lost grandson coming home. It's no problem."

By the time Jimmy finished talking to Clarke, he knew that if he didn't go do what Pendegrass wanted, then Clarke was going to be upset with him. That would be a problem.

Jimmy went home and prayed, did his shift with his mind only half on work, and went home to sleep. When he woke up, he knew he wanted to consult. He called Harry to talk it over. He told Harry, "It's like I'm being drafted. I told him I'd think about it. Drugs are not my thing. They did teach us what a marijuana plant looks like and I know the smell from college but I don't know the difference between meth and cocaine."

Harry said, "Can you stall them a while? Give you some time to think about it. Talk to your Grandma."

Jimmy went to Clarke and asked about getting a few days off to think about it. Clarke suggested a week and told everyone Jimmy was called home because his grandfather was seriously ill, possibly dying. It was one of the very few excuses for giving anyone a week off in the summer season.

Jimmy took it and booked a flight to Springfield. Harry was picking him up.

Jimmy told everyone in Missouri that he had a week's vacation and he had come to help Grandma finish painting the house and to do some work on the roof. An unexpected result of this was that suddenly several of the younger family members showed up to help. Jimmy was puzzled until Evangeline clued him in. She said, "Some of them are still stewing over you inheriting the place. They are trying to prove that they are just as diligent about taking care of it as you are. They're a bunch of brown-nosers but put'em to work. They ought'a been out here long before now."

The first evening he was home, he took Grandma off on a walk down to Spring Cave and talked to her about what drug enforcement wanted him to do. She remembered watching his father kill his mother and for the first time, she told him the details, how he shot her point blank in the chest and then put the pistol to the back of her head and fired again. She said urgently, "The man's a monster and getting anywhere near him is dangerous."

Jimmy could not bring himself to call Bo John Jones *Father,* much less *Dad.* He found himself thinking about what he would like to do to Bo John. If he went to Grand County, he might find a way.

He told Grandma, "You don't get omelets without breaking eggs. I'm the only one in a position to possibly get inside the operation and drugs are a big destroyer of lives. It does need to be stopped."

Wanda Wilkerson looked at the boy she had raised and said, "I maybe shouldn't have told you exactly how your father killed your mother. Desire for revenge is a normal reaction."

"Yeah," Jimmy admitted, thinking how Grandma could see right through him. "I need to do some praying about that."

On their way home from Springfield, Jimmy had discussed it with Harry. Harry had shaken his head. "Playacting is not your gig, Cuz. You've always been a straight arrow. I can't see you ever convincing anybody that you want to get involved with a drug operation."

"I know," Jimmy said. "That's one of my problems with this. I don't think I could ever convince anyone that I was into drugs. And I wouldn't dare actually use any. I don't even smoke so how could I smoke pot? And if I took any of that meth stuff, I might say the wrong thing and give the game away."

"Just tell'em no," Harry said.

"Yeah," Jimmy said. "That's what I want to do – but if I do, there's going to be a backlash. My boss is all gung-ho and sees no reason at all why I shouldn't go do it. If I say no, I think there'll be repercussions and you know being a park ranger is all I ever wanted to do."

Harry said, "I can't believe they put the squeeze on you like this."

The next day, up on the roof, Harry said to Jimmy. "I had a thought this morning." Jimmy looked up from the bucket of tar they were using around the chimneys on the tin roof and Harry went on, "We might talk this over with Evangeline. Women are smart in a way us men aren't. They think of things we'd never think of. And Evangeline's smarter than most. Look how she knew instantly why the cousins wanted to come help work on this house."

Jimmy thought it over. "Yes, remember how quick she spotted Hollaway at the school stealing. He'd been doing it for who knows how long and she saw it as soon as she started teaching there. She knows how to keep quiet, too. Didn't even tell you until it was wrapped up."

Harry nodded, "Evangeline is always nice, no catty remarks out of her, but underneath, she doesn't trust people. Partly, I think that it was that incident with the coach when she was a junior in high school but also it was our cousin, Carolyn."

Jimmy reflected on the past. Right after Harry graduated from high school, he had worked for a year to get money to go to college. Jimmy was a senior that year and he had an old car and took Evangeline home every afternoon. They both played basketball and usually they both had practice on the same afternoons. When they didn't, they waited for each other. One afternoon when Evangeline had practice and he didn't, he told her he needed to pick up something at the hardware store but he'd be back to get her. When he came back, he saw other girls from the team leaving but Evangeline was not among them. He went looking for her, found the gym empty, and finally approached the girl's locker room. He thought he heard a voice and he called out, "Evangeline, you in there?" He didn't hear anything. "Evangeline?" he called. He almost turned away but a noise reached his ears and he knew someone was in there. With the vision of someone slipping on a wet floor and getting hurt, he called out, "Evangeline, I'm coming in," and entered the locker room. He was so shocked, it took him a few moments to take in what he was seeing. The basketball coach was on top of Evangeline's naked body, holding her shirt stuffed over her mouth with her twisting and turning, trying to get loose.

Jimmy had broken the man's jaw and his own hand in the resulting fight, putting him out of basketball the rest of the season. The coach had maintained that what Jimmy had interrupted was consensual sex. He claimed Evangeline had seduced him back at the beginning of the season and they had been doing it ever since. Evangeline denied it strenuously and Jimmy knew she was telling the truth. Evangeline said that the day it happened the coach had kept her after the other girls went to the locker room so they were leaving as she was getting into the shower. The coach had stuck to his story and threatened to sue Jimmy but it was an empty threat. Parents, teachers, and community were all outraged regardless of whose story they believed and the coach lost his job. Charges were filed but Evangeline did not want to go to court and the coach left town.

The story with their cousin Carolyn went back for years. Evangeline and Carolyn had been in the same class at school. Evangeline was a top student and Carolyn was simply okay. She was jealous. When they reached junior high, Carolyn wanted Evangeline to help her cheat and Evangeline wouldn't. Evangeline was well liked by everyone but Carolyn only had her small click of friends. Their sophomore year, Evangeline was asked to the Senior Prom by one of Harry's classmates. Carolyn fed Evangeline a laxative to prevent her from going. Evangeline would never have figured out what happened if Carolyn hadn't been dumb enough to approach the guy and ask to take Evangeline's place. She had a dress ready and everything arranged. Evangeline never told the boy but used the incident to blackmail Carolyn into more reasonable behavior.

Harry, Evangeline, and Jimmy were such a tight trio that people started calling them 'The Three Musketeers.' It had persisted into college. Harry and Jimmy had started the same year, Jimmy on a scholarship. He played basketball and had helped get Harry on the basketball team, although at only 5 foot 9, Harry had not been considered an outstanding prospect. But Jimmy and Harry had played together in high school and Jimmy knew Harry made up for his lack of height with quickness, skill, and brilliant teamwork. By their next year, they were both considered first line players but opposing teams tended to ignore Harry, to their detriment. It was Harry who organized getting the ball to the right player at the right time to make a basket.

Evangeline joined them their second year and missed them terribly her last year when they had graduated, Jimmy to join the National Park Service and Harry to go back to Ellsinore to teach and coach the basketball teams. The next year, Evangeline had joined him, teaching Art and helping her brother coach the girls. Harry had discovered that high school girls did frequently come on to their coach and Harry being unmarried didn't help. He wanted Evangeline there, both to make sure the girls were safe and to serve as a chaperon for him. They joked about it but the problem was real.

Up on the roof, Jimmy said, "Yeah, fill Eva in and see what she says." He added, "Let's all three go out together this evening."

That evening, they took Grandma to Walmart in Poplar Bluff. Sitting in the back corner of the McDonald's in Walmart, the trio discussed the problem while Grandma did her shopping. It was a good place to talk. If they were seen, it was a normal place to be. At the same time, no one could listen in on what they were saying.

Evangeline, with her usual good sense, had checked that she understood the situation correctly. She asked, "You really tried to convince your supervisor that you didn't want to go do it?"

"Yes," Jimmy said, "and it was clear that he was all in favor of it and I could see that if I said no, there would be consequences."

She said, "If you go, your first problem is that you don't think you can convince these people in Grand County that you're interested in drugs. You need a motive. How about money? Could you convince them you want in for the money?"

Jimmy shrugged. "What do I need money for? My salary is more than what I need as a single guy. I'm building up a pretty good savings account."

Evangeline went on, "Another problem is that everyone here knows that all you have ever wanted to do was join the National Park Service. None of the family here would believe that you'd quit to go work as a deputy sheriff in Grand County, Tennessee. You need a motive for it that family here will believe."

Jimmy nodded. "That's what I tried to tell that drug enforcement man. Taking that job and moving to Tennessee is not going to make sense to anyone who knows me."

"Well," Evangeline said, "I've had an idea." Her idea needed Grandma's help but it might would work. When Grandma came and found them, they discussed it with her.

The first step was getting Grandpa Will Wilkerson to give the land and house to Grandma legally. Wanda surprised them by telling them that her father had already done that a few years back in order to avoid taxes and legal fees when he died. The land was an entire section, one square mile, 640 acres. It had been homesteaded by the Wilkerson family back in the 1830's. It was bounded on two sides by Mark Twain National Forest and it had three springs, a year around creek, and a cave. The house was an old two-storied wooden sided affair with porches front and back, a double parlor, and seven bedrooms. It had been kept in decent repair. They had run an electric line in and now had running water and lights. It had a large barn, also in good condition, and other assorted outbuildings. The place was worth at least 600,000 dollars and Aunt Audrey thought it was worth 750,000. For plain hill people, that was a lot of money.

The next step was for Wanda to make a Will that she would show to everyone. In the Will, she would say that when she died, Jimmy would get the place if he paid 800,000 dollars for it. The money would be divided among her four brothers, or if a brother had predeceased her, then it would go to his children. If Jimmy could not raise the money within three months, then the option of buying would move to her oldest brother. If he did not want it or could not raise the money within three months, then the option to buy would pass to the next brother. It would move on down the line. If none of the brothers bought it, then it went on the open market.

Jimmy no longer being heir to the Wilkerson place would serve as a motive for Jimmy to become more interested in his Tennessee family. If he was able to set it up to get in to the operation there, then they would tell the family here in Missouri that his grandfather in Tennessee was promising an inheritance. That was a motive that Aunt Audrey would buy.

Wanda asked Jimmy some practical questions about the operation. He had to tell her what happened to drug enforcement's last agent. Grandma Wanda didn't like it. She said office workers and bureaucrats did not understand danger. How was he supposed to communicate information? In small towns, strangers were noticed and newcomers watched. Phones could be tapped and cell phones listened in on. Sheriffs could get phone records, even cell phone records.

Jimmy returned to his park ranger job at Sequoia National Park with an agenda. He told Clarke to tell Pendegrass that he was seriously considering taking his offer but he needed to ask another question or two. When Pendegrass called, he asked about communication. Pendegrass said he'd be given a phone number to call. Jimmy countered with sheriffs being able to get phone records. Pendegrass said that he would be given a cell phone with an out-of-the-area number to use only for communication with drug enforcement. Jimmy said it was a non-flier. He wanted communication routed though someone in Ellsinore that he knew he could trust. Calls to Ellsinore would be considered normal.

Pendegrass didn't like it. Jimmy said, "I think you don't understand the danger. Your last guy got killed. I don't intend to follow him. We either set up a communication line that I'm happy with or I don't do it."

"Okay, okay," Pendegrass said. "We'll work something out."

It took about a month for Wanda Wilkerson to get her part set up. She told Jimmy on the phone that actually her four brothers had all said that she could leave the place to Jimmy if that was what she wanted. She told Jimmy, "Harold said that his wife is greedy." Aunt Audrey's general discontent with everything was well known. Jimmy suspected that if anyone had come along that looked like a better deal than Uncle Harold, she would have quickly left. But Uncle Harold was a successful insurance agent and they had an amazing place out from Ellsinore with a greenhouse full of orchids which were Aunt Audrey's passion.

So Jimmy packed his few personal belongings and Clarke announced to everyone that Jimmy was going on an extended leave of absence due to the health of the grandparents who had raised him. Schools were starting and the number of tourists was abating. No one questioned his going.

❀ ❀ ❀
Chapter 4: Home

At home, Jimmy reflected on how much he loved the place and his Grandma Wanda and Grandpa Will. He remembered when he first arrived at age 5, he had been scared of Grandpa Will. But he had learned that Grandpa was patient. He expected obedience but focused on teaching Jimmy what to do rather than on punishing him when he made a mistake. Back in those days, Grandpa had still farmed about 30 acres of his land, using a small Ford tractor and planting corn, beans, and wheat. He had rotated his crops and kept a couple of dogs to help with the predications of the wildlife. He taught Jimmy the ways of the animals with which they shared their land. He had taught him how to hunt, both with bow and gun. He and Grandma had taught him how to live. Be kind. Tell the truth but always in love. Stealing was both unkind and dishonest. Don't gossip. Do your share of the work but have some fun. Help others when they need it and ask for help when you need it.

Harry and Evangeline were both teaching school but they showed up together the first afternoon he was home and the three of them went for a walk down to the cave. They sat on rocks and it was Evangeline who looked at Jimmy and said, "Jimmy, what do you think about cousin marriages?"

"Well," Jimmy answered, "I thought that bunch of Joneses down in Tennessee all marrying their cousins were a little bit weird. And I sure wasn't going after that 15-year-old."

"And second cousins? It's legal even here in Missouri to marry your second cousin."

"I guess that would be a little different," Jimmy said. "I got all you second cousins here and it's not like we're brothers and sisters but I sure wouldn't want to marry Carolyn."

Evangeline said, "One point I've been thinking about on this Grand County deal is communication. Your grandma raised a good point on that. I was thinking you might run communications through the two of us and Grandma. I was thinking you might tell those crazy people in Tennessee that I'm your girlfriend and Harry's your best friend. That would do two things. It would make phone calls to us normal and it would keep those Tennessee people from trying to pair you off with one of the cousins there. They all marry their cousins so they would think me being your girl was normal."

They sat, silent for a minute, thinking. Then Jimmy said, "I think it's great. I was thinking Grandma would be the natural person for communication but Grandpa's memory is slipping, so if I do this, she needs to keep him from finding out. Splitting it up would make it a lot less obvious. Saying you're my girlfriend would make it normal for me to call you often and anytime, day or night."

Then he added, "I have wondered if Gramps has any ears here in the Ellsinore area."

"Do you think so? How could he?" Harry asked.

"Well, if he's giving me a job as a deputy, it would be considered routine for him to check on me with local law enforcement here," Jimmy said.

"We could ask Sheriff Barnett to let us know if he does," Harry said.

Evangeline shook her head. "I don't think that's wise. Sheriff Barnett would know something was up. He'd say the right thing to Sheriff Jones but he'd likely talk about us asking him to let us know and gossip might get back to Tennessee." Evangeline paused and then said, "Jimmy, would you mind everyone here thinking you and I had something going?"

Jimmy looked at Evangeline and said, "No."

Harry suddenly hooted. "This is going to be fun," he said. "I can just hear what Aunt Audrey and Dee Dee and Carolyn are going to say."

Rather than outright lying, Evangeline proposed a prank. She had heard that Cousin Carolyn was going over to the Drive-in Movie Theater on Highway 21 that evening. She suggested that Jimmy take her, just the two of them. In the past, such an outing would have included Harry and the movie chosen would have been a lot cleaner. They went in his truck and chose a spot where they knew Carolyn would see them. With a lot of 'How do they do this?' and laughter, they finally got settled comfortably, cuddled up together. Evangeline entertained Jimmy by telling him that couples normally went to the Drive-In in sedans with back seats that were much more suitable for canoodling. They saw other people they knew at the Drive-In Theater as well as Cousin Carolyn and when someone they knew came by for a better look, they tried kissing. It wasn't long before Carolyn showed up. They were watching and saw her coming. They got real cozy and Carolyn rapped on the side of the truck to get their attention. Her greeting was an inelegant demand of, "What are you two doing?"

Jimmy grinned at her. "I think it's called kissing."

"Does Aunt Wanda know?" Carolyn demanded.

"Yes," Evangeline said.

Carolyn said, "I can't believe it," and wondered off looking bewildered.

Evangeline buried her face in Jimmy's shoulder and laughed so hard she was gasping for breath. She finally said, "That was so much fun. Harry was right. This is a hoot."

Jimmy was also laughing. He whispered in Evangeline's ear, "And this kissing business is fun, too."

Evangeline said, "Is it? All the girls in school used to talk about how shy you were about kissing. They said that you would always give them a goodnight kiss if they wanted it but you never wanted to park somewhere and kiss for a while."

Jimmy explained. "When I was about 12, Alice Anne Dunlap wanted to kiss. I didn't know how so I asked Grandpa."

Evangeline laughed, "No! You didn't!"

"Did," Jimmy said laughing too. "So I got my talk on the birds and the bees from Grandma and Grandpa."

"Both of them had go at it?"

"Together," Jimmy confirmed.

"That's different," Evangeline commented. "What did they say?"

"Grandma did most of the talking," Jimmy told her. "She said we all have hormones that make us want sex real bad. She said they were tricky things and when you kissed a girl, they kicked in and if you weren't careful, they would completely take control. She said if you didn't watch out, you'd find yourself having sex and that produced babies and other complications."

Evangeline laughed. "You must have told Harry about it. My mother just told me not to do it, that I could get pregnant. It was Harry who told me that if I let a boy kiss me too much, we'd both go crazy and do it." She stopped and then added, "After that scare with the coach in my junior year, I was afraid to kiss a boy at all."

Jimmy nuzzled her neck and said, "Now that I've kissed you, what I really want to do is kiss you again. I was thinking maybe we should leave. Carolyn has got her gossip and if we leave now, she'll just think we're looking for a little more privacy."

Down the road, with Evangeline over on the other side of the truck, Jimmy said, "I think part of it, too, was knowing about Grandma going off to college and getting pregnant. It made me think she knew what she was talking about."

"You knew about that at 12!"

"Oh, yes," Jimmy said. "Compliments of Cousin Carolyn. She told me one day when I was about 8 that my mother had been a bastard and that made me one, too. I asked Grandpa what it meant and he was clearly mad but instead of explaining, he just stomped off. But the next day he came and told me that he was sorry he didn't answer my question. So he explained what a bastard is. He told me that it wasn't nice of Carolyn to call me names." Jimmy paused and then said, "I asked Grandpa what I should do if she said it again and he told me the best defense against taunts and insults is to pretend not to care. So the next time Carolyn said it, I just said, 'So what.' After I did that a few times, she quit saying it."

The next day, Jimmy told Harry, "The manure has been flying. Grandma has had phone call after phone call."

Harry answered, "Tell me about it. Mom got phone calls before Evangeline got home last night. Mom was astounded and didn't really believe it until she got another call. But Mom's cool. She just said, 'Really. That's interesting.' By the time Aunt Audrey called, she had got her breath back and she said, 'Well, it's about time. I thought that girl never was going to get on with it.' I wish I could have seen the look on Aunt Audrey's face."

"What did your dad say?" Jimmy asked, obviously uneasy.

"He said Evangeline could look a lot further and do a lot worse. Cuz, you may find it was easier to get into this than it will be to get out. I think Mom is already planning the wedding."

What Jimmy said was, "Grandma knows. It'll be okay." But what he felt was a kind of strange longing. Was it just hormones?

Later, he asked his Grandma Wanda, "How do I pick out a good wife?"

She looked at him keenly and said, "Was kissing Evangeline that much fun?"

He blushed and admitted, "Yes."

She smiled and said, "A wife is not just a lover, she's a partner. When the hormones have faded, will you still want to spend time with her? Evaluate her value system. What does she see as important? Ask what she wants out of life. Are the two of you going to be working toward the same things? Getting married is rather like getting into a canoe with someone. If you work together, everything is fine, but if you don't, you turn the canoe over."

Jimmy repeated, "Value system. What she sees as important. What she wants." He looked at Wanda and smiled, "You're real helpful,

Grandma."

She squirmed and said, "I've made my share of mistakes."

Jimmy said, "Yeah, but the function of parents and grandparents is to pass on the wisdom that comes with experience."

She smiled and said, "Yes, but some kids listen and learn and some have to learn the hard way."

Jimmy said, "That stuff Paul wrote about hardships producing character came from experience. Maybe Bo John Jones breaking my arm made me more willing to learn things the easy way."

Wanda shook her head and said, "Maybe, but here you are, going to Tennessee. I know why you're going and I understand but this whole business gives me the heebie-jeebies."

"Evangeline suggested something. She said maybe we should set up a code so that I could communicate things on the phone without others suspecting. She said not something elaborate but something simple like mentioning a fire of any kind would be an urgent *send help immediately* message. She said she'd think about it and make a list, not too long, but just about things I might need to communicate when I was not alone."

Wanda said, "That sounds good to me."

❈ ❈ ❈
Chapter 5: Scouting Trip

On his way to Tennessee, Jimmy reflected on how much help it had been to talk things over with Grandma, Harry, and Evangeline. He was on his way for a brief visit to check things out. If he just suddenly called Gramps and said he'd changed his mind, Gramps might be suspicious. Also, he might work for Gramps for a year or longer before he was trusted enough to be let in on the drug operation. The discussions had produced a strategy that he would try. If it didn't work, he would tell Pendegrass he couldn't get in.

Pendegrass had not been at all happy about Jimmy's communication arrangements. Jimmy had just said, "Take it or leave it. If you want me, that's how it is. These people are all keenly motivated to keep me alive." Pendegrass had muttered about amateurs but in the end had agreed.

Jimmy had not called ahead and he checked into the same motel where he stayed before. He went over to the Sheriff's Office, where he actually had never been the last time he visited. He walked in and found the the office manned by a tall red-headed female who was clearly a Jones. He said, "I'm Jimmy Wilkerson. Is the sheriff here?"

The woman looked at him and said, "They told me you looked just like Robby Lee. I've seen him without his beard and you could be his twin brother."

Jimmy smiled and said, "And you are?"

"Myrna Jones, your pa's sister." Jimmy caught something in her voice when she said *your pa* which made him think Bo John might not be one of her favorite people.

He bobbed his head politely, and said, "Aunt Myrna, nice to meet you."

"I'll call Dad and tell him you're here," she said.

Her dispatchers cubicle was large and glassed in so he could not hear what she was saying. From his information via Grandma, Jimmy knew she was 40, Bo John's younger sister. Unlike most of the other female Joneses he had seen last time, she was neatly dressed, with her hair nicely done, and light makeup. She was tall and lanky, not a raving beauty, but still nice looking. With a smile on her face, she might be quite attractive.

She came out and said economically, "Five minutes, maybe ten. Where you staying?"

"Starlight Motel," he said.

She nodded. "You staying long?" she asked.

"Don't know," he said. "I'll discuss it with the sheriff."

"Surprised you're back," she said. "Heard you liked working for the park service."

"I did," Jimmy said, "but maybe I'd like it here just as well."

The woman looked at him and then said, "Felicity said you're a wet firecracker."

Jimmy grinned. "Underage girls are not my thing. Besides, I've got a girl in Missouri."

"How come you're not in Missouri?" she asked.

"Just checking things out," he said mildly with another smile, trying not to sound rude.

As he said this, he heard "Myrn, you there?" from the open door of the dispatcher's cubicle and she said, "Nose to the grindstone," and went back in, shutting the door.

Jimmy was considering the amazing sound-proofing and large size of her cubicle when the sheriff bustled in, and holding out his hand, said, "Jimmy Joe, this is a surprise. Why didn't you call? Let's go get coffee over at Gina's."

Jimmy said, "Well, I'd prefer somewhere a little more private."

The sheriff looked at Myrna and then moved toward his office door saying, "Come on in, boy. It's good to see you."

The office was large, with an impressive deer head, a cougar's head, a large mounted fish, a moose head, even a bighorn sheep head and a lot of framed photographs on the walls. It reeked of cigarette smoke and Jimmy decided not to waste time. He started in with, "That family I lived with all these years in Missouri own some land. To be exact, they own a square mile of mostly forest land adjacent to Mark Twain National Forest. The land has a creek, three springs, and a cave. It has a house that would probably qualify for the historical registry. Up until this came out about who I really was, I was slated to inherit it all. Now, some of the family have been agitating and there's a new Will."

Jimmy handed a copy of the Will to Sheriff Jones and waited while he read it. He read it through and then went back and skimmed through it again. He finally looked up and said, "So now you're only going to get it if you pay 800,000 dollars for it."

"Yes," Jimmy said, "and Grandma just retired after teaching school for 30 years. She's got health problems. She's not telling the rest of the family but she's got cancer. The doctors want to do a bunch of treatments but after looking into it all, she's decided it's not worth it. She's got a year, probably not much more, maybe less." Jimmy looked down while he said this, trying to project sadness but not confident of his ability to carry off an outright lie.

"That's too bad, boy," the sheriff said. "You're going to need money."

"Yes," Jimmy said. "I talked to the bank people and they aren't willing to loan me that much money on the land. It's located in the middle of nowhere and in recent times, there's only been about 30 acres under cultivation and even that has been abandoned for the last six years."

"So you're here to ask for a loan," the sheriff said.

Jimmy was secretly happy with the track the sheriff's mind was following. "Well, I thought it wouldn't hurt to ask but I did have another idea."

"Well, what was you thinking?"

Jimmy shifted position and looked at the impressive deer head on the wall. "I was considering your offer of a job." He paused and then looked at the sheriff. "The last time I was here, I noticed a few things. I may not have grown up here but you all are still blood kin and that counts for something so I'd never say anything but I figured out that somebody's growing marijuana and I suspect someone's making meth. They couldn't be doing that without you knowing." Jimmy saw that the sheriff was looking worried. He went on, "I never said anything to anyone and I don't plan to say anything, regardless, but I need money and I wondered if I could get on on the action."

"I would never have thought you were into drugs," the sheriff said.

"I'm not," Jimmy said. "I'm into money. I want that place in Missouri."

The sheriff was silent for minute, thinking, then said, "Well, I'm not too sure I want to help you do something that'll keep you in Missouri."

Jimmy was ready for that one. "I'm not expecting to have 800,000 dollars by the time Grandma dies but I was thinking I'd learn the business and we might can set up a branch in Missouri. I got a girl there, second cousin, or we would be if I was really Jimmy Wilkerson. There's a lot of family. If I marry Evangeline, I'd be considered part of the family again. On this drug thing, I'm not thinking a big operation but just a nice little business bringing in a nice steady income on the side."

"Would the family go along with it?" the sheriff asked.

Jimmy said, "I would keep it small and involve only a few that I can trust." He paused and said, "Also, if I work here a while as a deputy, learn the ropes, I could probably get taken on there by Sheriff Barnett. That would be a big help in keeping secrets. If I keep a clean image I might can even eventually become sheriff there. Sheriff Barnett will retire someday and there's no obvious successor at this point."

"Boy, I think you got the Jones brains. But I don't like being pressured."

"No pressure, Gramps," Jimmy said. "If you tell me no, I'll go away and never say a word about what I smelled here in Grand County."

"I gotta think about this," the sheriff said. "Where you staying?"

Jimmy said, "At the Starlight. I'm planning on going back to Missouri tomorrow. If you can't decide that quick, you can phone."

But it was only about three hours later before the sheriff came by to take him for a spin. He stopped on an overlook by a river. The first thing he did was light up and Jimmy asked if he minded opening the windows. The sheriff started off with, "I want to know where and how you spotted the marijuana and the meth."

"Marijuana smells," Jimmy said. "If someone has been smoking it, the smell gets in their clothes and in their hair. If you normally don't even smoke cigarettes, the smell is pretty obvious. I caught the scent at several houses."

They talked for a while and Jimmy knew by the sheriff's reactions that he hit a nail every time. He went on to say, "And that wild child, Felicity, offered to get me some. Somebody needs to corral her before she causes some serious trouble. On the meth, I was more guessing. Felicity mentioned it but out at that house with all the horses and two junk cars in the front yard, someone was going to show me a horse when there was a smell. They suddenly reversed directions and took me somewhere else. They acted nervous and I acted like I didn't notice anything but I think someone was cooking meth."

"Dope-heads!" the sheriff said. "Stupid morons!"

Jimmy said, "One of the things I was thinking I might could help you out with is letting you know who's giving the game away. Stupid morons is about right. Lots of people know the smell of marijuana. If you're going to do something illegal, at least take a precaution or two."

"Why didn't you run to the law with this?" the sheriff asked.

"I told you, I may not have grown up here but I'm still blood kin." Jimmy paused and said, "I want nothing to do with my father and I only talked to him that one time but I wondered if he's got a drug problem. He has that look about him."

The sheriff sat looking at Jimmy with his mouth open. "Son, you're good. How come drug enforcement hasn't recruited you?"

Jimmy's heart thudded but he shrugged and said, "Druggies are always going to find drugs. You can't stop them. I might as well be on the side of the problem that makes the money."

The sheriff laughed. Then, he asked, "Okay, son, what are you expecting?"

Jimmy relaxed a little and said, "Money. It's why I want in. As far as work is concerned, I need time to sleep and eat but not much else. I want a clean reputation, no rumors following me back to Missouri. Setting up there requires that no one suspect I'm involved in a drug operation. I expect to work as a deputy 40 hours or more a week and learn to do the job right. But that leaves time for other things. I could easily learn to make meth. I've operated farm machinery. I can learn to drive a truck. And you can trust me to keep my mouth shut and stay out of the goods. I want money but I'm not stupid enough to steal from you all."

The sheriff nodded. "Before we talk turkey, you need to know that the narcs have tried to find out what we're doing out here. About six or seven years ago, one of our buyers squealed. He was hushed up before arrests were made, but not by us. We weren't sure he had talked about us until they sent in an undercover agent. We were watching, spotted him right away, and run him off before he learned a thing. Then, they tried sending in a woman but we were on to her just as quick. After that, they sent in a guy that wormed his way in far enough to be trouble but the man died in a traffic accident." The sheriff paused and looked at Jimmy. "They think we did it but I really didn't know until he was dead and I had his cell phone. We are quite sure he reported things before he died."

The sheriff paused, clearly expecting Jimmy to comment, so he asked, "Do you think they've got someone in here now?"

"No," the sheriff said. "We tightened things up, bought some high tech equipment, and never ever let any outsiders get involved. A lot of the family know about the marijuana but they don't see it as serious. Only a very few know about the meth and even fewer anything about how our product is made, sold, or transported."

"Sounds smart," Jimmy commented.

"We've had a couple of family members, potheads, who couldn't keep their mouths shut. One of them had a fatal accident. I think it was just the natural consequences of driving when he 'uz smoking but I used it to put the fear of God into loose tongues. I need to warn you, boy, that if anyone in the family thinks you're double crossing us, you're dead."

Jimmy shrugged. "I'm not that stupid."

The sheriff considered him for a minute and then said, "As you probably know already, everyone involved except Bobby Ray's Mexicans, are family. The Mexicans grow the tomatoes in greenhouses and sometimes marijuana but a lot of it is grown by different family members in small hidden plots. The big money maker is meth. It's fairly easy to make and easy to sell. It's very profitable. We've been approached to expand our business to cocaine and heroin coming out of Mexico but refused. I think some of those offers were being arranged by drug enforcement. We've hoped our refusal has made them question if we're still operating. One of the biggest mistakes people in our business make is being greedy."

The sheriff paused and Jimmy asked, "You worried about me being greedy?"

"You want money," the sheriff said, his tone challenging.

"I want money but what I really want is a future. Money is just a means. I will not do anything to compromise my future."

"You're not going to get 800,000 dollars in a year."

Jimmy smiled. "I don't need that much in a year. The bank will loan 400,000. You saw in that Will that Grandma left me everything she has except the house and land. She has a 100,000 tucked away and I'll get it. My girl thinks her family will let her have another 100,000. That's 600,000. I know I probably won't get 200,000 here in a year but I thought if I was going to set up in Missouri, you might loan me the rest."

The sheriff smiled. "I can see that you're a planner. That's good. When could you start?"

"Three days. I need to go back to Missouri, pack a few things, see my girl."

"What about your job with the park service?"

"When I told them about Grandma, I was able to arrange an indefinite leave. She has no living children or grandchildren so as an adopted grandson, I'm next of kin. If everything pans out, I won't go back. But if things don't work out, I still have a job," Jimmy explained.

"What was your pay with the park service?" They discussed pay and agreed on an amount that wasn't as much as the park service but more than what the other deputies were getting. The sheriff said, "Everyone will think I'm grooming you for my job when I retire. My three deputies are part of the family but none of them have any college education or the brains to take over my job. Marvin Jones is my best deputy but he can barely read."

He went on to tell Jimmy, "What we really need right now is someone reliable to cook meth. You'll start as a deputy and we'll let you get settled in before we start you making meth. Once you start cooking, you'll get paid by output, and we can market everything you can make."

Jimmy said, "I do have one other thing you need to know." When the sheriff nodded, he went on, "The family in Missouri need a good reason for me taking a job here. Grandma making a new Will gave me an idea. I thought I might tell them that you have promised to put me in your Will if I come work for you. Later, if everything pans out and I return to Missouri, I'll say you gave me a loan. It would explain where I got the money."

"Boy, you've put a lot of thought into this," the sheriff said.

Jimmy nodded. "I make plans. They don't always work out, but then I make another one."

The sheriff said, "I think this is going to work."

❀ ❀ ❀
Chapter 6: Stranger in a Strange Land

So Jimmy found himself headed back to Tennessee very early on Sunday morning. Gramps had arranged for him to stay at the Lilac Bush Bed and Breakfast while he made other living arrangements for him. Jimmy had adamantly refused to stay under the same roof as Bo John. The Lilac Bush was ran by a widow named Lilac Jones. Her husband had been part of the family but had died in a work accident years ago. Gramps warned Jimmy that she knew nothing about the drug operation and he was to make sure it stayed that way. Jimmy was in Big Creek by 3 in the afternoon and unloaded his clothes and the few personal possessions he had brought.

He was coming back down the stairs to ask about breakfast arrangements when he met a young woman, who demanded, "Robby Lee, what are you dong here?"

She had the Jones height and brown eyes but her hair was not the fiery red of Jimmy's but darker, auburn. She was beautiful, a real head-turner, and being angry did not alter that. Jimmy smiled. "I'm not Robby Lee," he told her. "I'm Jimmy."

"You can't be!" she said and then added, "I heard you looked just like Robby Lee but I can't believe it!"

Jimmy laughed. "I haven't met this Robby Lee yet but I can't believe it either."

"I'm Rose," the woman said, "Rose Jones. Mom told me you were staying here but I really can not believe it. You really do look like Robby Lee."

"Well," Jimmy told her, "apparently we aren't alike otherwise. That kid, Felicity, called me a wet firecracker."

"Did she?" Rose said, obviously appraising him. "That actually is a good recommendation in my book."

"Is it?" Jimmy responded. "I was on my way to ask what time is breakfast,"

"When do you want it?" Rose asked.

"Is 7 too early?"

"No," Rose responded. "It's actually quite convenient. I eat at 7 so I can get to work by 8. Anything else?"

"Well," Jimmy hesitated, "can you give me a rundown on the churches around here?"

"Churches!" Rose exclaimed. "You really aren't Felicity's type, are you?"

Jimmy ended up going to church with Rose and her mother. They attended something called Love and Truth Worship Center which Rose had described as somewhat Pentecostal and one of the bigger churches in town. Jimmy found Rose over and over saying, "This is not Robby Lee. His name is Jimmy. Isn't the resemblance incredible?" And over and over he saw looks of surprise and disapproval change to surprise and relief.

The church was one of those new metal structures and big. The music was a mixture of modern songs with some older favorites like "How Great Thou Art." They had a great worship team and Jimmy tried to keep his mind on the worship and not on critiquing the musicians. After all, their purpose was to worship God, not produce a performance for his entertainment. They had a time for people who needed prayer and the sermon took 40 minutes, had some life in it, and was followed by an altar invitation. Back at the Lilac Bush, he was given his choice of coffee or hot chocolate with cookies. He had liked the church and said so.

Jimmy asked exactly who was Robby Lee and found out that he was the grandson of Gramps brother, Bobby Ray Jones who had the tomato farm. His mother was Bobby Ray's daughter, Jennifer, but she had married a man from out of the area who now was the main supervisor at the lawn mower plant and his last name was also Jones – Robert Jones. Robby Lee was only a few months younger than Jimmy. He drove a truck and also played with a band that provided entertainment in bars. He was known as a rebellious troublemaker, a womanizer, and a brawler.

He was also a player of pranks, some actually funny, most of them inconvenient, and some downright destructive. The squirrel he let loose in a service at the Baptist Church was mostly considered funny. The snake he had left in the girls' locker room in high school was a mixed bag, depending on whether you were a girl or a boy. The red dye he had put in the church baptistry at Love and Truth had elicited no laughs from the congregation. He was a known source of fake dog turds, illegal fireworks, and false alarms.

Rose's mother commented, "Robby Lee looks like all his mother's family but his younger sister and brother look like their father. Their father's family was military and his mother was from Korea or somewhere so they have black hair and look sort of Chinese. Funny how these things work. Because Robby Lee looks like his grandfather's family, Bobby Ray has favored him. I don't think it's done the boy any good."

Rose had gotten her looks from her mother who was still a nice looking woman with a pleasant disposition. She told Jimmy to call her Lilac instead of Mrs. Jones. He asked if she minded if he made it Aunt Lilac. She was his mother's generation. He said, "I'd feel odd calling you just by your first name."

She said, "Aunt Lilac is fine. You're very polite. Tell us about these people who kidnapped you."

Jimmy smiled and said, "They didn't kidnap me. I call the woman *Grandma*. She actually saw Bo John kill my mother. She had just seen my mother tell me to stay in the car, so she grabbed me and run." Jimmy smiled at Aunt Lilac and her daughter. "It wasn't a kidnapping. She was just helping me hide. When we talked it all over, I decided I wanted to stay with her, so I did."

Lilac Jones shook her head and then said, "What were you? 5? Smart even then. Why in the world would you come back now?"

Jimmy looked down and knew he was facing his first real test. Lilac Jones was a good woman and he was going to have to lie to her. He didn't like it but it was necessary. He looked vaguely at a picture of an old man praying over his food that was hanging on the wall and said, "Grandma's got cancer. She can't leave me anything when she dies. She told me it'd be better for my future to come work for Gramps." Jimmy looked at Lilac and said, "Also, Bo John has been threatening to file kidnapping charges. Grandma doesn't need that right now."

"Well," Lilac Jones said, "I like you a whole lot better than Robby Lee. If you need to know anything, just ask."

Jimmy suddenly had a feeling that Aunt Lilac was thinking he might make a good son-in-law. "Do you mind if I give your phone number to my girl in Missouri?" he asked. "I have a cell phone but if she can't reach me on it, can she call here?"

"You've got a girl?" Lilac asked and Jimmy talked about Evangeline happily.

Later, when her mother had gone up to bed, Rose said, "I'm glad you have a girl. I just finished college this spring and Mom thinks it's time for me to get married. Years ago when I was in high school, Robby Lee went after me and Mom told me to never, ever hook up with any of the Jones family. I think Mom might have been thinking you could be an exception but I have other plans."

"You've got a fellow?" Jimmy asked.

"Back in high school, when I turned Robby Lee down and dated someone else, the boy got a broken leg in gym class. I thought it was bad luck but then Robby Lee beat up the next boy I started seeing. Then, the next one told me Robby Lee warned him off. I quit dating. When I went off to college, Robby Lee came around and warned off a guy I was dating there. He kept showing up and got in a fight with another guy I dated. After that, I kept things to myself."

"Smart," Jimmy said. Later, that night he thought about it and decided that he probably was not going to like Robby Lee – and he probably was going to have to pretend that he did.

The next morning, Jimmy inspected the town with interest. Like most farming areas, it was up and moving early. It had a central square with a large stone courthouse. Around the square were businesses. A combination hardware and feed store and a cafe were already buzzing. He saw a few cars in front of a Dollar General that had replaced a Newberry's. They still had a Ben Franklin store. There was a grocery store fronting on the square, already open. He glimpsed a parking lot behind it. There were the usual offices of lawyers and insurance agents. The court house square even had a gas station with a car repair business off the back. The sheriff's office was a block off the square down a side street in a newer building with what was clearly the jail at the back. It wasn't all that big and Jimmy thought they must not house long-term prisoners.

The town had no Walmart and no shopping center other than downtown.

At 5 till 8 Jimmy reported in to the Sheriff's Office. His uniforms were waiting. ("It'll come out of your first paycheck.") He changed in the restroom. Aunt Myrna was again on duty. He learned that she and her much younger sister, Lisa Marie, handled the office. It was closed from 10pm to 7am from Sunday through Thursday nights and midnight to 7 on Friday and Saturday nights. Myrna normally took mornings with Lisa Marie taking over mid-afternoon but they switched up as needed. Someone was always on call. He was issued a new phone, a high tech smart phone that he had to learn how to use.

He found out why the dispatcher's cubicle was so big. Not only were there radio and phones but computers and a row of screens that were fed from traffic cameras. The traffic cameras took photos and reported the speed of every passing vehicle. The photos were not just of license plates but also of car drivers. It was a sophisticated, high resolution, expensive set-up. The cameras were not located at the edge of town but out by the county lines on each of the paved highways that came into the county. The sheriff's office saw every vehicle that came and went from Grand County unless they used an unpaved route. Gramps grinned as he saw Jimmy figure it out. "Yep," he commented. "Got her sewed up tight. Nobody comes and goes around here without us knowing about it."

Jimmy commented, "Wow, you know what you're doing," and succeeded in making his voice project admiration. He was thinking furiously to himself about the possibilities of high-tech surveillance equipment.

The county patrol cars were equipped with the usual radios but Gramps told Jimmy, "These radios can be heard by anybody who has the price of a scanner. You'd be surprised at how many bored people buy one. Never say anything on them that you don't want publicly announced."

So Jimmy spent the next week learning about law enforcement, Grand County style. His introduction included the fact that Grand County statistically had very little crime compared to other counties. "Keeps the State people out of our hair," Gramps said.

He also learned that the judge who presided in the courthouse was a Jones on his mother's side and the young prosecuting attorney's father was related to the Jones family and Gramps had helped put him through law school.

Tennessee State Troopers came into the county but when it happened, they knew. Myrna said, "We can pretty much keep track of them. If we have anything on the move, we make phone calls and all the rabbits find a hidey hole."

Lisa Marie was another surprise. She was about two years older than Jimmy and their resemblance was so strong, she could have been his sister. She commented, "Robby Lee and I look a lot alike but you two could be twins." Jimmy had learned over the years that to people who didn't mind red hair, he was considered handsome. But now he was looking at a female version of himself and saw that Lisa Marie was attractive, not the knock 'em dead gorgeous that Rose was, but nevertheless quite appealing.

It was only a couple of days before Robby Lee turned up. He was waiting for Jimmy when he returned to the Lilac Bush to sleep. He climbed out of a huge chrome infested pickup truck and stalked over to confront Jimmy. He was a tad taller but slightly stockier and carrying a little more weight. His face was a little wider, or maybe just looked that way due to a thick, virile looking beard, but his eyes were exactly the same. Even after all the comments, Jimmy found himself astonished by the degree of resemblance. Jimmy read the angry aggression in the man but waited quietly, smiled politely and said, "You must be Robby Lee," and held out his hand.

Robby Lee was startled into shaking hands but Jimmy was not surprised to find it turning into a bone crusher. He gave as good as he got. When Robby Lee finally disengaged, he said, "Shit, 'dey tole me ya's my twin but I didn't believe 'em."

Jimmy noted the crude by-word, extreme hill-talk speech, and macho dress in tight jeans and tight t-shirt with an anti-social message. He thought Grandma would not have approved and neither did Aunt Lilac. But Jimmy simply smiled pleasantly and said, "Yeah, I didn't believe it either. Felicity said you drive a truck."

"Yeah," Robby Lee agreed. "Gone a lot. Come by ta warn ya dat Rose what lives here is mine. Keep your hands off."

Jimmy kept his pleasant smile while gently shaking his head. "Got my own girl in Missouri," he said.

Robby Lee said, "Ya keep it dat way! Ya hear?"

Robby Lee's beard was slanted at an aggressive angle and suddenly Jimmy had an urge to laugh but controlled himself. "No problem," he said mildly and with one last fierce scowl, Robby Lee stalked off back to his truck and Jimmy noticed his fancy cowboy boots with heels that gave him a little more height. In their stocking feet, Jimmy was possibly a hair taller.

Aunt Lilac was hovering just inside the front door. "I saw him waiting out there," she twittered nervously. "Was he warning you to stay away from Rose?"

Jimmy grinned. "Yes," he told her and started laughing. Aunt Lilac looked at him in disbelief. Jimmy explained, "He was just like a cartoon character, beard sticking out and muttering 'Keep your hands off my girl.' Honestly, does he think this is still the dark ages? Rose can chose who she wants and he can't stop her."

Aunt Lilac looked distressed. "You don't understand. He beats people up, maybe even arranges accidents."

Jimmy smiled at her and said, "I know. Rose warned me."

"But . . . you're laughing!" Aunt Lilac spluttered.

Jimmy nodded. "I'm as big as he is. I hope I'm smarter. I work as a sheriff's deputy. And I've been warned. I'm not some poor unsuspecting kid or a nerdy college student. I told him I got a girl in Missouri but I'll keep my eyes swiveled anyway." He grinned again and said, "I may even get some fun out of this."

Aunt Lilac shook her head, still looking worried. "Rose never goes anywhere alone, not even in the daytime. She works at Dollar General. People she works with pick her up and bring her home. They all know that if Robby Lee shows up, they need to whisk her out immediately."

Jimmy nodded. "I'll talk to Gramps."

Jimmy spent his training days riding shotgun with the three other deputies. They were all either kin or married into the family, or both. They were all fairly young, big, and didn't breathe without asking Sheriff Jones first. Jimmy learned that a lot of things were dealt with unofficially. Drunks who got out of line were apt to wake up with a lot bruises, maybe even a broken bone or two. Traffic tickets were for serious offenses and persistent offenders.

At the end of his first week, they had a major domestic situation. A man called Duncan Wagoner beat his wife. Grand County didn't have a hospital but did have two doctors, a married couple, who had a small clinic with three beds and emergency medical care. One of the doctors called the sheriff. Gramps had Marvin Jones and Jimmy meet him at the man's house. They just knocked briefly and walked straight in.

Wagoner was sound asleep in a recliner in the living room with the alcohol fumes so thick, Jimmy hoped no one lit a cigarette. They dragged him to the kitchen and dunked his head in the kitchen sink.

When they had him awake, the sheriff started in on him, "Duncan, you shit-assed moron, you broke your wife's jaw."

The man mumbled something about her nagging him.

The sheriff replied, "We all know women is dumb and one of the dumb things they do is nag. You're a man. Take it like a man."

The man started to mutter something else but Gramps said, "I warned you the last time."

Then, the sheriff took out his night stick, put his left hand in the man's hair to hold his head still, and whacked Wagoner on the jaw. The man doubled over in agony. The sheriff just calmly waited until his screaming died down and then said, "We'll be dropping you off at the clinic. You'll tell the doctor that you stumbled and fell down some steps. Slapping your wife around a little when she's a nag is understandable but breaking her jaw and knocking out half her teeth ain't. Is that clear?"

Marvin and Jimmy dropped Wagoner off at the clinic. Afterwards Jimmy said, "And none of this will officially get reported."

"Right," Marvin said. "Saves a lot of paperwork."

Later, as Jimmy dropped off to sleep he wondered about what happened with Bo John and his mother all those years ago. It had been before Gramps became sheriff 17 years ago, so he would not have been in charge then. But was there a different set of rules for the Jones family? Jimmy had not seen Bo John yet. He lived at Gramps place out in the country and nobody had even mentioned him to Jimmy.

After just a few days at the Lilac Bush, Jimmy was moved to a place out back of beyond. The road was so bad, Gramps parked his vehicle and rode in with Jimmy through fields where he saw cattle. It was clear he was going to need the 4-wheel drive on the truck. A mobile home on the place had burned in the not too distant past. A scrapper had removed what could be sold and Gramps had the remains bulldozed and buried. An old hay-filled barn was in reasonable repair and Jimmy was told there had once been a big house but it had been gone for years. A very old two room log cabin had survived and they had added an electric line. It had a tin roof and a tin bathtub on the back porch along with a hand pump for water. The rest of the amenities was a pit toilet located a good distance from the house.

Gramps told Jimmy, "It's biggest advantage is that no one can get here without being seen. We've got a warning buzzer rigged out on the gate. My last cook we had living out here blew himself up last winter. He decided the barn was too cold and he was cooking in his trailer, the dumb git." Gramps was shaking his head.

Gramps also thanked him for the heads-up on the meth maker he had spotted when he was visiting. Gramps said, "He had helped Hank some and he was using so he decided to make his own. His family was upset but didn't know what to do. When I went out there to talk to them, they wanted my help. We've sent the boy to a rehab program and we'll keep an eye on him." It left Jimmy with questions in his mind about just what the rules really were around here.

After he was moved to the cabin, Gramps invited Jimmy out to his country place for a Sunday afternoon barbecue. Jimmy asked, "Will Bo John be there?"

"Boy," he said, "you're going to have to face him sometime. Might as well get it over with."

Jimmy thought, *Yes, sometimes you have to take the bull by the horns.* He said, "Why did you let Bo John get away with what he did to my mother and to me?"

Jimmy saw Gramps shift uneasily and then say, "I wasn't sheriff then and I didn't think it was serious until your mother took you and left. Bo John says you fell and broke your arm and she blamed it on him so he slapped her around a little."

Jimmy shook his head. "I still remember it clearly. He was hitting her with his fist and I tried to stop him. He grabbed my arm and twisted. My mother took the x-rays into court there in Bakersfield and some doctor testified that the break in my arm was caused by twisting and that you don't get that kind of break from a fall."

Sheriff Gramps shook his head and said, "You was only 5. It's what you's told."

"No," Jimmy said. "It's what I remember. I remember a lot from back then. I remember the house we lived in. I happened to drive by it a couple of days ago and it hit me like a lightening bolt. I recognized it. Nobody could have taught me that. I don't know about now but back then it had wall paper in the living room with flowers on it, blue and yellow ones. My mother painted the kitchen yellow. My bedroom was painted blue and there were glow stars on the ceiling." Jimmy paused then looked Gramps. "Bo John drove a red truck that had a confederate flag painted on the hood and a horn that tooted 'Dixie.' He wrecked it. Shall I go on? For my fifth birthday, there was a cake with Scooby Doo on it. I got a puppy for my birthday. Bo John got mad and kicked it and it died. I think that happened very shortly before the incident where he broke my arm. I was thinking he was going to make my mother die, like the puppy."

Jimmy looked at Gramps. Gramps looked shocked, his mouth slightly open and his expression pained. Jimmy said, "When Bo John killed my mother, he shot her pointblank in the chest and after she collapsed, he leaned down and put another bullet in the base of her skull. And now you want me to be nice to this man, feel sorry for him, eat with him." Jimmy stood up and said, "No." He walked away.

Jimmy had been ending his shift. As he drove home, he found himself shaking. He had never intended to confront Gramps with Bo John's violence. He had intended to play along, avoid Bo John as much as possible, but be quietly pleasant when necessary. Recognizing that house had been a kick in the gut. All those memories had come flooding back, the ones he had mentioned and more. He knew he may have just blown the whole undercover operation. He realized it would be a relief.

Jimmy had felt like he was being constantly watched from the moment he had returned to Grand County. There were always people around and part of the sense of being watched came from how carefully they were not watching him. He was learning that some people called Gramps or Myrna to pass on all kinds of observations. There were a lot of others who seemed never to see anything. People at home in small town Ellsinore watched newcomers and gossiped but there was something extra here, something a little beyond small town curiosity and lack of other entertainment, some edge of secrecy or fear, maybe both.

Jimmy considered what was possible these days with surveillance. He wondered if his room at the Lilac Bush had been bugged. He suspected his cabin and truck were. He had come to Big Creek with a hidden Tracfone. It had no name on the caller ID. He had bought it in Nashville. He made some calls on his personal cell phone but he knew Gramps might be having those calls traced and logged. He had hid the Tracfone and was very careful about where and when he used it.

When he got home that night, he left his phones on the table in the cabin and went for a walk, first to the outhouse and then, on up the mountain behind his cabin. He had found a faint path where he had seen animal tracks. It was dark and he didn't go up very far before he sat on a rock and looked at the stars. "God," he prayed, "I don't know what to do." He sat quietly for at least half an hour before using his Trackfone to call Evangeline.

"Eva," he said, "I may have blown it."

"What happened?" she answered and they talked for an hour. Most of it was about his outburst with Gramps but then Evangeline told him that Pendegrass was really getting snarky about the communication setup. "Yesterday, he called us *damned amateurs* and I told him I was not going to stand being sworn at. He started in on saying that was just what he was talking about and I didn't know shit about how this was supposed to be done. I hung up on him and refused to answer his return calls." Jimmy felt angry but then heard Evangeline laughing.

"What does he think he can do? Have me arrested?" Then she told him, "I told Harry and he called Pendegrass and told him that his Aunt Wanda and his sister were ladies and he'd better control his potty mouth if he wanted to hear anything directly from them. Harry says he's foaming at the mouth for direct communication."

Jimmy said, "No way. I've got enough to worry about without having him on my back."

Jimmy hung up, somehow feeling a lot better and went back down to the cabin. His fancy smart phone wanted his attention and there were messages on his personal phone as well. They were all from Gramps. When Jimmy called him, he jumped all over him for not answering his phone. Then demanded, "Where the Hell were you?"

Jimmy said calmly, "I went to the outhouse. Then, it's such a lovely clear night, I was looking at the stars. Then, I started praying. I guess I didn't realize how long I was out there."

"Praying?" Gramps voice was incredulous.

Jimmy's mind scrambled around thinking what was he supposed to say but couldn't think of anything.

After a long silence, Gramps went on, "I'll talk to you tomorrow morning at the office."

Jimmy reflected on how he felt like a stranger here, a stranger in a very strange land.

Chapter 7: Decision Time

The next morning, Jimmy was up early after a restless night. He was at the office before 8 and found Lisa Marie on duty. When he asked after Myrna, Lisa Marie said she was under the weather. "Dad's waiting for you in his office." She was looking at him rather intently and he wondered if Gramps was going to fire him.

Jimmy went in and closed the door but remained standing. Gramps looked at him and motioned, "Sit, boy. Sit." Then he asked, "What's this praying business?"

Jimmy shrugged. "I pray sometimes."

"But you still want in on this drug business?" he asked.

Jimmy shrugged. "I don't see a problem. Like I said, some people want them and you can't stop them. They're going to buy regardless. I can't stop them." Jimmy paused and then said, "If you think our arrangement isn't going to work out, I can just quietly leave. I won't say anything."

"No, boy," the Gramps said. "I don't want you to leave. Frankly Bo John is a problem. He's using drugs, cocaine when he can get it and other stuff when he can't. I'm trying to shut off his supplies but it ain't easy. I tried to set up that Sunday barbecue because he's demanding to see you."

"Can you arrange for him to get arrested?" Jimmy asked.

The sheriff shook his head. "He knows too much. Before I realized he was a drug addict, I told him too much about our business. I tried to help him get off the stuff he's using and he cut back some but he didn't quit and he's slowly built back up. My cleaning lady will only go out there when I'm going to be there."

Jimmy looked at the old man and found himself feeling sorry for him. His only son was a hopeless drug addict. He knew it was justice but he still felt sorry for him.

In an effort to give some kind of comfort, Jimmy said, "You've got your two daughters."

The sheriff said, "Like Hell. They're only here for the money. They're both banking it off-shore. In a few years when I'm too old for this, they'll follow their money."

Jimmy said, "So you want me to stay around and take care of you when you're old?"

The sheriff looked at him and snorted, "Boy, you look like a lot better bet than the rest of what I've produced."

There was a knock on the door and Lisa Marie stuck her head in, "Clarence is here waiting for Jimmy."

Clarence had been up all night dealing with a runaway teenager and he gave Jimmy a rundown before he went home to sleep. It was another incident which probably would never appear in the official records. For the first time, Jimmy was on duty alone. He dealt with one minor accident in front of the hardware store and a kid stealing candy at Swandale's Grocery. Lisa Marie called and had him shadow one strange car. He followed it to a house and sat watching it until Lisa Marie called again and told him it was one of the house owner's relatives from Memphis come to visit. He spent the rest of the day drifting around, getting to know the roads, the traffic patterns.

When he handed over to Marvin that afternoon, he said to Sheriff Gramps, "You should be banking money off-shore too. Pick your own paradise. Retire to Barbados or somewhere else where living is cheap and the weather is nice. Marry a local woman who'll look after you."

Sheriff Gramps laughed. "Boy, you do get ideas, don't you?"

Then Gramps said, "Tomorrow morning be up and ready to learn something by 8 o'clock. I'm sending you a teacher."

That evening, Jimmy carried his smart phone up the mountain trail. He left it on a rock and moved far enough away that he could hear it ring but too far for it to be used to pick up what he was saying. Jimmy had some suspicions about that fancy phone.

Before he left his cabin, he had briefly called Grandma and Evangeline on his personal cell phone. Grandma had been a "How are you doing?" call. He and Evangeline had been soppy, saying how much they missed each other, just in case anyone was listening.

Here away from the cabin, he used the secret Tracfone and talked to Evangeline for an hour before calling Grandma and Harry briefly. He had taken to calling them every night. It made him feel anchored, orientated, knowing who he was, feeling like he had his head on straight rather than being an odd animal in a bazaar zoo.

The next morning at 2 minutes to 8, a woman showed up who only gave her name as Sally. She was mid to late 30's, maybe 40, and her hair was blonde but with her brown eyes and skin that tanned, she looked like a Jones. Once it occurred to Jimmy that her blonde hair came out of a box, then he was fairly sure.

She was all business. Even though they worked together for the next two days, she never chit-chatted. She had a smart phone and she was on it a lot. If it rang while they were busy, she ignored it but then later walked away to make calls. He heard parts of some calls including one in which he heard her say she was in Nashville. She also did a lot of texting.

She had arrived in a box truck full of equipment and boxes. The equipment all went into the loft of the old barn where someone had stored some old furniture as well as a lot of bales of hay. Jimmy decided the hay could be arranged to hide the equipment. There was a rickety looking old ladder but the loft had outside doors with an old rusty pulley arrangement for dealing with hay. Sally produced suitable rope and they used the pulley to move the equipment and some boxes to the loft. There was also a cellar whose entrance was nicely concealed. Sally said it could be used to store supplies and that's where they put the new rope and more boxes. If the lab was found but with no supplies, Jimmy could deny knowledge of its existence.

He made notes as they went along. She told him, "Writing stuff down is dangerous." He showed her his notes and she laughed. Between his omission of key words and his use of personal abbreviations, his notes were useless to anyone but him. "Uncle Johnny said you were smart," she commented.

They worked all day on a large batch of the stuff with the doors open for ventilation but she also produced masks for them to wear. She had brought a sleeping bag and slept in the barn that night. At the end of the second day, she left with the results of their work weighed and packaged, ready for market. The process also produced waste and she had a container for it as well. It was toxic and he wondered where she was disposing of it but didn't ask.

As he helped her pack up, she said, "You've caught on faster than anyone I've ever taught before. You've got brains and you don't act like a user. Why are you doing this?"

He smiled at her. "Money," he said.

They discussed delivery of supplies and product. He discovered her husband was a veterinarian. She helped him but had two children and he had other help. She warned him that her husband had no idea what was going on and it had better stay that way. He asked her why she was doing this.

She smiled and said, "Money." He had to laugh.

She promised him a cat for his mouse infested cabin.

After that, he generally worked four days a week as a deputy, usually 10 to 12 hours, and cooked methamphetamine the other three days. He tried to make church at least once a week. When Gramps noticed it, he asked about it. Jimmy said, "A clean image is good and I enjoy it."

"Enjoy it?" Gramps said.

"Sure," Jimmy said. "Music. People. Ideas. I like it. Of course, you usually go to that church in the middle of town. Try the one I'm attending. It's a lot more lively."

"Roll in the isles and jabber nonsense, do they? Not my idea of church," Gramps said.

But Gramps started scheduling him so that he often could attend church Sunday mornings. Jimmy usually ate Sunday lunch at Gina's cafe where Gramps frequently joined him.

Jimmy stored away his supplies in the cleverly concealed cellar when he was not making meth. It was work putting stuff away but it was wise. He also worked out an arrangement up in the loft so that someone climbing up for a casual look would not see anything suspicious. There was even a broken board in the floor of the loft near where he placed the ladder which would discourage exploration. It was necessary to move the ladder to a different location to reach his lab.

One day when Jimmy met Sally somewhere to get supplies, she said, "Your grandfather had me go out to your place when you weren't home to check it out. If I had not known what goes on out there, I would have never suspected anything. You're good," Sally told him, "the best we've ever had."

Jimmy filed away in his mind her allegation that Gramps had sent her out to look. He doubted that very much. He suspected that Sally might be one of those people who often attribute their own motives to other people.

Jimmy had passed the information up the pipeline to Pendegrass that he was cooking meth but he still knew nothing about how they got supplies in unless Sally was doing it. And how was it getting to customers? After his scouting visit, Jimmy had told Pendegrass about the tomato operation and suggested maybe stuff was going in and out with the tomatoes but Pendegrass had said they had inspected trucks repeatedly using dogs. They had never found anything.

Jimmy had decided he would not ask questions but just wait for information to float his way. That had been Grandma's idea. She said nothing gave a spy away like wanting to know everything. Grandma was smart. After several weeks, Gramps said to him, "Jimmy boy, you've never asked how we get supplies, how we find customers, or how we get stuff out to our buyers."

Jimmy shrugged. "I'm making money and I figured when I need to know, you'll tell me." He looked Gramps in the eye and said, "Or maybe you won't, because you hope to keep me here forever."

Gramps had looked startled. "Crickets, boy, every time I begin to think you may be playing games with us, you come up with a zinger like that. I know if you were planning to double-cross us, you'd never say this kind of thing."

Jimmy laughed. "Gramps, I'm too far in this to double-cross you now. I'm making money a lot faster than I expected." Then he said, "Can I get a couple of days off to meet my girl in Nashville?" Jimmy wanted to pass over detailed notes, money, and photos. He also felt strongly that he needed a break from Grand County.

At first, he planned to meet Harry but they decided if would be safer if he met Evangeline. In the interest of lying as little as possible, and knowing that Gramps might be spying on him, Jimmy met Evangeline in Nashville where they booked a motel room, making sure it had two beds. Jimmy left his smart phone at home but took his personal phone for which Gramps had the number. When he chided Jimmy for not taking the smart phone, Jimmy said that he didn't think he needed it since he could not be called in for duty and he was afraid it would get stolen in Nashville.

On the way to Nashville, Jimmy did some thinking. He could just not go back. He could name Sally and testify against her. He knew Gramps was protecting her. He had money for evidence and he could tell them where to find the meth lab. He knew Pendegrass would want a lot more but did that really matter? Sally could say he was lying and how could he prove otherwise? Gramps would probably go to jail and Sally get off with probation on a plea bargain if she would implicate Gramps. It was decision time. Settle for what he had or go on with the investigation?

In spite of his indecision, Jimmy had a great time with Evangeline.

They went to the Grand Ole Opry and saw all the sights. They walked hand in hand and Jimmy had his arm around Evangeline more often than not. Only once they were in their room, he never touched her.

They discussed his problem. Jimmy reluctantly decided that he needed more evidence on Sally.

Jimmy gave Evangeline the money he had accumulated along with a list of serial numbers. They made copies. Jimmy passed over notes and a card from a small digital camera with a lot of photos Jimmy had made but he told Evangeline not to pass them on to Pendegrass yet. He told Evangeline to rent a large safety deposit box at the bank when she got home and keep them there.

Jimmy told her, "Rent that box and we'll talk about it on the phone as where you are putting the money. You need to go through all the motions as though you're being watched."

"Jimmy, you're paranoid," Evangeline said.

"Maybe," he answered, "but someone who tracks every single vehicle going in and out of his county is paranoid and I need to be just as careful or he'll catch me."

Jimmy had talked about the traffic cameras before and now Evangeline laughed, but agreed that they should take every precaution.

Jimmy had told Grandma, Harry, and Evangeline not to tell Pendegrass he was meeting Eva in Nashville. They wanted to find out if Pendegrass was spying on them.

Jimmy returned to Big Creek feeling refreshed and happy. Myrna noticed. She said, "Jimmy Joe, you looked pleased with yourself. You had fun with your girl."

Jimmy gave her a wide grin and just said, "Yes."

She shook her head and said, "No details?"

"No details," he agreed and went on duty still grinning.

Chapter 8: Stupidity

Gramps had made no further effort to get Bo John and Jimmy together. However, Jimmy was not surprised when Bo John walked into Gina's Cafe on Sunday while he was eating. Bo John walked over to Jimmy's table and sat down. Jimmy felt a violent physical reaction and stopped eating as soon as he saw Bo John. He knew he could never eat with Bo John there so he put his fork down and waited.

After a silence, in which Jimmy realized that everyone in the place was watching them, Bo John said, "Aren't you even going to say hello?"

Jimmy said, "No."

Bo John said, "You're my son. Can't I even eat a meal with you?"

Jimmy said, "No."

A waitress brought coffee and a menu. Bo John said, "Bring me the pork chop plate."

"Well, boy," Bo John said, "Eat."

Jimmy was swamped by a memory. He was 5 years old again and Bo John was yelling at him to eat and he was refusing. Jimmy tossed money on the table and stood up, saying, "I'm not 5 years old any more," and turned and walked out of the cafe. He heard Bo John coming behind him. It reminded him of playing basketball but then knew this was more like football. At the right moment, he turned and drove his fist into Bo John's face. Bo John fell against a car and slid to the ground. Jimmy looked down at his bloody nose and then turned and walked to his truck. As he pulled out of the parking lot, he saw a knot of people gathering around Bo John.

He was not on duty at all that Sunday and stopped at Swandale's to buy a few supplies and ice before heading home. He drove with his right hand in the bag of ice.

He reported for duty the next day with his hand bruised but usable. It was Lisa Marie on duty and she greeted him with, "Well, you got the whole county talking. Myrna thinks we should give you a reward."

Jimmy smiled at her. With their age difference being only about two years, he didn't call her aunt and she treated him more like a brother than a nephew. She was divorced and looking for another husband but had privately said, "None of this cousin stuff for me."

She had thought him calling the sheriff Gramps was cute and now she indicated his mood by saying, "His Grumps wants to see you before you go on duty."

Jimmy went into the sheriff's private office with no idea what Gramps was going to say. What he did say was, "Boy, laying Bo John out like that was stupid."

Jimmy just shrugged and said, "Was it?"

"You don't understand. Now you need to watch your back."

Jimmy looked at Gramps and knew he was right. "You're afraid of what Bo John may do."

Gramps hesitated but then admitted, "He's mean when he's on a toot. He may come after you."

"I'll keep my eyes open," Jimmy said.

The next afternoon, Myrna called him back to the office. She said, "We've got a stranger over at the Starlight and Gramps says he's a Fed. Recognizes him."

Jimmy looked at the screens. The car was a rental but still the type favored by Feds. Myrna pushed buttons and the driver's picture appeared. It was Pendegrass. Jimmy felt a wave of dismay. He knew he had re-acted and was glad he was looking over Myrna's shoulder and she could not see him. "I think Gramps is right," he said.

"I've called the Starlight and told them to call when he leaves his room. We'll bug it," Myrna said. "Dad was waiting for you to get here. Take your truck and park where you can watch the Starlight. Be ready to move in if Dad wants you."

Jimmy went out to his truck. He did not have time to set up a safe place to use the Tracfone. He parked down the street from the Starlight and used his personal phone to call Grandma. "Hey, Gran," he said, "I'm on surveillance. It's boring. How you doing?"

"Boring subject," she answered. In the code they had worked up, *boring* meant a problem.

"Grandma, you were right about that cat I got. He don't know a mouse trap when he sees it. Stuck his foot right in it." When they had made that code, some things they had not anticipated. Mention of a *mouse trap* meant he thought they had guessed and were setting a trap. "I may have to hang up any time. This surveillance is a stranger, middle-aged man, looks suspicious. Gramps thinks he recognizes him from some deal way back. Nobody knows what he's doing here in Big Creek. When you get a chance, call you-know-who and tell her I love her. I gotta go."

He hung up and hoped Grandma got it. *Call you-know-who* meant call Pendegrass. He was hoping that a middle-aged stranger would remind Grandma of Pendegrass himself.

After a few minutes, Jimmy saw Pendegrass come out of his room and put his suitcase back in the trunk of his car. As he started to leave the parking lot of the Starlight, he found the sheriff's vehicle blocking his path. Jimmy's smart phone rang and Myrna said, "Dad wants you to join him."

He pulled his truck around and parked behind Pendegrass. Gramps climbed out of his car, so Jimmy climbed out to join him.

Gramps walked right up to the car and Pendegrass put down his window. Gramps said, "Well, fancy this. What was your name? Pendragon or something like that? What brings you back in our neck of the woods again? You think we got a drug problem?"

Jimmy's mind was spinning but he tried to keep a blank face. Gramps had definitely recognized Pendegrass. His heart sank down to the soles of his feet and was looking for a place to run. He found himself automatically putting his hand on his weapon. This might be it. The end. If Gramps was onto him, there was no way he could get out of the county without getting caught or resorting to violence.

Pendegrass said, "Good afternoon, Sheriff. Have I met you before? I'm sorry I don't remember."

Gramps said, "Well, now, that's too bad. It's normal procedure for Feds to check with us local law enforcement before coming in. Just barging in like this is rude."

"I'm sorry," Pendegrass said. "I made a mistake. I just called in and I'm in the wrong town. I'm suppose to be in Big Spring, not Big Creek. I did call ahead and now I'm not where I was expected." Pendegrass was so nervous, he was almost stuttering.

"Well, we won't keep you. You've got a long drive and no dragon to fly you there," the sheriff was almost laughing.

Gramps went into the Starlight office and Jimmy followed him. Mrs. Grafton said, "Well, that was interesting. I knew something was wrong about him. He said he was a pharmaceutical salesman. We only got the one small clinic with two doctors and the only pharmacy. Why would he need to stay overnight?"

"Well, whatever he was doing, he's gone now," Gramps said. "I thought we'd check and make sure he didn't leave anything behind."

Jimmy followed Gramps back to the Sheriff's Office, trying not to shake. He knew Gramps might be on to him. What would he do?

But Gramps was laughing. "I can't believe he thought we wouldn't recognize him. He's gone gray but he still wears the same hairstyle and the same suit."

Gramps hung at the office watching until they saw Pendegrass leave the county. He was speeding. Gramps called the next county and told them what highway he was on.

Then he said, "Myrna, who's new in the area? That guy wouldn't be here unless they've sent in a undercover." Jimmy was almost paralyzed. He wanted to talk about something to distract Gramps and Myrna but was afraid his nervousness would show.

They made a list. They had one new teacher from out of the area. She was just out of college and talked constantly about her upcoming wedding. Her fiancé had already applied to teach here next year. "We try to hire local. I'll check on them some more but I don't think it's her," Myrna said. The one manufacturing plant in the county where they made lawn mowers had gotten a new accountant from out of the area about three months back. Myrna said, "I've heard he's already trying to get another job. His wife and kids hate it here." Some guy named Jack Fowler had married a woman from out of the area. "Do you think the Feds would go that far?" Myrna asked. "Jack's dumber than a box of rocks so it wouldn't be hard for a woman to get him to marry her."

Gramps had laughed and said, "They're living with his family and they're all thicker than two planks and poorer than Job's turkey. Let's check her out. She must have some reason for staying."

Myrna made a phone call and then reported. "She pregnant, very pregnant. Jack's mother did some math and called their preacher to the house and was ranting and raving about them fornicating. Not even the Feds would go that far."

Myrna told them that was all the recent newcomers.

Jimmy could not believe the county had so few new residents. He was trying to think of some way to widen the pool. He said, "What about returning college students like Rose? I know it's not her but are there others? The Feds could recruit someone who's already local."

Myrna said, "College students is a good idea. They're young and the adventure of being an undercover agent would appeal to them. If they want a future career in law enforcement, it would be a wonderful opportunity. But we don't have that many kids here who go to college." She was making a list, starting with Rose.

Jimmy's heart was pounding but he said it anyway. "What about me? I'm a newcomer." It had crossed his mind that they had already thought of it but just hadn't said it out-loud.

The look Myrna gave him showed that she had thought of it. But

Gramps snorted. "Boy, if you's going to play undercover agent, you'd have let Felicity lead you to the marijuana and you'd have cozied up to your dad and found out where he's getting his stuff. You also would have been asking a lot more questions than you have and doing a lot more prowling around. I've watched undercover agents at work and you aren't one."

Jimmy felt the tight band around his chest relaxing but he told himself he wasn't out of the woods yet. Pendegrass may have done something really stupid that would come to light or be remembered later.

He hung at the office while Myrna checked on a couple of possibilities. He was watching for signals that they wanted him to leave but he wasn't seeing any. After a couple of hours, they reviewed their findings. The best possibility was a young man named Jason Howard who had left college after three years and was working at the lawn mower plant. He was studying engineering. He had said he was going to work a year and go back and finish. They sent Jimmy with a bug to put in his truck and were going to put Lisa Marie up to dating him. She would get bugs into the house where he lived with his parents and three younger siblings. His father was a Jones relation so he might know something about the marijuana, although he had a reputation of being uninterested in it. That upped Jason's score as a possible snitch.

Jimmy considered trying to make a quick phone call while he was out on his errand but decided to wait. He knew Grandma would be extremely worried but to call, he would have to move away from his truck and if he did that, it might be noticed. He had tried to check and had found what he thought were bugs in his truck, his cabin, the barn, even the pit toilet but had continued to act like he didn't know.

When Jimmy returned to the office, Gramps and Myrna were still at it, like a dog worrying a bone. They had another suspect. A local girl named Juliet Harris had finished two years at a community college and been hired last year at the high school as a teacher's aide. Last year, she had wanted to organize a lot of anti-drug education and had had a few seminars. This year, she had not said much about it and they wondered if she had a reason. She rented a small apartment over a relative's garage near the school. They would get bugs in place.

Gramps commented. "Used to be easier. Everybody had a phone that was a land line. Their phone would quit and we'd send in a repairman. Bugs in the phone and a few other places. Simple. Now lots of people have gone to cell phones so we have to think of something else."

Jimmy was eventually sent out on patrol only because someone called in an accident. Old Man Crawford was drunk again and had scraped another pickup truck in the parking lot of the Robber's Roost. The people at the Robber's Roost said, "Don't blame us. He was arriving, not leaving."

Jimmy reflected that Grand County wouldn't be a bad place to live if it weren't for the drug industry and the lack of work. Maybe there was a correlation between the two.

What with dealing with the angry truck owner, Old Man Crawford and his family, and another discussion about who could be their stool pigeon, Jimmy was late getting off duty. On his way home, he called Grandma on his personal phone. She would know it was a public conversation. Jimmy said, "Grandma, you doing okay?"

"Yes, Honey," she said, "and you."

"Busy day but I'm on my way home. I'll call you later."

At home, he called her again while he started putting supper together. He just chatted casually about Old Man Crawford. He asked her about people at home and they got off. He ate and headed out to the toilet. Up the path behind the toilet, he laid his official phones on a rock and went on up the path.

He called Grandma on the Trackfone and said, "Grandma, I assume you called Pendegrass."

"I did. What was it all about?"

"First, tell me what you told him," Jimmy said.

"I told him that you had just called and said to call him. I said I knew you were having to be careful what you said because you could be over-heard but it was something about a problem, a trap, and a middle-aged man. Was that right?"

"Grandma, you're a genius!" Jimmy said. "That was exactly right. If you weren't such a nice lady, I'd tell you to call that so-n-so and cuss him out good. He is dumb beyond belief."

"What'd he do?" Grandma asked.

"He showed up here in Big Creek. I told you about the traffic cameras. Gramps recognized him from one of the previous incidents. He's gone now but they decided he was here because he's got another undercover agent in place. They're busy trying to figure out who it is."

"Jimmy, come home," Grandma said. "It isn't worth you getting killed."

"Gramps is sure it's not me," Jimmy told her. "They are focusing on a couple of other people. So unless Pendegrass did something totally stupid that I haven't found out about yet, I'm okay."

"What could he have done?" Grandma asked.

"Asked someone where to find me," Jimmy said. "I really couldn't think of anything else. But he is so stupid, the motel people were already wondering what he was up to and he had only just checked in. He hadn't even had time to unpack. He told them he was in pharmaceuticals and Big Creek only has two doctors, a married couple, and their clinic has the only pharmacy. No pharmaceutical salesman would stay overnight here."

"Well, I'll call the bozo and ream him out," Grandma said. "Call Evangeline. She's been praying ever since I let her know something was wrong." Jimmy hung up thinking how his team was also his prayer support. He told God how grateful he was.

Jimmy called Evangeline. Harry was there. They discussed the incident and Harry said he was calling Pendegrass and giving him heck. "After all he's said about security, he does something this stupid? No wonder this country has such a drug problem with idiots like him in charge of dealing with it!"

Harry went off somewhere to call Pendegrass and Jimmy and Evangeline chatted a few more minutes. Evangeline said, "Jimmy, I had no idea how nerve racking this would be."

"I know," Jimmy said. "I didn't either."

Jimmy called Grandma back and she said, "Pendegrass swears he didn't ask anyone where to find you. I hope he's telling the truth. I told him what a stupid idea saying he was a pharmaceutical salesman was. The man makes me mad enough to cuss. He kept trying to convince me I was overreacting!"

Jimmy called Harry again. Harry told him that Pendegrass did make him mad enough to cuss. Harry said, "When this is all over, I'm going to find out who his boss is and I'm going to tell him just what a dumb ass he's got working for him."

Jimmy knew Harry normally didn't used that kind of language. He was mad, really, really mad.

Grandma had suggested a new addition to their code list. If Pendegrass ever did anything so stupid again, Jimmy was to talk about a cat going potty in inappropriate places. Grandma said if his cat was a male and not fixed, he would mark his territory with urine.

Jimmy laughed and said, "I think I need to get another cat. It's a male and it has been fixed and it's hopeless as a mouser. I saw a mouse and tried to get him to chase it and he kept trying to get me to pet him. Whenever I come home, he's all over me wanting to be fed."

The next morning, Jimmy was not on duty and was planning to play cook but he called into the office at 8, just to check. Myrna said, "Everything is quiet. You can stay home and get something done out there."

Jimmy ducked up the path and called Harry on the Tracfone. Harry said, "I think we've arrived at an understanding with Pendegrass. Aunt Wanda's dressing down did more to get through to him than my ranting at him. I think it's all those years in the classroom. He was talking down to her and you don't do that to Aunt Wanda. He's promised he'll behave himself. I hope he keeps his word.

❀ ❀ ❀
Chapter 9: Robby Lee

Jimmy sat up his equipment and started cooking. He had asked for more equipment, had fallen into a rhythm with it, and could turn out quite a lot of product in a two or three day stretch. But in the middle of the afternoon, the buzzer sounded that signaled a vehicle coming in. No one had called.

By the time Robby Lee pulled up to the cabin, Jimmy had things under control and was pouring himself a glass of iced tea. Robby Lee got out of his truck and looked around. "If'n I didn't know better, I'd think nothin' ever happened out here."

"Not much," Jimmy said. "To what do I owe the honor of your visit?"

Robby Lee said, "Ain't cha gonna offer me a drink?"

"I didn't figure you for an iced tea man."

"Beer," Robby Lee said. "Right outa da bottle's fine."

"No beer," Jimmy said. "Iced tea or coffee. Glass of milk if you're really in the mood for it."

"Dang," Robby Lee said, "if I hadn't heard how ya laid out Bo John, I'd take ya fer a pansy."

"My grandma grew pansies," Jimmy replied, smiling. "Hardy things. Don't mind cold. I've seen them bloom with snow on the ground."

RobbyLee spit and then laughed "I'll take iced tea."

When Jimmy came back out, Robby was coming out of the barn. "Nothin' showin'," he said. "You're good. Uncle Johnny said ta lay off you. He said the story 'bout the girl in Missouri's true. Said if'n I wanted Rose, I oughta take lessons from you."

Jimmy handed him his iced tea and they sat in the rockers on the porch. Tommy, the orange striped non-mouser, jumped up into Robby Lee's lap and to Jimmy's surprise, Robby Lee started casually rubbing the cat's ears. "You just come out here to be friendly?" Jimmy asked.

"No," Robby Lee said. "Grandpa tole me ta come check ya out. He says Uncle Johnny's talkin' 'bout ya like da sun shines outa yer arse."

Jimmy shook his head. "If I was really a nice person, would I be doing what I'm doing?"

"I reckon not," Robby Lee said, "but cha sure know how ta keep Uncle Johnny happy. If Bo John ain't careful, Uncle Johnny's gonna let him lose his parole."

"I asked Gramps about that and he said Bo John knows too much about the business."

"Shit," Robby Lee said. "I like my beer but dat other stuff is fer morons. Somebody oughta shot Bo John years ago."

"Yeah," Jimmy said. "When he turned up out there in Bakersfield, my mother should have shot him instead of calling the police."

"I hear'd Uncle Johnny talkin' ta Grandpa 'bout Bo John shootin' your ma. Uncle Johnny said 'at he got aholt a da police reports 'n' what you tolt him was how it was. Said he understood why dat woman grabbed ya 'n' run. He said Bo John lied to 'im about what happened."

"If Bo John got out on bail, why didn't he run?" Jimmy asked.

"Da bail was a huge amount a money. Uncle Johnny put up everything he had er could borrow. He got some a da rest a da fam'ly ta help 'im too. I don't know what Bo John done but my Grandpa 'uz real mad at 'im 'n' wuddn't help wid 'is bail. If he'd a jumped bail, Grandpa wudda helped go after 'im. When Bo John was comin' home, Grandpa tolt Uncle Johnny dat if Bo John gave any trouble now, he's gonna shoot 'im hisself. Uncle Johnny said dat he's tryin' his best ta keep Bo John away from Myrna. He say anything like dat ta you?"

"No," Jimmy said, "but I know Aunt Myrna don't like Bo John."

Robby shook his head. "Well, dere's never been any love lost atween 'em. Der mother was Aunt Jody. Her folks lived up Lexin'ton way in Kentucky. Tall red-head but green eyes, not brown like us. Dey say she was a real looker and her family had money 'n' she was gonna git it – only child. Da family says she wert snooty, lookin' down her nose at us. What I been tole is Myrna 'uz her favorite 'n' Uncle Johnny favored Bo John. Dey tell me she useta take Myrna 'n' go visit her family all da time. Dey say Uncle Johnny couldn't afford ta divorce her 'n' she didn't want da scandal. Den when Bo John 'n' Myrna 'uz teenagers, Aunt Jody got pregnant with Lisa Marie 'n' everybody thought it weren't Uncle Johnny's kid. She took Myrna 'n' stayed 'bout da whole time wid her family. Everybody 'spected a divorce but when da baby 'uz born, it shore looked like a Jones. I hear'd some mention a DNA tests. Musta been Uncle Johnny's kid 'cause dey didn't divorce. And you 'n' Lisa Marie 'n' me could all be twins.

"After Lisa Marie 'uz born, Myrna 'uz sent off ta a fancy boardin' school. Aunt Jody 'ad a nanny ta take care a da baby 'n' she was always goin' up ta see her folks. Den Aunt Jody drowned. Nobody talks 'bout it much. Somethin' about bein' out fishin' which I cain't imagine but I was real little when it happened. Bo John was there 'n' Uncle Johnny but Myrna was off at school when it happened. Aunt Jody's folks raised Lisa Marie. They's gone now but it turned out dey both got cancer 'n' spent all der money on doctors." Robby Lee paused and then said, "Life's a shit sometimes."

Jimmy commented, "Who was it that said nothing is certain but death and taxes?"

Robby Lee laughed. "Whoever it was had it right."

Jimmy asked Robby Lee if he wanted more tea. After a trip to the little house out back, Robby Lee said, "I been thinkin' 'bout somethin'." He looked at Jimmy like he was trying to x-ray him. Jimmy just waited. "You 'n' me look so much alike, I thought we might have some fun with it."

"What kind of fun?" Jimmy asked.

"Well, I thought you could ask Rose ta da movies or ta pick her up from work er somethin'. Den I shave my beard. She'd be in da car wid me afore she know'd it weren't you."

Jimmy shook his head. "I'm not playing tricks on Rose."

"Oh, come on," Robby begged. "If she got ta know me a little, she'd like me. I'm real good wid da women. Dey all likes me."

Jimmy shook his head. "Sorry, but you're on your own."

Robby Lee shook his head. "Felicity said you's a wet fire-cracker."

Jimmy laughed. "Yeah, she told me."

"I like having fun," Robby Lee said. He looked at Jimmy and grinned. "Providin' distractions is fun."

"Distractions?" Jimmy asked.

"Sure," Robby said, still grinning. "When somethin' is a goin' on we don't want saw, dere's nothin' like a good distraction. Like a magician. Dat's what dey does. Dey gets ya lookin' at somethin' so's you don't see what dey's really doin'."

Jimmy grinned. "Now that sounds like it might be fun. Give me an example. It can be theoretical if you like."

"I don't know no the'reticals but here's how it works. When we's a movin' somethin' we don't want saw, we sends an escort. If da law decides ta stop da vehicle fer some reason, da driver calls 'n' da escort does a distraction. Of course da driver tries not ta get pulled over fer nothin' but sometimes dem cops are bored 'n' invent reasons. We's only had it happen a couple a times but when Grandpa sends a big shipment, we's ready. One time I went flying by doing about a hundred miles an hour. Law never caught me. Another time, the driver called afore the law pulled 'em over so I passed 'em honkin' my horn 'n' flipped off dat officer. I ducked off da road 'n' hid but that smokey was good. Found me. I tolt him I wuddn' flippin' him off but 'uz aimin' at da driver a da vehicle he's a followin', dat he's my cousin 'n' he swiped my girl 'n' I's mad at 'im. He wrote me a ticket fer disturbin' da peace. How's flippin' somebody off disturbin' da peace? We's thought of a couple more now. I got a cousin, Coop we calls him, 'at fell offa da porch when he's a little tyke 'n' got ep'lepsy. Sometimes we carry's him along. If we gets another situation, we pulls over 'n' calls 911 'n' say he's a havin' a real bad fit. He can fake it real good 'n' dere's a doctor ta back us up. 'Nother one is ta run a car in da ditch 'n' call 911 'n' say you's hurt your back. Nobody can tell 'bout a back. Dose kind a calls ta 911 'll pull a officer offa stopping a vehicle."

Jimmy laughed and said, "It sounds like fun. This cooking the stuff is boring but somebody's got to do it."

Robby Lee said, "Better you dan me. Tricky business, cookin'. Gota get everything just right."

Jimmy said, "Yeah, not a job to tackle buzzed."

"Ya sure ya won't help me wid Rose? She sure is a looker. She was looking good at 14 'n' now she's a knockout. She seems ta like you okay. How come?"

"Maybe because I'm not after her. I don't think she likes being pursued. Scares her. I really don't think she's your type," Jimmy said.

"I tried goin' ta church but da preacher come 'n' talked ta me. He said I weren't allowed ta sit by Rose. And I had ta quit cussing in church. He said otherwise, I's welcome. Well, if'n I cain't sit by Rose, what's da point a goin'?

Jimmy remembered what Grandma had said about marriage. He said to Robby Lee, "You know getting married is like getting into a small boat with someone. If you work together, you can get somewhere. But if the two of you are paddling in different directions, it doesn't work very well. You don't get anywhere and if you get to fighting, you turn the boat over."

"Dat's so. But I ain't getting' in no boat wid Rose. I don't wanna marry her, just take her fer a roll in da hay."

Jimmy shook his head. "There's your problem. Rose isn't the type for a roll in the hay."

"Why not? I'm good. Dey all tells me so."

Jimmy realized that Robby had no concept of abstinence. He didn't give Jimmy the willies like Bo John did, but he was rather like Tommy, pleasant enough but with no boundaries, no morals, a nuisance, just doing what felt good.

Jimmy decided it might be time for a change in subject. Maybe he could learn something. He said, "When you were talking about Gramps and his . . . well, I guess she was my grandmother, it sounded to me like they were paddling in different directions."

Robby Lee laughed. "Dey sure was!" he said.

"So what do you want out of life? What direction do you want to paddle your boat in?" Jimmy asked.

"Drivin' a truck's okay," Robby Lee said. "I ain't wantin' ta settle down. Enjoy life, dat's my d'rection. So what's yourn?"

Jimmy smiled. "I want to buy a piece of land in Missouri. I need money to do that. Then, I'll marry my girl and raise some kids."

"Dat's a drag, man, a real bore."

"To each his own," Jimmy said. "You drive trucks and provide distractions. I cook."

Robby Lee shook his head. "Ya know, Jimmy Joe, I's really out here ta see how I could arrange a accident but I reckon I don't need one." He suddenly gave Jimmy a piercing look. "Course, ya might be lyin'. Pro'bly shouldn't a warned ja."

After Robby Lee was gone, Jimmy went back to his interrupted job in the barn. He was turning over in his mind what Robby Lee had told him about Gramps and Bo John. So Gramps had believed Bo John's lies back then but he didn't now.

And Gramps brother, Bobby Ray, had threatened to shoot Bo John. Jimmy wondered why.

And Myrna's feelings for her brother were a deep, dark pool of abiding aversion.

It was a real cozy family.

Jimmy was aware again of feeling like an alien here. He thought of his family in Missouri and started praying as he worked.

Chapter 10: Lisa Marie and Myrna

At the office, Jimmy had gotten acquainted with both Myrna and Lisa Marie. Myrna was moody, often morose, and generally very busy. She was the one leading the search for their undercover agent. She monitored the comings and goings from the county and what was coming in on the bugs. She tracked gossip and she handled the money. She treated Lisa Marie more like a daughter than a sister. Given the gap between their ages and that their mother had died when Lisa Marie was so young, it was understandable.

Somewhere along the way, Jimmy learned that Lisa Marie played the piano but Jimmy said nothing about his own musical ability. He had decided it would be a distraction to the operation, so he kept quiet.

Jimmy knew that Myrna disliked her brother, Bo John, intensely and she loved Lisa Marie. But he really felt like he knew very little about her personal feelings otherwise. After Gramps' comment about the girls both leaving, Jimmy had watched. Myrna was businesslike with her father but there were no signs of affection.

Lisa Marie had initially clearly regarded him with caution but had then relaxed. She was much more open than Myrna. She chatted. She treated her father like a lot of people treated their dogs, vaguely affectionate but not as an authority figure. Once that idea crossed Jimmy's mind, he realized that even with stuff related to their work, it was mostly Myrna telling Gramps and Lisa Marie what to do. In fact, Gramps seemed not to spend that much time with either of his daughters. As the two women lived in Gramps' place in town, it took Jimmy a while to realize it. Gramps did sleep there at times but he seemed to take most of his meals at Gina's Cafe and he often went out to his country place where Bo John lived.

One evening when he was still on duty, Lisa Marie sent him out to a farm where they had just discovered a theft. He took the report. It looked like the main objective had been stuff that could be sold as scrap metal. The farmer said, "How come Johnny didn't come out here. He'll know who took the stuff."

Jimmy called Lisa Marie and she said to tell the farmer that her dad would be consulted. When he dropped his report back to the office, Lisa Marie said, "I've identified our thieves. They took the stuff out of the county to sell it."

Jimmy had nodded. "Shall I go arrest them?"

"No," Lisa Marie told him. "Dad likes to do all the arrests for thievery. It puts him in a good light with the voters. I'd call him tonight but he's got that Barbara out at the ranch.'

"Barbara?" Jimmy asked.

"Dad has a whole string of women," Lisa Marie said casually. "He always takes them out to the ranch. I don't know why they put up with it. They all know there's others. I asked Myrna once and she said 'trading favors.' I asked what favors but she wouldn't tell me. Jimmy, you're smart. What do you think?"

"Drugs?" he asked.

"No," Lisa Marie was shaking her head. "I know it's not drugs. Dad keeps a real clean image, other than his women, and mostly people think that's funny."

"Money?" Jimmy suggested.

"Maybe gifts," Lisa Marie said. "at least some of them. But I don't think that's all of it."

"No parking tickets?" Jimmy grinned.

"Blackmail?" Lisa Marie suggested.

"Maybe he's just good in bed," Jimmy countered.

By then they were both laughing. Lisa Marie said, "Jimmy, I do really like you. Everybody else involved in what we're doing is more or less shady, but you don't seem that way and you joke about stuff. Nobody else does that."

"I'm finding it a little lonely. Myrna and Gramps never just talk. It's all business. Robby Lee came out to my place the other day but you're the only person I really talk to.'

"Robby Lee!" Lisa Marie exclaimed. "What in the world did he want?"

"Says his grandpa sent him out to check on me," Jimmy responded. "I couldn't figure out if his grandpa doesn't trust me or if he's just jealous because Gramps likes me."

Lisa Marie considered. "That's funny. Why shouldn't he trust you? And what's to be jealous about? You've been making us a lot of money – oh, I just realized. Uncle Bobby Ray is the marijuana side of things. Less risk but less money. Maybe he is jealous."

"You don't socialize with them much?"

"No," Lisa Marie shrugged. "I like him and Aunt Jeanna okay but they're . . . I don't know how to explain. We don't have much in common."

"What was your mom like?" Jimmy asked.

"I hardly remember her," Lisa Marie said. She paused and then said, "She was classy. Her family were old money – you know, rich and educated but quiet, not brassy. She played the piano, classical music and old ballads that she sang. I don't remember her ever playing anything else." She hesitated again. "After Mom died, I lived with Mom's parents so they are who I remember. I only started living here after my divorce. I married before I finished college. Mom's parents got sick. They hid it for a long time. I got a divorce and that's when I found out. I wanted to help take care of them but they didn't want me there." She shrugged. "They said they didn't want me to have to suffer along with them. But I wondered too if part of it was the divorce. They didn't like scandal of any kind. They didn't like the divorce but it was such a mistake. What else could I do? I was young and stupid and I married the guy without any of the family meeting him. Dad said I should of at least told him first and let him check on his background." She looked up at me and said, "The guy thought my family had money and he wanted on the gravy train."

Jimmy nodded. "A mistake. Who wants a lazy moocher?"

"What's your girl like, the one in Missouri?" Lisa Marie asked.

Jimmy smiled. When he thought of Evangeline, he couldn't help it. "I've known her since first grade. If I were really Jimmy Wilkerson, she'd be my second cousin. Her brother was a grade ahead of me in school and when I started, he played big brother and looked after me. Then, when Evangeline started, we both looked after her." He went on talking about Eva for several minutes and then it occurred to him that maybe that wasn't wise so he stopped.

Lisa Marie said, "I can tell by how you talk about her that you love her." He heard longing in her voice and he knew she wanted a man who loved her.

"There's a lot of good men out there, Lisa, but Big Creek is not that good of a place to look."

"That's what Myrna says," Lisa Marie responded. "She said the good ones here either marry young or leave the area."

Jimmy found himself thinking that was true of Ellsinore as well. "Have you thought about moving out of the area? You could get a job somewhere else."

She said, "Yes. Myrna and I are making plans. We're thinking of moving to somewhere in the Caribbean. You ever been down there?"

"No," Jimmy said, "but I was told Grand Cayman has a lot of banks. And Gramps? Is he going to move there, too?"

Lisa Marie shook her head. "I don't think so. Sometimes I feel sorry for Dad."

"Why?" Jimmy asked.

"Well," Lisa Marie seemed to be sorting things out in her mind. "Who really loves him? Myrna certainly doesn't and he was hardly involved in my life as I grew up. I had a nanny that I loved but she's dead now. I loved Grandmother and Grandfather but I barely knew Dad. When I was divorced and broke, Myrna wanted me to come here and help her with the office. Myrna cares about me and I needed money, so I came."

"Did your mother love him?" Jimmy asked.

Lisa Marie shook her head and said, "I remember so little about Mom. Isn't that strange? I was 8 when she died. I should remember. I remember a lot of other things from then but not her. I asked Myrna once about Mom and Dad and she said she thought Mom must have loved him, otherwise why did she put up with things? I suppose she meant the other women. I don't know."

Jimmy looked at her sadness and thought how fortunate he was that Grandma had taken him away with her, taken him home and loved him. And so had Grandpa. He had grown up secure and loved, happy living with people who knew what family was supposed to mean.

Jimmy had been cautious about talking to Myrna from the beginning. Something about her said 'Do Not Enter.' He had figured out that she was the brains of the operation, the manager, the one who kept everything in order. But she never chatted. She never talked about the operation. He learned stuff as it passed in front of him.

One Sunday, Lisa Marie invited him to their house for dinner. "Sometimes I cook," she said.

Jimmy was straight forward. "Is Bo John going to be there?"

Lisa Marie looked at him in surprise. "Of course not," she said. "He's not allowed to come to our house."

Jimmy smiled at her. "I didn't know that. I'll come."

He was interested in seeing their house. People's houses often told you a lot. As he parked, he saw Lisa Marie's car, Myrna's jeep, and Gramps pickup. He wondered how many people were coming.

He rang twice before Lisa Marie appeared. "Sorry, we're out on the patio." As he walked through the house, he had an impression of a rather normal, comfortably out-of-date suburban family home. It was a ranch style, brick, mid 60's, probably three bedrooms he estimated. It was generic. No one appeared to have wanted to stamp their personality on the place. The only interesting thing he saw was a piano but it was one of those short spinet type chosen by people who know little about pianos. During the afternoon, he found out that Gramps had bought the house at an auction years ago, complete with the furnishings.

Out on the patio, Gramps was doing steaks. He said, "The women want theirs burned. Boy, how do you want yours?"

"Medium well," he answered. He had not met rare steaks until he left home. Backwoods people knew all about the hazards of raw meat. He was given a baked potato and someone had made a great-looking salad. Myrna opened a cooler and held up a beer. He shook his head. "Coke," he said. "I'm on duty later. Who's minding the office?"

"Locked the door and transferred the phone here," Lisa Marie said. "That's what we do at night."

Gramps was muttering about wasting good meat and Myrna said, "I can't stand the sight of blood." Myrna was drinking beer and as they ate, Jimmy realized that Lisa Marie and Gramps were both watching her like they were a little worried. Lisa was drinking Sprite. Gramps finished a beer and changed to Dr. Pepper. At one point when Myrna went after another beer, Gramps said to her, "Honey, do you think that's wise?"

Myrna said, "You're too late. You should've locked up the beer when I was 12."

Lisa Marie chattered and he did his best to assist her in keeping conversation moving but underneath, it was not a jolly success as a social event. When he left to go on duty, Lisa Marie said, "I'll be at the office later."

He dropped in the office at 10pm when he was going off duty. Lisa Marie said, "Sorry that was such a dud. Dad and Myrna both seem to like you so I thought it might be fun. I should've known better."

"What's with Myrna and the beer?" Jimmy asked. "I've never smelled alcohol on her at the office and she's never acted drunk."

Lisa Marie looked pained. "She's had a problem in the past so we never keep any in the house. Mostly she never touches the stuff but once in a while she goes off the wagon. Yesterday, I bought some for Dad. He doesn't really get drunk but if he's not going to be driving, he gets buzzed. Otherwise, one's usually his limit."

"Myrna doesn't seem like a happy person to me," Jimmy commented.

"Yeah," Lisa Marie says, "she's not. I don't know what this 'when I was 12' deal is but she's made cracks about it before. Every Tuesday afternoon, she goes all the way over to Batesville to see a psychiatrist." Lisa sighed. "I was happy when I was a child and I was enjoying life until I met that loser I married. I guess I could go through life blaming him but really, several of my friends warned me about the guy, so I guess it was as much my fault as his."

Jimmy said, "Most of us would get through life better if we listened to what people who care about us try to tell us." Jimmy shook his head. "But all of us do dumb things sometimes."

Lisa Marie looked at him solemnly and said, "Jimmy, get out of this game while you can."

On his way home, he considered Lisa Marie's well-meant advice. If he were really in this just for money, he'd take it. He considered pulling out anyway. He loved working for the National Park Service but now that he had gotten closer to Evangeline, he was entertaining other ideas. After that couple of days in Nashville, he thought he might have a chance with her. The thought sent him off in a daydream and later that night, he spent a long time on the phone with her.

The next day, when he went on duty, Myrna was in the office. "Jimmy," she said apologetically, "I'm sorry about yesterday. I'm a bad socializer."

Jimmy grinned at her and said, "I've seen worse. You didn't puke on anything and you didn't cuss anybody out and you didn't try to take off all your clothes."

After a brief pause, Myrna laughed. "Jimmy, you do brighten things up around here."

"Good," he said. "Now how's our witch hunt going?" Jimmy was thinking that when Myrna smiled, she was actually a very attractive woman.

Still smiling, Myrna said, "Not good. Lisa Marie got our Jason at the lawn mower plant to take her to the movies. She really likes him and said if he wasn't four inches shorter than her with a face like a mule, she'd seriously consider marrying him."

"Granny's apple pie, is he?" Jimmy said.

Myrna nodded and went on, "Our anti-drug activist, Juliet, has found a Romeo so that's where all her thoughts, time, and energy are concentrated. Too bad he's married."

"Married!" Jimmy exclaimed.

Myrna shook her head. "Some people are dumber than dumb. He's a teacher whose father-in-law is on the school board. They're making bets on how long before she's fired."

"You mean everybody knows! Haven't either one of them got any sense?"

"Apparently not," she said. "How old were you when you found out about sex?"

"Twelve," Jimmy said, "but I already knew about illegitimate babies."

Myrna stared at him. "Okay, how old were you when you found out about illegitimate babies."

"Eight," Jimmy told her. "At school one day, one of my cousins told me my mother was a bastard and that made me one too. I found out that Grandma, that is the woman I called Grandma, had had my supposed mother without being married."

"She told you about that!" Myrna said.

"No," Jimmy said, "I asked her father what was a bastard and he told me about her going off to college and coming home pregnant."

Myrna gave him an odd look and said, "Okay, when you were twelve, what were you told about sex."

Jimmy grinned and said, "A girl at school wanted me to meet her somewhere to kiss. I didn't know how to kiss so I asked Grandpa. So he and Grandma had a talk with me about sex. Grandma told me that if you do too much kissing, your hormones get all stirred up and you go crazy and end up having sex. They told me that sex made babies and also you could catch diseases. After that I was real careful about kissing girls."

Myna was laughing. "That's hilarious," she said.

Jimmy was grinning. "Yes, but a lot more practical than what most kids are told."

Myrna suddenly sobered up. "That's true," she said.

Jimmy sensed some deep emotion under the surface and he changed the subject. "So who else is on our suspected witch list?"

"Jack Fowler's wife just produced twins and it's definitely not her. Everyone's expecting a divorce." Myrna looked at Jimmy and paused before she dropped the bomb. "The twins are obviously black. Not even Jack's that dumb."

Jimmy shook his head, thinking about the uneducated, not too bright, poor redneck Fowler family. "Yeah, that'll produce a divorce. So who's left on our suspect list?"

"No one," Myrna said. "Only Rose and nobody's suspecting her but we planted bugs anyway. Don't tell anybody but she's got someone she met at college that she's planning to marry. If it gets back to Robby Lee, he'll arrange an accident, so keep it a secret."

Jimmy agreed without telling Myrna he already knew. Instead he said, "Yeah, when Robby Lee came out to my place, he said he's been considering arranging an accident for me so if it happens, you know who to blame."

Myrna stared at him. "Robby Lee actually told you that."

"Well, he said he'd decided he didn't need to," Jimmy explained, "and then he said, unless I was lying to him." Jimmy shook his head and said, "He's obsessed with Rose but he doesn't want to marry her, just take her for a roll in the hay."

"That's authentic Robby Lee," she said. "He even tried to seduce Lisa Marie." Jimmy heard the note of anger in her voice.

"Myrna, how long before you plan to split?" Jimmy had said it before he thought. He knew immediately he probably should not have asked.

"Soon," she told him. "Right now, with you cooking, our output has more than tripled. We're raking it in hand over fist. But you're not here forever. I think when you go, I'll go."

In the following silence, Jimmy considered what she had just said.

"Jimmy," Myrna said with an odd note in her voice, "I shouldn't have told you that."

Jimmy looked her in the eye and said, "I won't tell anyone."

She continued to look at him in silence and then said, "If we can't find our witch, we may all be out of here sooner than we thought.'

"I had an idea," Jimmy said. "Maybe when that man was spotted, he pulled his undercover out. Has anyone left the county unexpectedly?"

Myrna considered. "It's a thought," she said.

As Jimmy went about his duties as a deputy sheriff, he pondered on the fact that he was getting attached to people here. He wouldn't mind at all seeing Robby Lee in the hoosegow and Gramps had it coming but he really didn't want to see Lisa Marie locked up. He sensed something deep in Myrna that felt broken, like an old tragedy, long buried, but the pieces unmended, its ghost still haunting her.

❈ ❈ ❈
Chapter 11: Pendegrass Again

Two days later, Myrna called Jimmy back to the office mid-afternoon. Gramps and Lisa Marie were also there which wasn't normal at all. He immediately was uneasy, wondering what was going on.

But Myrna smiled at him and said, "Jimmy, you do have good ideas. When I checked, Jeremy Anderson suddenly quit his job at the clinic and decided to look for work in Louisville where he went to college. He had a good job for this area so I tracked him down and talked to him." Jimmy looked at all three faces and they were all smiling. Myrna said, "When we talked to him, he said our man, Pendegrass, approached him and asked him to do some undercover work for him last year when he was still at college. Jeremy told him no but Pendegrass contacted him again recently. Jeremy says Pendegrass was asking him about you."

Jimmy's heart froze. He knew it showed on his face and he should say something to cover up but he couldn't think of a thing to say.

Suddenly, Lisa Marie laughed. "Jimmy, the shocked look on your face is hilarious. Relax. That Fed is not really on to you. From what he said to Jeremy, we think he maybe thinks he can recruit you to work for him."

"What!" Jimmy exclaimed.

"Yeah," Lisa Marie said, "we thought it was hysterical."

So then Myrna repeated to him everything Jeremy had told her about his conversations with Pendegrass. It sounded to Jimmy like Jeremy knew there were murky waters in Grand County and he had no desire whatsoever to find out what was lurking in them.

They discussed the thing for more than an hour. Then, as he was leaving the office, Gramps clapped his hand on his shoulder and said, "Jimmy Joe, if the Feds approach you to work undercover, you tell them *yes*. Then we'll let you find a few marijuana plants and you'll tell the Feds that's all there is. It'll be fun."

Jimmy left the office but decided he would wait until he was home tonight before calling his team in Missouri. It would be easier and much safer. So he hit the three night spots in town as usual, checking that all was quiet before returning to the office to check out at 10pm.

It was Myrna at the office. She said, "I entertained Lisa Marie with your story about finding out about sex. Those people who raised you, they sound like nice people. Way back then, unmarried women did not have babies. It must have taken a lot of nerve. She could have done something else, put it up for adoption, got an abortion, hid it somehow. But she went home and had her baby and everybody knew. I think she was brave. She made a mistake, faced the consequences, and got on with her life."

Jimmy nodded and told her, "She has four brothers and they wanted to go after the guy who got her pregnant but she wouldn't let them. After she and her father talked to me about sex, she told me that her parents had not told her enough. She said they had thought that her innocence would protect her. She told me she knew because she made the same mistake with her own daughter. Her daughter married the man who got her pregnant. She was supposed to have died in an accident but Grandma has always thought he killed her. When they found the remains of her grandson, they told her he showed signs of having been beaten repeatedly. Her daughter would have been a whole lot better off doing exactly what her mother did, going home and having that baby solo."

Myrna had a sober look on her face. She said, "I think when we make a mistake, we're probably better off just facing the consequences and getting on with life. Sometimes, trying to hide something causes more trouble than the mistake itself."

With a sudden flash of insight, Jimmy knew it was not his grandmother's mistake she was talking about. What mistake had she made, and covered up, that had hurt her so badly? And he thought again of old sins, long hidden, but still casting shadows.

Jimmy remembered how once he and Harry had been playing with matches and had set the hen house on fire. They tried to put out the fire but couldn't. Grandpa heard them and came running and he said, "Get all the hens out." After it was all over, the adults discussed how it could have happened. Some of the relatives smoked. They thought someone had been careless with a cigarette. They said one could smolder for hours, even overnight, and then flare up. Grandma had said how brave he and Harry were for rescuing the hens. When they rounded them up, one was missing. Grandma said maybe it had gone into the woods and a fox got it. But the evicted hens had all dived happily into the kitchen garden where they normally were never allowed. Jimmy knew the missing hen had been brooding, sitting on a clutch of ten eggs. He had personally grabbed her and threw her out of the hen house but because of her eggs, she might have gone back.

That night, he had trouble sleeping. The next day, when they checked the rubble, the missing hen was found where her nest had been located. Grandpa had shook his head and said, "Mothers. They don't abandon their young."

During the night, Jimmy woke up screaming from a terrible dream in which he had been trapped in a burning building. Grandpa had come and sit by his bed, waiting for him to go back to sleep. But he couldn't sleep again and finally he said, "Grandpa, the fire was my fault. I got some matches from the kitchen and Harry and I were playing with them in the hen house."

Grandpa said, "Son, are you ever going to do it again?"

"No," he said. Then, after a while he asked, "Are you going to spank me?"

Grandpa said, "I reckon you'd feel better about it if I did. It'd be like you paid for it. But I expect that dream you had was worse than any spanking I could give you."

Jimmy had cried for a while and then fell asleep. He knew if he had not told Grandpa what really happened, he would have kept on having bad dreams.

He had the idea that Myrna had a lot of bad dreams.

Back at his cabin, Jimmy went up the path and called Grandma. "That idiot, Pendegrass, has done it again," he said. "Grandma, you call him up and tell him if he doesn't stay out of this, he's going to get me killed."

He had a longer talk with Harry. Harry told him Pendegrass was demanding that he pass orders along to Jimmy. "He wants you to call him directly. He wants recordings and photographs and lists of dates, times, amounts, etc. that he can take into court. He wants me to pass on a list of questions he wants answered. He wants you to set it up to intercept a big shipment."

"Harry, it's no wonder Pendegrass's agents have all gotten caught. The man's a juggernaut. Tell him he has created so much suspicion that I am afraid to ask anything. I may even have to pull out. Tell him that his talk with Jeremy Anderson has made them think he may be trying to recruit me. I need to watch every word I say. Tell Pendegrass that if he doesn't quit, I may have an arranged accident."

He considered the accident possibilities. Cooking methamphetamine was dangerous and an accident would not be carefully investigated. He began leaving small markers to let him know if anyone had been messing with anything when he was gone.

He did some serious praying.

❀ ❀ ❀
Chapter 12: Promotion

After Jeremy's revelations, things were quiet. Jimmy asked Sally about finding a cat that would catch mice and she said, no problem. There were a lot of them around. She'd drop one off at the sheriff's office for him.

Jimmy had slowly picked up information on Sally. She bred dogs and had her kennels on the property where her husband's veterinarian clinic was located. She was involved in the SPCA and she went to dog shows. She always answered her phone but she was often out of town.

Myrna and Gramps decided that Pendegrass had been here to talk to Jeremy Anderson. Jeremy had quit his job and moved, rather than be subjected to more pressure to help drug enforcement. They relaxed and Jimmy realized that they had been laying low, worried that someone was watching.

In the meantime, normal sheriff's office business had been ongoing. Some man named Jeff Davis showed up at the sheriff's office and wanted to file charges against Felicity. He had caught her and his son, who was only 14, in the loft of his barn, both of them totally naked. Gramps explained that as Felicity was not quite 16 herself, she could not be charged with statutory rape. Gramps promised to talk to her parents.

After Davis was gone, Gramps said, "That girl has been nothing but trouble from the day she was born. She calls me 'uncle' but actually her mother's mother is my half-sister and her father is a distant cousin. He has always said the girl isn't his. He farms. He's got several patches. He and his son turn out good stuff." Jimmy realized that 'farms' meant growing marijuana. "His wife belongs to that church out near the county line that handles snakes. She's always at church. He figures the girl's his wife's responsibility." Gramps looked at me. "Got any ideas?"

"Take a shotgun and make Robby Lee marry her?" Jimmy said and Myrna burst out laughing.

But Gramps shook his head. "That's one female Robby Lee hasn't had a tumble with yet although it's not from lack of willingness on her part. He got arrested once for bucking an underage girl and he's been careful ever since."

"Is there anyone else she fancies?" Jimmy asked.

"Things was easier when I was young," Gramps complained. "Then girls like her were married off and had at least one baby by her age."

Gramps left and Myrna said, "Things are pretty quiet and Dad said to show you the ropes here in the office."

With that introduction, Jimmy was shown the secrets of Myrna's cubicle. Not only were there traffic cameras on the highways, Gramps had more. He kept track of movement in and out of Bobby Ray's tomato farm. He had two cameras out near his brother, Billy Bob's place, and Jimmy was puzzled. Myrna laughed and said, "What did you think all those barley fields are for? They sell a lot of barley to a distillery over near Lynchburg but all the Jones family used to make moonshine. Billy Bob still does." And there was a camera positioned to catch traffic in and out of the gate to Gramps country property. "He had that installed to keep track of Bo John," Myrna explained. Myrna showed him how they worked. The system stored information and he learned how to call up and find what he wanted to see.

Since Myrna had mentioned it, he asked about tracking Bo John. Myrna said, "It's not only the camera, he has Bo John's phone, his truck, and his room bugged. He can track his phone. Dad wanted to know where he's getting drugs."

When Jimmy's only response was, "Oh," Myrna said, "He's found out and is trying to think of a way to get his supplier busted without getting Bo John nabbed, too."

Jimmy said, "That might take some thought."

Myrna commented, "Jimmy, there you go again doing exactly what you wouldn't do if you were a snitch. You haven't asked who or anything else."

Jimmy laughed. "I'm not nosy enough, huh? Why do I need to know? If Gramps needs my help to deal with it, he'll ask."

Myrna said, "Jimmy, you're so easy to work with. No undercurrents, no second guessing what you're thinking."

Jimmy thought about how he was really double-crossing all of them and felt guilty.

Sally got him another cat. She came with a litter of kittens. The kittens had gotten Mama Cat evicted from an apartment. Jimmy found her a real tiger. She thought his mouse infested cabin was paradise. He had found it necessary to prevent Tommy from climbing up into the loft when he was cooking but Mama Cat hated the meth operation and wouldn't get near it. Jimmy found it interesting that she was so smart. But he spent so little time with her, that her kittens started getting wild, and he began eating more at home. They got a lot more friendly when he started giving out pieces of his hamburgers and sharing his tuna salad.

Another day Jimmy learned all about the bugs. He learned that if someone had a land line telephone, like Lilac Jones at the Lilac Bush Bed and Breakfast, it was easy to bug the phone. Other bugs were small and battery operated so they had a definite life span. They also had only a certain range within which they could be picked up so their use was limited. There were also bugs that could be wired into electric lines but they also had a limited range. Out at the ranch, they had installed an antenna so they could listen to Bo John from the office and everything was recorded.

Jimmy had already found bugs at his place but now that he knew exactly what to look for, he checked again. He found two in the cabin, one on the front porch, several in the barn, and one in the outhouse. He even checked the path where he regularly went to make calls but it was clean. He discovered that one of the lightening rods on the barn was really an antenna which allowed what the bugs picked up to be heard at a much greater distance. He followed its wiring and found some equipment. It had a battery but was also connected to the electrical system. Maybe the battery was back-up. He suspected that what happened out at his cabin could be heard in the sheriff's office. He left everything in place but asked Myrna about them the next day. She laughed and said, "I knew you'd look. Why did you leave them in place?"

He shrugged and said, "What have I got to hide? You know about the meth."

"Jimmy," she said, "you've been so absolutely boring, I quit even bothering to really listen, just check once in a while." She was not denying that she could listen in from the office.

"Shall I bring you all those bugs so you can put them somewhere more interesting?"

"No," she said. "I thought if you get any unauthorized visitors, they might be a help."

Jimmy learned that his suspicions about the smart phones issued to the sheriff's deputies were accurate. All their phone calls were recorded. They could, of course, be tracked but they also had a bug so that as long as they were on, whatever was said nearby was recorded. Myrna said it was partly to protect deputies from false accusations. But Jimmy thought it also protected Gramps from being betrayed by one of his own deputies. Then, Myrna causally told him that when she first set up the system, she had discovered that one of the deputies had been collecting protection money from a number of people.

"What happened?" Jimmy asked.

He expected to hear a tale of someone being fired or scared straight but Myrna said, "He had an accident. Fell off a ladder while he was working on his roof. County had a big funeral. Dad passed the word that he was there to protect people, was elected and paid for it, and anyone else trying to get paid for it, better think twice." Myrna paused.

"I think it was just an accident. I know Dad didn't do anything but maybe someone else did. We had a deputy after that who accepted a bribe for not writing a ticket and Dad fired him. He tells his deputies to go easy on handing out traffic tickets and its okay to let people talk them out of issuing one – but no bribes."

Myrna and Lisa Marie were the surveillance experts. Myrna bought the equipment but they both did set up. Myrna said, "I spend most of my time monitoring surveillance. It's a bore but I don't intend to do any jail time, so it's necessary."

Myrna warned him, "Nobody but me and Lisa Marie and Dad know about this stuff. He doesn't trust anyone else, not even his brother, Bobby Ray."

Jimmy practiced using the equipment. Myrna gave him information on where to buy all the fancy gizmos She said a lot of theirs were out of date now but they didn't want to spend the money to upgrade. She warned him, "Dad is trying to think of a way to keep you here."

Jimmy shook his head. "My girl likes her family. She'll help me with a side income but she won't move down here. She knows I'll not stay here without her."

"Jimmy, I still can't figure you out," Myrna said. "You're straight. You even go to church. But you're the best cook we've ever had."

"Those dope-heads are going to find the stuff anyway so I might as well make some money. But this meth is bad stuff. The weed doesn't bother me as much. My grandpa told me the Indians used it for medicine and now they're finding out it does have some medicinal uses."

"Yeah," Myrna said, "and now it's even legal some places. Uncle Bobby Ray has been talking about moving to Colorado."

Jimmy eventually found out about phone records. His suspicions about that were also on target. They had a way to get phone records. Myrna explained that she called a certain phone company employee and tipped her fifty dollars in cash. The phone company employee did not feel that she was doing anything wrong because it was the sheriff's office asking. Jimmy was really thankful he had been so careful. If someone's cell phone was not the main phone company, it took longer, but somehow that phone company woman could get the information, as long as she had a phone number and knew the carrier. And she got a bigger tip for that.

Jimmy had been talking to his team about most of what he was learning but they were passing on to Pendegrass only what he directed and he was seriously holding out. They never told Pendegrass about Bo John's drug problem. He was afraid Pendegrass would jump on it. He had told about the traffic cameras when Pendegrass had come that time but now he never mentioned them again. They didn't tell Pendegrass about the bugs, the phones, or the phone records. He did tell Harry to tell Pendegrass that he was catching wind of arranged accidents but he gave no names or details. Harry reported that Pendegrass had spewed demands for who and when and how.

During their witch hunt, Lisa Marie told him it was actually unusual for law enforcement to use people who were not already in law enforcement for undercover agents. She said all three of the people they had spotted before had worked somewhere in law enforcement. Jimmy wondered how Lisa Marie found out about the law enforcement backgrounds but he didn't ask.

Lisa Marie also told him, "I think they're trying to recruit someone local because they've had so much trouble getting anyone in here undetected." Jeremy said when that Fed contacted him the first time, he offered good pay." Jimmy began to speculate. Pendegrass had not offered him any pay. Why?

Jimmy asked Harry, "Has Pendegrass ever mentioned anyone he works with?" and the answer was no.

Jimmy said, "I want you and Grandma and Evangeline to start recording every conversation you have with Pendegrass. I'm beginning to wonder if he's playing Lone Ranger." Jimmy told Harry what equipment he needed and where to get it.

Lisa Marie made a trip to Florida. She went about every three mouths, leaving on a Friday evening and returning the following weekend on Sunday night. She went to visit a friend of hers from college. The woman and her husband had a sailboat and they always sailed for a week in the Caribbean.

Jimmy took over her shift in the office while she was gone. It gave him a chance to really check out what all the surveillance could do. He had thought he was being excessively cautious, maybe even paranoid, when he came down here. He discovered he wasn't.

Myrna was very pleased to have his help. "This is nice," she said. "Usually, when Lisa Marie is gone, I'm run ragged trying to keep up with everything. We often have to defer normal activities until she gets back. Right now that would be very inconvenient. It's a busy time with the farmers and we've a lot of stuff to move."

"Couldn't Lisa Marie wait a few weeks?" Jimmy asked.

"No," Myrna told him "She has to go on her friend's schedule. The friend's husband is also stashing money in Georgetown but he doesn't know that Lisa Marie is. He sends his wife and Lisa Marie to the bank so Lisa Marie has to go on his schedule. He thinks she's great cover for his wife and has no idea."

Myrna then gave him a speculative look and said, "You do realize that you can't just produce a lot of cash out of nowhere and not arouse suspicions."

"Yes," Jimmy said, "I have realized that. When I went to Nashville, I took what I had then and passed it to my girl. She's rented a safety deposit box at the bank. But I'm thinking I'll get Lisa Marie to tell me all about how to bank off-shore for later. But if I put the money I'm getting now in a bank on Grand Cayman, how can I have it easily available to buy that land?"

Jimmy did have some concerns about money being stolen. He was paid in hundred dollar bills so even a large amount of money was not bulky. He made a record of all serial numbers and stashed the money in a small metal cash box. At first, he had hid it up the path from the outhouse but then he made a place in the stone wall of the cellar of the barn where he stored his meth making supplies. He was also keeping a record of the meth he made, dates and how much.

During the week that Lisa Marie was gone, Jimmy begin to get his first inkling as to how meth making supplies got into the county and meth got out.

Jimmy had thought they must be moving stuff at night but that wasn't it. Neither was it being done in the tomato trucks. He had wondered if Uncle Bobby Ray was bringing in supplies along with fertilizer and other things for his tomato operation, but he wasn't.

When Jimmy went into the office his second day to take over, Myrna said, "Good. You're here. I was up most of the night with a bar fight and I can hardly hold my eyes open. Lilac Jones has gone to Nashville with a dog for Sally." Jimmy had learned that Sally bred some kind of Australian shepherd. She had a good business selling the pups and she attended dog shows all over. "I got word that the Smokies are out in force over that way so I warned her to stick to the letter of the law. Actually, she normally does anyway. That's why they use her to deliver dogs. She's bringing back another dog and a load of supplies for Sally. She's supposed to call when she leaves Nashville. If she has a problem, she'll call. Call me if that happens."

After Myrna was gone, Jimmy wondered why Lilac Jones was calling the sheriff's office instead of Sally. Sally had a cell phone. Was it broken or something? And why should he call Myrna if Aunt Lilac had trouble?

Aunt Lilac called when she left Nashville and Jimmy chatted with her. He asked if she was supposed to call Sally or was he? She said, "I don't know. I always call the sheriff's office when I start home and then I call Sally when I hit the county line and she tells me where to meet her." Jimmy thought to himself, why would Sally meet Aunt Lilac anywhere? Why wasn't whatever she was bringing being taken to the animal clinic or the dog kennels?

Jimmy just said, "I'll call her and tell her you're on your way home.

Then, she'll know what time to expect you."

Just to be consistent, Jimmy did call Sally and she acted like it was normal. He wondered why the normal system was to call the sheriff's office rather than to call Sally directly. He backed up the traffic surveillance system and watched Aunt Lilac on her way out. She was driving her old station wagon. The dog carrier was in the front seat with her and the back of her car was full of boxes. Why? What was in the boxes?

When she re-entered Grand County, Jimmy was watching. Again, her car was loaded with boxes and the dog carrier again in the front seat. Jimmy speculated.

Jimmy spent a lot of his office time while Lisa Marie was gone watching traffic and listening to what was coming in on the bugs. It was interesting and by the time she returned, he had a whole list of names and ideas, not only about the meth but also the marijuana and the moonshine.

Jimmy waited until Lisa Marie was back before he tried to find a chance to talk to Aunt Lilac. When she asked him to her house for Sunday dinner, it was a good opportunity. Rose had gone to visit a friend from college and Aunt Lilac had a married couple staying and she was doing Sunday dinner. "They're staying a week," she explained. "Their granddaughter lives here and they came to see her but she and her husband are living with his folks so they can't put them up and they don't like her husband's family much, anyway. So they asked me if I could do Sunday dinner for them. Frankly, Jimmy, I thought you might be a help talking to the men."

Jimmy checked in with Myrna who was running the office that Sunday and asked her if she would like for him to retrieve the bugs they had planted to check on Rose. It was possible that they might be found. Myrna told him where to look.

Jimmy was reasonably successful in diluting the atmosphere but he could see why Aunt Lilac had asked for help. The granddaughter's husband was Billy John Jones, grandson of Billy Bob, the moonshine maker. Jimmy didn't know if the granddaughter knew, but if she did, she was keeping quiet. She was pregnant and the women discussed that while he talked to the grandfather. He asked the old man what he did and discussed farming with him and Billy John. When that topic was exhausted, there was a brief silence and then the old man asked Jimmy about working as a sheriff's deputy. He told a story about stopping a drunk. He'd asked the man to do one of the standard field sobriety tests and the man had said, "I can't count backwards when I'm sober so I sure can't do it drunk." Billy John laughed and told about some dumb thing one of his friends had done when he was drunk. Then, the old man told one that happened when he was young and they laughed. The women asked what was so funny and then, Aunt Lilac told one. That carried them through to the end of the meal and Aunt Lilac shooed the men into the front parlor and gave them coffee. When they were settled, Billy John said to Jimmy, "I heard that you laid Bo John out with one blow in the parking lot of Gina's Cafe. Is that true?"

Jimmy grinned. "Enjoyed it too," he said.

"My dad told me Bo John's a mean son of a bitch and to avoid him like the plague. He also said to never under any circumstances leave him alone with any of the women. Is he really that bad?"

Jimmy sobered up and said, "Yes, he's that bad."

"Who's Bo John?" the old man asked.

Billy John shifted uncomfortably, suddenly realizing that Jimmy might find that an embarrassing subject but Jimmy calmly said, "My father." The old man looked shocked, so he explained, "He killed my mother when I was five years old, shot her. A woman who saw him do it grabbed me and run." The girl's grandfather looked appalled and Jimmy said, "It happened in California so a lot of the family here never heard what really happened."

"Why did they let him out of jail?" Billy John asked.

"Paroled," Jimmy said. "There wasn't anybody to show up at the parole hearings and protest. Since I came back, I found out that even Gramps didn't know how bad it was. Bo John had told him some story and he didn't know what really happened until I told him."

Billy John nodded. "Dad said to stay clear of Bo John and if he showed up somewhere, to leave. He said he's a bomb looking for a place to explode and I wouldn't want to be there when it happened. He said if Bo John did anything at all, even just frowned, I should call the sheriff's office."

Jimmy smiled at the young man. "Good advice," he said. "Gramps told me his house cleaner won't even go out to the ranch unless he's there."

Billy John said, "But she's an old woman, 50 at least!"

Jimmy said, "Well, if anybody shoots him, just make sure it looks like self defense and call me to investigate."

The grandfather looked at Billy John and said, "Son, how would you like to come help me farm? I'm getting old and none of my kids want to do it."

In the ensuing discussion, Jimmy and Billy John learned the man had 160 acres with crop land, pasture, and good hay fields. He had been hiring help but it wasn't working out very well. When the old man went to visit the restroom, Jimmy said to Billy John, "He's got 160 acres he owns free and clear but none of his kids want to farm. It's hard work but it's an honest living and he offered you a small house. Ask your wife what she thinks. Do you all really like living with your parents?" When the old man got back, Jimmy could tell Billy John was considering it.

When the young couple left and the old couple when up to have a rest, Jimmy took Aunt Lilac outside to admire her flowers. He had left his phones in his truck. He asked her, "How often do you deliver dogs for Sally?"

"Lately, its been every Monday regular but it used to vary more. Once in a while, I can't go and she gets someone else, either my friend, Ethyl Shilling, or her sister, Edith Barnes."

"What are those boxes that go with the dogs?" Jimmy asked.

"Sally makes a special dog food which she sells to the pet shop where I deliver the dogs."

"And what is it you bring back?" Jimmy asked.

"Supplies for her husband's animal clinic," Aunt Lilac told him. "Sally is a good arranger. She always has a load going both ways. She sends dogs back and forth for breeding purposes so there's always a dog along. I've asked why they don't get a truck but she says she doesn't trust the kids who work for them to deliver the dogs."

Jimmy admired Aunt Lilac's yard with its neat shrubs and flowers blooming even this late in the fall. She said, "That flower bed in front of the sheriff's office is a disgrace. Daffodils and crocus are easy to care for. We could make it look nice."

So Jimmy discussed the flower bed with her before going on duty. When he came into the office, Myrna asked, "What took you so long?"

"Helping Aunt Lilac with a sticky social situation," he said. "Then, we were discussing the flower bed in front of the office here."

Myrna shrugged. "Why plant flowers when you're not going to be around to enjoy them?"

Jimmy said, "Maybe to make people think you have every intention of staying around."

Myrna looked at him oddly, and said, "Jimmy, sometimes I wonder about you."

Jimmy felt a cold chill go up the back of his neck and told himself he had to be more careful. This undercover agent business was difficult. You never knew when the most innocent remark could give you away.

Chapter 13: A Visitor

Aunt Lilac brought some daffodil and crocus bulbs and Jimmy dug up the flower bed in front of the sheriff's office. The bulbs were put where Aunt Lilac directed and stones were placed to mark the empty parts of the bed. Next spring, daylilies and windflowers would be planted. Aunt Lilac told Jimmy quietly that Rose had come back from her visit out of town upset. She and her beau had split up. Aunt Lilac said, "She won't talk about it much yet."

Jimmy was coming off duty and the sun was going down but when he stopped at the gate, he knew immediately that someone had been through the gate since he left that morning. The gate had a chain that looped over a post to hold it shut. One link of the chain was bent and Jimmy always left it in a certain position. He also always left the gate just slightly unaligned with the fence. He tried to check for tire tracks but the ground was too dry. He thought about calling Lisa Marie but his first suspicion was that his visitor was Pendegrass.

He drove slowly down the track to the cabin. It was not dark yet but getting there. His headlights were off but he knew that the sound of his truck would signal his arrival anyway. There was no way to approach the cabin unseen without hiking some distance. He thought of the bugs at his cabin and tried to think what to do if Pendegrass was sitting on his front porch making fatal phone calls.

When he could see the vehicle in front of his cabin, it was a pickup truck with local plates that he didn't recognize. He couldn't visualize Pendegrass driving a pickup but maybe he had gotten smart enough to at least try not to look like a Fed. As he drove slowly on up to the house, he couldn't see anyone on the porch. He circled and parked his truck near the barn with its nose out and waited. No one appeared. There was no light inside the house but then it wasn't fully dark yet. He slowly exited his truck and went into the barn, through it and around to the back of the cabin. He would like to have called Lisa Marie at the office and asked her what she could hear on the bugs but if it was Pendegrass in there, that would be disastrous.

Mama Cat was in the barn. She followed him out but acted skittish. When he approached his cabin, she stopped and waited, studying the cabin intently. He decided she didn't know whoever was in there and was uneasy. Tommy was not nearly as smart and was probably inside bugging whoever it was, wanting to be fed.

He checked his back porch. No one was waiting there. He unholstered his gun and took off the safety. He approached slowly, silently, like Grandpa had taught him to do when they were hunting. He knew if he stepped on the back porch, it would creak. It didn't have just a squeaky board or two, but the whole porch was creaky. So instead, he moved around the cabin to the other side where a window looked into the sitting room and kitchen part of the cabin. He left that window open all the time with one of those sliding screen things to keep the bugs out. He had rigged a cat door in it. He looked through the screen and could see a figure sitting in the comfortable wing-back chair with feet up on the footstool in front of it. From this angle, he could not see the figure well but as he studied it, he became more and more sure whoever it was was holding a long gun, maybe a rifle but probably a shotgun.

Jimmy waited. He wasn't sure how long but finally the figure moved. "Shit," the man said, "what's that boy up to?" The man rose and moved to the front door and opened it. Jimmy moved to the corner of the cabin and watched the man step out onto the front porch. The gun was a shotgun and the man was Bo John.

"Bo John," Jimmy said, "drop that gun."

Bo John did not drop the gun. He turned to point it to where Jimmy had been but when he started to turn without dropping the gun,

Jimmy had ran. He circled around the cabin and from the other side, saw Bo John stalking around the other corner of the cabin, cussing and yelling for Jimmy to come out.

Jimmy ran for his truck and had it started and took off as he saw Bo John emerge from behind the cabin. He hightailed it for the gate but knew that if Bo John were quick, he would catch him when he stopped to open the gate. But Bo John did not appear and he closed the gate and looped the chain around the post.

When he was far enough away that he thought it was safe, he pulled over and called the sheriff's office number on his smart phone. Lisa Marie answered the phone. He told her what happened. "I'll check," she said.

Jimmy just waited silently for her to call back. Eventually she did. "Bo John left the ranch midday. He's been to buy drugs and visit a prostitute. We were tracking him. When he started home, we got busy with other stuff and assumed he would go on home, like usual. Obviously he didn't. I'm sorry, Jimmy. If we'd have tracked him, we'd have known he was out at your place. He's still there. Dad's on his way out. Watch for him and follow him in case he needs back up. If Bo John's on a roar, not even Dad's safe."

Gramps came in a 4-wheel drive vehicle which was his but had been done up with the sheriff's department emblems and had lights and a siren. Gramps stopped at the gate and had Jimmy get in with him.

Bo John's truck was where it had been before and lights were on in the cabin. Gramps roared up to the cabin and slammed to a stop. They both jumped out of the vehicle and unholstered their guns. Gramps left the safety on his. Jimmy didn't.

Jimmy kept a can of kerosene for when the electricity went off, which happened about every time they had a good storm. Bo John had made a big pile of furniture and bedding which he was dousing down with the kerosene. When they came through the door, he dropped the can and pulled a cigarette lighter out of his pocket. Jimmy pitched his gun back out the open door, knowing it might go off, and tackled Bo John. He grabbed the arm with the lighter and they both went down onto the floor. Bo John rolled but Jimmy didn't turn loose. Bo John was on top and he was heavier than Jimmy. He was hitting Jimmy with his left fist but Jimmy held on to the arm with the lighter. Gramps turned his gun butt out and hit Bo John several times before he turned loose of the lighter. He was stunned and Jimmy helped Gramps cuff him before he came around, which he did almost before they got the cuffs on him. He started screaming at his father, cussing the stars out of the heavens, but Jimmy helped Gramps cuff his ankles together anyway.

Jimmy retrieved his gun, put the safety on and snapped it into its holster. He found the lighter and opened both doors and all the windows to the cabin, turned out the lights, and rode out to the gate with Gramps and Bo John. Gramps was taking Bo John to the doctors. Jimmy noted that in spite of Bo John's ranting, Gramps had left the cuffs on.

When Jimmy returned to the cabin, he inspected the damage. Among other things, Bo John had taken the photos Jimmy had on display in the bedroom. There had been the one of his mother which Grandma had given him when he was a child. He had had one of Grandma and himself and another one of he and Grandpa made when he was 10 and got his first deer. He'd had one of he and Harry and Evangeline and another one of Evangeline. Jimmy knew they were somewhere in the kerosene soaked pile in the other room.

Jimmy looked at the heaped up jumble. Bo John had piled all the furniture together, then added the mattress and all the bedding, all the clothes from the dresser drawers, all the linens including the kitchen towels, and even some of the curtains from the windows, leaving the rods broken and hanging. Jimmy sorted out the mess, carrying all the kerosene soaked linens and clothing out to his truck. The mattress was unsalvageable and he dragged it out back away from the cabin. He stacked the furniture on the back porch and surveyed the remains of his family pictures with sadness. Bo John had ripped them out of their frames and torn them to pieces, piled the pieces in a basin and poured kerosene on them. Jimmy guessed that Bo John had done that before he came home and planned to light it in front of him as a taunt.

Jimmy needed to sleep. He called the Lilac Bush and when Rose answered, arranged a room for a night or two until he could get things cleaned up. He asked her to keep quiet about what Bo John had done. He walked up the path and made a short call to Evangeline. As he was leaving, he realized that Mama Cat and her kittens had disappeared and he hadn't seen Tommy at all, which was weird. Tommy was always under his feet, wanting to be fed or petted. He put out a dish of dried cat food by the hand-pump, knowing that if Tommy didn't eat it soon, the raccoons would.

At the Lilac Bush, Rose talked to Jimmy about breaking up with her boyfriend. She told him, "He had invited me to visit his family. The purpose of my visit was for me to meet his family and to announce our engagement. When I got there, I discovered his family were all out of town which made me uncomfortable. He was pressuring me for you-know-what. He said if we were going to announce an engagement to his family, then it was time to take it to the next level." Rose was shaking her head. "I know it's how a lot of people think but I just felt like a target being hit on. He kept smooching all over me and slipping his hands where they didn't belong. I was supposed to stay another day and meet his family when they came home." Rose stopped and then said, "When I told him I wouldn't have sex with him, he finally put me in his parents' bedroom. It gave me the creeps. The sheets hadn't been changed and there were dirty clothes scattered around. It was clear no one had expected me to sleep there. Then, in the middle of the night, he came into the room. I woke up. He tried to claim he was walking in his sleep – like I'm going to believe that! After I got him out of the room, I packed my things and came home."

Rose asked me, "Jimmy, are all men such turds?"

"No," I told her, "but a lot of them are and Big Creek doesn't have much selection."

Rose smiled and then joked, "If I get really desperate, there's always Robby Lee."

The next morning, Aunt Lilac told him to leave the mess with her. The clothes would need more than a normal wash. When she asked what had happened, he'd told her about Bo John but asked her not to talk about it. She shook her head and commented, "Bo John makes Robby Lee look like a mischievous kid."

She directed Jimmy to a second hand furniture and junk dealer where he found a reasonable mattress and loaded it into his truck. He headed back out to his cabin, knowing he had a lot of cleaning to do before moving back in. He parked by the barn. He wanted to check that Bo John had not messed with things in there.

Jimmy checked everything carefully but saw nothing to indicate Bo John had been there. Myrna, Gramps, and Lisa Marie had all assured him that Bo John did not know that Jimmy was making meth for them.

Satisfied that everything in the barn was secure, Jimmy started to the cabin. Near the house, something caught his eye when two large black birds flapped into the air. As he took a closer look, his blood froze. It was the orange striped cat, Tommy. His death had not been easy. Jimmy could see a trail where the injured cat had dragged himself from the front porch. It was clear that he had a broken back leg but that was minor. His belly had been sliced open and his intestines were strung out behind him. The birds had been pecking at the entrails.

Jimmy knelt beside Tommy's body and touched his head. Tommy opened his eyes and Jimmy was horrified to see that poor animal was not dead. He was sure Tommy could not survive but he could not bring himself to shoot him. He phoned the animal clinic and asked if there was some kind of injection to kill an animal painlessly. There was. He arranged for Gramps to pick it up and bring it out to the cabin. When Gramps balked, Jimmy said, "Gramps, you got Bo John paroled. You're responsible for him being loose. You deserve to see what he's done to this poor animal."

Jimmy brought an umbrella from his truck to shade Tommy and then dribbled water in his mouth which Tommy licked and swallowed. Jimmy wished he had found him last night. At that point, he might have been savable.

When Gramps arrived, he looked at Tommy grimly and silently injected the needle. Then, he walked away while Jimmy quietly stroked Tommy's head as he died. When Tommy's breathing stopped, Jimmy went after a shovel. He dug a really big hole near the corner of the front porch and buried him deep. He stood over the grave for a silent prayer.

Gramps was sitting on the front steps. "Thanks for bringing that injection," Jimmy told him.

When Gramps looked up, he saw tears in his eyes. He said to Jimmy, "Boy, what am I going to do?"

Jimmy realized the tears Gramps were shedding were not for Tommy but for Bo John, his son, who was a monster. Gramps said, "Bo John was such a fine looking boy, like you. He was great at sports, on all the teams at school. Then, he got your mom pregnant and had to get married. I paid him to finish school and your mom's folks helped out, too. Her mother kept you so your mother could finish. I wanted your dad to go to college but he started driving a truck. Then, your mom's family got killed in that wreck up near Nashville and your mom took you and left. All those years Bo John was in prison, I waited for him to come home. I thought he could start over, find a wife, get married, have some more kids. He's not too old. But all he wants to do is drugs and prostitutes. I keep thinking, what did I do wrong? Years ago, I blamed his mother, I blamed Myrna, I blamed your mother, I blamed everyone else, but I didn't blame Bo John."

Jimmy looked at the white puffy clouds sailing merrily across the blue sky, and then looked at Gramps and said, "And now, you're blaming yourself instead of Bo John."

"Well, boy, you said on the phone I was responsible for him being loose. What am I going to do?"

Jimmy shook his head. He wanted to say, *shoot him,* but Bo John wasn't an animal that you could just give an injection, dig a hole, and bury him.

Gramps left and Jimmy buried the remains of his family pictures beside the big rock up the trail behind the cabin. He spent the rest of the day scrubbing down the furniture and cabin floor. When it started to get dark, he loaded the wing-back chair, it's footstool, and the cushions from the rockers into the back of his truck. They would have to be redone. He'd rolled up a large rag rug and thought he'd ask Aunt Lilac if it could be saved. The sofa he dragged away from the house and turned over onto the mattress. It wasn't worth saving and tomorrow he would burn them both.

After another night at the Lilac Bush, he found an upholstery man Aunt Lilac had recommended. The man examined the chair and footstool and declared them to be, "Good furniture, worth saving." Jimmy's look at possible replacements yesterday had produced the same conclusion. "Don't build this stuff now like they used to," the man said and named a fee that Jimmy thought reasonable. Aunt Lilac had tut-tutted over the rocker cushions and said to leave them with her.

Jimmy had asked Aunt Lilac where to get daffodil and crocus bulbs. He planted them on Tommy's grave.

That night, he slept back at the cabin and Mama Cat and her kittens finally reappeared. They weren't particularly hungry and he decided they must take after their mother and enjoyed catching their own food. They liked his bits of hamburger but thought the dry kibble Tommy had eaten was definitely for the raccoons.

Jimmy went up the path and spent a long time talking on the phone and praying.

When he told Grandma about Gramps tears, she said, "I understand. If his son died from an illness or in an accident, he would have his good memories to comfort him. But he's grieving over the loss of his hopes and dreams for his son. That is more heartbreaking than a physical death."

Chapter 14: The Computers

Lisa Marie was the computer expert. Somehow this surprised Jimmy. Lisa Marie said, "Why is it that all men think that if a woman is attractive, she must be dumb? I was studying computer technology at college. That loser I married was studying fun and games. I was hired to tutor him through a basic math class. He couldn't add two and two and get four, so why I thought he'd make a decent husband, I cannot for the life of me think?"

Jimmy said, "Hormones?"

Lisa Marie laughed.

"Yeah," she agreed, "but now-a-days every girl knows how not to get pregnant. He was the first man I'd ever done it with and I thought I had to marry him. I was naive."

"Naive is not the same as stupid," Jimmy said.

"Myrna said you're an idea person. Sometimes you come out with some good ones," she said. She was showing him how to use Skype. She had a computer at home and Myrna was there. They made contact and then disengaged several times until Jimmy understood how it worked. Then Lisa Marie said, "Now you can talk to your girl at home face to face."

Jimmy said, "I don't think she's got the right kind of computer."

"Almost all computers can do this now-a-days," Lisa Marie said. "Call her up and we'll try it."

Jimmy looked at the clock and said, "She teaches school. She's working right now."

"The school will have a computer that can Skype for sure," Lisa Marie said.

"But will it show later in the usage records?" Jimmy asked. "The school monitors computer use carefully."

Lisa Marie said, "If I was there, I could take it out of the record."

"Show me how to do that," Jimmy said.

So Jimmy spent time learning to Skype and learning how to remove the record. But he never actually said anything in his conversations with Evangeline that was not for Lisa Marie's ears. He did not trust her not to be spying somehow. With an illusion to maintain, he could get soppy. He talked about Evangeline's beautiful warm brown eyes and how he wished he could run his fingers through her gleaming midnight hair. The family had a good dose of Indian ancestry and he called her his Cherokee Rose. He talked about walking in the moonlight and wishing on falling stars.

At home, up the path he told his team to tell Pendegrass that his last meddling with Jeremy Anderson had the drug enterprise on high alert and they had shut down the meth lab for a while. Pendegrass needed to quit trying to interfere and give things some time to get back to normal.

He also warned Evangeline that because they had used Skype, Lisa Marie could now probably get into the computer Evangeline had been using. It had been a school computer and Jimmy also speculated that Lisa Marie might could get into the other school computers. Evangeline and Harry canceled their internet service at home. Their parents both had internet at work but were puzzled about the cancellation of service at home. The two conspirators spun their parents a tale about students hacking into the computers of teachers.

In the meantime, Harry was having fun getting Pendegrass to admit that he had maneuvered Jimmy into working for him. Harry brought up Pendegrass's attempts to interfere and the negative consequences. Pendegrass maintained that if he had direct communication with Jimmy, there were not have been any problems and things would be moving along much faster. He didn't seem to realize that his words were confirming the truth of his attempts to interfere. Harry had it all recorded.

Jimmy had gotten his cabin put back together and he was cooking meth every minute he wasn't working, on the phone with his team, sleeping, or eating. He had took to watching Mama Cat every time he came home. She had known Bo John was waiting in there and had been leery.

Jimmy never got access to the surveillance system in the office without Myrna or Lisa Marie there but Evangeline was finding out things for him from the computer teacher at her school. Things like that if a computer had Skype capability, then a good hacker could turn on the camera and watch people. She told him where to find the small light that gave it away but said that many people did not know about it so they didn't notice if it was on. She said a good hacker could get into other people's computers and read their passwords and access their e-mail and anything else they had on their computer. Jimmy thought it all was a bit scary. He wondered who Lisa Marie was spying on.

During a teaching session, Jimmy asked about people accidentally leaving their system on and getting watched when they didn't know it. He phrased his inquiry like he had just thought about people being careless. He wanted to see how much Lisa Marie would tell him.

"It happens," she said. "My ex did exactly that when I was supposed to be attending class. I watched him with another woman."

Jimmy said, "I guess I need to be really careful I shut everything down when I've been talking to Evangeline. She said the computer lab teacher asked her what she had been doing on his computers and then he said she needed to be really careful to shut down properly."

Jimmy was waiting for Lisa Marie to tell him that a good hacker could turn the system on and use it to spy on people. When she didn't tell him, he knew she was doing exactly that. She had probably been watching him when he was running the office. He was ardently thankful he had been so careful. Lisa Marie had been spying on him and now she thought she could trust him. He wondered who else she spied on.

When he first moved out to the cabin, Lisa Marie had suggested he get a laptop and internet service. He had said he didn't need it. It would require a satellite and they were expensive. Lisa Marie told him that with a satellite he could also get TV. He told her he didn't have time for TV.

Jimmy was slowly confirming who were the drivers transporting meth and marijuana out of the county and meth making supplies back in. The meth and the marijuana were being handled by two totally separate groups of people. None of the meth carriers had any idea what they were carrying out or in. All three were older women, Aunt Lilac being the one used most often and the other two only when Aunt Lilac was too busy to go. There were always the boxes of supposed dog food and a dog going to Nashville. Usually, there was a dog for the return trip and Jimmy had the idea that sometimes the dog returning was the same as the one which went.

The marijuana was bulkier and required a lot more carriers. The drivers knew what they were carrying. Most of them were growers. One man had pigs and the truck he hauled them in had a hidden compartment. The pigs were so smelly, no one wanted to look very carefully. Jimmy caught on because he never sold the pigs, just hauled them out of the county and then back in. One man sold mulch. The plastic bags he used were even partially transparent and it seemed that no one had ever suspected that not all of them contained what they said. Another man was a junk dealer. The next county had an open air market every Saturday and he always took junk to sell. He had a cousin who was also a junk dealer and always met him at the market and took the marijuana onward. An old couple had a station wagon from which the seat cushions had been removed and they used the space to carry marijuana. They always had other stuff in the back of the car and no one ever checked them with a sniffer dog. All of these people were carrying out fairly small batches. It was an untaxed side income.

The biggest grower was Uncle Bobby Ray. He was not sending his stuff out with the tomatoes or using any of his tomato operation trucks.

It was going out in assorted vehicles driven by assorted relatives, never by any of the Mexicans. A lot of the drivers were women and they took small children along. When Robby Lee was around to escort, they sometimes sent bigger shipments but mostly it was pickup trucks and SUVs.

The most risky loads going out were the moonshine. Jimmy worked it out that they used a different vehicle every time and they always had an escort which was never Robby Lee. They set it up with the sheriff's office before hand. They had not moved anything the week Lisa Marie had been gone. It was not a high volume business. No one ever talked about it at the office and Jimmy never asked questions.

One thing Jimmy very much wanted to know but decided he shouldn't ask was where Sally cooked her meth. It was not at her house or her husband's clinic which was where her dog kennels were located. Jimmy waited patiently, knowing that any sign of curiosity would be a mistake. Asking Sally would make her suspicious. One day in the office, he learned that neither Myrna nor Gramps knew where her cooking location was, either. Jimmy knew then that he probably was not going to find out. But it crossed his mind that Lisa Marie with her computer spying knowledge might know.

One night when he was checking out before going home, Jimmy asked Lisa Marie if Sally was a Jones. Lisa Marie laughed. "Of course," she said. "She's a natural redhead but she keeps her hair blonde. She's had it blonde for years and she says her husband likes it. She's a tricky person and I don't totally trust her."

"Really?" Jimmy asked, "Do I need to be careful what I tell her?"

"No," Lisa Marie said. "She likes you. You're making her money. But don't be standing in her way if she wants something. Things happen to people who get in her way."

"What kind of things?" Jimmy asked.

Lisa Marie considered and then said, "I've been told that in high school she was manipulative and vindictive. She had ways to get what she wanted. She wanted to be a cheerleader and was. She wanted a certain role in a school play and got it. She wanted to be homecoming queen and made it. She went away to college and when she came home, she got a job working for the veterinarian she's married to now. I've never been sure what happened. Her husband had a wife and she had health problems and committed suicide. I'm sure they didn't have anything going before his wife died but with her out of the way, it didn't take Sally any time at all to land him. I didn't think anything about it until Hank blew himself up."

She stopped and Jimmy waited. "Hank was the cook who lived in the trailer out by your cabin. It was about three days before anyone went out to check on him. He was not nearly as reliable as you are and Sally used to go out there often to check on him, sort of encourage him to get things done, keep him honest. He was using and Sally suspected he was selling on the side and I think she was right. Trying to fire a meth cook isn't easy. He can just go to drug enforcement and get a reward for getting fired." She paused again and then went on, "Him blowing himself up was convenient. He hadn't answered his phone for three days and I find it hard to believe Sally hadn't been out to check on him. She said her kids were sick and sent Dad out to check what was going on so it was Dad who found him." Lisa Marie shook her head. "I have never been sure. But I've discovered that if Sally wants something, she gets it."

Harry reported that Pendegrass was getting greatly aggravated about the lack of progress and was demanding that they arrange for Jimmy to come out to Nashville or somewhere that Pendegrass could meet him. Jimmy said, "Tell him they are relaxing and I think we'll be back in operation soon. Tell him when we do, I have some ideas for finding out how supplies are coming in and how they are getting product out. Tell him Uncle Bobby Ray has a small airplane he flies himself. When I think he might be taking out a load, I'll pass the word."

In reality, Jimmy knew that Bobby Ray never used the plane to transport product. It was too obvious. Pendegrass took the bait and the next time Bobby Ray flew out, he was searched. Jimmy sent word back through Harry that Pendegrass had blown it again. He had not waited to get a word from Jimmy and now they would probably never use the plane to transport stuff again.

Jimmy talked with his team trying to evaluate where they were with the investigation. He thought he had enough information to make arrests but they were never going to get all of those *farmers*. They decided that when Lisa Marie made her next trip to Florida might be a good time to try to wrap it up. Jimmy talked about his reluctance to see Lisa Marie and Myrna in jail.

Jimmy talked to Evangeline a lot about the people. She asked if anything more had come up with Myrna about what happened when she was twelve. Jimmy told her no, but talking about an unmarried woman having a baby had hit a nerve with her. Evangeline wondered if she had had an abortion and was still dealing with remorse.

Jimmy found himself praying for Myrna, for Lisa Marie, for Gramps, for the whole situation.

❈ ❈ ❈
Chapter 15: Accident

Five days after the incident with Bo John, Jimmy returned home from work to find that someone had been through his gate. He called the sheriff's office number and got Lisa Marie. He asked her where Bo John was and she asked why. He told her someone had been through his gate. He waited while she checked. Bo John was home where he was supposed to be. She said, "I'm listening to your bugs but I don't hear anything. I'll backtrack on the recording." Jimmy found it entertaining that she was not even pretending they did not record everything said out at his cabin.

He drove in with his lights off but found no vehicle there. Mama Cat came and greeted him but he when he moved near the cabin, she complained. He circled the cabin to look in the window where he had looked before. The window was shut. He had left it open with the screen with the cat door in it. He felt his hair standing on end. He tried to look through the window but could not see anyone. He moved away and Mama Cat quit complaining. If someone was inside, they would have heard his truck arrive. Were they laying in wait for him? Why close the window? It was no longer summer and maybe whoever it was had gotten cold.

Jimmy went back to his truck and called Lisa Marie again. She said her Dad was out at the ranch and so she knew Bo John was there. But Dad had taken a woman home with him and Lisa Marie was reluctant to call him. She said that Myrna had taken a sleeping pill so she didn't want to wake her up. She had listened back through the recording and heard some noise but it was just doors opening and closing, maybe windows going up or down, small noises like that. Also, a man's voice mumbling like he was talking to himself, but nothing understandable except a few cuss words. She didn't want to send Marvin or one of the other deputies because she was worried it might turn out to be something they didn't want one of them to see. She asked if he wanted her to come and he said no, he thought he would check a little more first.

Jimmy got to wondering if it was Pendegrass waiting for him. If so, he didn't want Lisa Marie out here. So he told her he'd look around a little more and call her back. He approached the house again on foot. He circled around to the outhouse and left his smart phone and his personal phone there. He had to be sure it wasn't Pendegrass. He didn't go to either of the doors but he had remembered that one of the bedroom windows had no lock on it. He didn't know if he could get it up without making noise but he would try. He got a screw driver and a putty knife and slid them under the window and it moved easily. He pushed up on the frame and it slid up an inch. His screw driver fell to the ground and he bent over to pick it up. He smelled gas. Mama Cat was back some distance away complaining. He had turned the putty knife sideways to hold the window cracked open. He put his nose to the crack. Gas. No mistake.

Jimmy moved away from the window and joined Mama Cat. Between his cabin and the barn was a large propane tank which fueled his cook stove and a gas heater for winter. The propane gas had a distinctive odor. A spark of any kind would set it off. If his cabin was full of gas, it could explode. Had someone rigged something to make a spark when he opened his front door?

Propane tanks like this one had shut-off valves at the tank so Jimmy shut it off. He went back to the window and carefully eased the wooden frame up and propped it up with a stick. He went around to the other side of the cabin and checked the window where the screen had been. Whoever shut it, had not locked it. He eased it open and propped it with a stick. He could smell the gas.

Jimmy called Lisa Marie and told her what he'd found. She told him to leave the cabin to air out and come sleep at their house tonight. "Dad's gone. You can have his bed," she said.

The next morning, he was up early and did bacon, scrambled eggs with cheese, fried potatoes, biscuits and gravy. When Myrna got up, she faced him and the feast with bewilderment. He was telling her about the night before when Lisa Marie appeared. It was clear she usually slept in but she dug into the food with enthusiasm and said, "Who could sleep through this? I should have suspected you might know something about cooking. Too bad you're too close kin. I'll have to think of some other way to keep you here."

They discussed the event and the names which come up were Bo John and Robby Lee. Lisa Marie had listened to the whole section where someone was in the cabin but all she heard was a few mutters sounding like a man's voice talking to himself while he was doing something.

Lisa Marie said, "I've checked and it wasn't Bo John. I'll talk to Robby Lee. If it was him, he'll tell me."

Myrna looked concerned. "Lisa Marie, don't let him get you into bed."

"Don't worry," Lisa Marie told her. "He's got the morals of a tomcat. But he's not a sneaky conniver. Now if Sally were mad at you for some reason, I'd suspect her but she's real happy with you."

Myrna went off to the office and Jimmy went home. He checked everything in the barn carefully before approaching the cabin. When he went to the window for a look inside, Mama Cat jumped up on the sill to greet him. He climbed in and looked around. The trigger was a simple device, battery operated, designed to produce sparks when the front door was opened.

He thought it might have fingerprints on it so he got a paper bag and gently pried out the batteries. The device had been taped to the door-frame and he bagged it as well. He was debating running it into town or just letting it wait. He had planned to spend the next couple of days cooking. He started to town and Lisa Marie called so he pulled over to talk to her.

"It was Robby Lee," she told him. "I called his house and his mom answered. I asked if he was home and she said he was still sleeping. She says he came home from a run yesterday and then he got a phone call. She said there's a rumor going around town about you and Rose and someone called and told him. She says he yelled and cussed and slammed out of the house and then came home late last night drunk. She's worried. She said he hasn't come home drunk like that in a couple of years. I talked to Myrna. She says the gossips have been talking about why you were at the Lilac Bush and why you were buying a new bed, a new sofa, and having other furniture redone. Rose's mother is redoing your rocker cushions. Everyone is speculating that you and Rose are getting hitched. I hadn't heard the gossip or I would have warned you. Myrna had heard it but it was so silly, she hadn't bothered to talk about it."

Lisa Marie said, "I called Jennifer back and had her get Robby Lee on the phone. I told him you and Rose do not have anything going. I told him a skunk got in your cabin and your cats tackled it and created a disaster." She paused and then said, "Bo John is a skunk, isn't he?" Jimmy couldn't help laughing.

Lisa Marie went on, "Robby Lee's not nearly as dumb as he sounds with all that hill-talk he does and he's pretty straight-forward, doesn't hide things. You should talk to him."

"Lisa Marie," Jimmy said. "Robby Lee could have killed me. I wondered if he's done it before."

"I thought of that," Lisa Marie said. "I asked him and he swore he hadn't killed anyone. He said he knew who had but he wasn't talking."

Instead of going into town, Jimmy went out to Robby Lee's. His mom answered the door and looked at him in total shock. Jimmy knew Robby Lee and he looked a lot alike but he had never seen him without his beard. However, if he gave his mother such a shock, he decided they must really look alike.

Jimmy said politely, "Ma'am, is Robby Lee home?"

Robby Lee was still in bed and his mother invited Jimmy in but was so flustered, it was almost funny. She was clearly a Jones, tall, brown eyes, skin that tanned without freckling, fiery red hair, Jones face features. While she went to tell Robby that Jimmy was here, he studied a large family photograph on the wall. Robby Lee was about 10 and looked just like Jimmy at that age. It struck Jimmy that his own mother had looked similar to the Jones women. Her hair had been a lighter red and her eyes hazel but she had been tall. Robby Lee's father had black hair and brown oriental type eyes. Robby Lee looked nothing like him. The family group showed a younger boy, maybe 4 or 5, and a girl, maybe 2 or 3. The two younger kids both had dark hair and looked like their father. He saw another framed picture of a family group sitting on a table. It included an Asian woman and a tall man with brown hair. Grandparents? Jimmy remembered what Aunt Lilac had said about Robby Lee's father being half Asian but faced with the dramatic differences in appearance, Jimmy's thought was that Robby Lee had a different father than the two younger children.

After maybe 10 minutes, Robby Lee appeared carrying a big mug of coffee. "Let's go get breakfast at Gina's," he said. Jimmy figured out he did not want his mother hearing what they were going to discuss.

Outside, Robby Lee said, "Look, Jimmy, I'm sorry. Lisa Marie says all this gossip is hogwash. She said you got a skunk in your cabin and your cat tackled it and it was so bad, you had to burn your sofa and your mattress."

Jimmy noticed Robby Lee had dropped the hill-talk accent. He still sounded rural south but not completely illiterate as well. Jimmy found himself laughing. "Robby Lee, you're a fraud," he said. "You act like a dumb country hick but you're not really stupid. Who told you Rose and I were getting together? Lisa Marie says the gossip was going around but people would have been careful to not tell you."

Robby Lee looked thoughtful. "Bo John," he said. "He called me and told me. I should have suspected. Bo John ain't never called me before. First time ever. Why now?"

Jimmy looked at Robby and said, "Well, that skunk who got into my cabin was Bo John."

"What?!" Robby Lee said.

"I came home one night and he was waiting for me with a shotgun. I ran and he piled up everything in my cabin and was pouring kerosene on it when Gramps and I got back. He was high on something and it took Gramps and me both to get him cuffed."

Robby Lee was staring at Jimmy with his mouth agape. Jimmy waited and he finally shook his head and said, "Somebody should shoot him."

"Yeah," Jimmy agreed, "but I don't want to go to jail for it so I think I'll let someone else do it."

Robby Lee started laughing and then held his head. "This getting drunk is for idiots." He looked at Jimmy assessingly and said, "You're as slippery as a eel. Bo John didn't catch you and I didn't either." He shook his head and groaned and added. "I can't believe Bo John set me up like that!"

So then Jimmy asked Robby Lee who he knew had arranged a fatal accident. Robby Lee sobered up and said, "I reckon I owe you. It was Sally. Sally did that Hank in. But he was using so it wasn't hard. She tried to get me to do it and I wouldn't." He paused and said, "Even with you, I figured that gas would blow up and knock you back out the door and you'd survive. It was meant more to warn you off than kill you."

"Robby," Jimmy asked, "why Rose? You seem to get women easily. You don't want to marry her. Why Rose?"

Robby shook his head. "Honestly, I don't know," he said. "Maybe just because she won't have me."

"If the only way you could get her was to marry her, would you do it?" Jimmy asked.

He shook his head, groaned again, and then said, "Probably."

"Robby, has it ever occurred to you that what you really want is a good woman?"

"No," he said. But he looked uncertain, like he wasn't sure.

Jimmy followed him to Gina's. On the way he remembered he had not asked him not to tell anyone about Bo John so in the parking lot at Gina's Jimmy talked to him again. Robby Lee said, "You all are not going to tell anyone I tried to blow up your cabin so I'll not tell anyone about Bo John trying to burn it down." As he was turning away, he stopped and asked, "Jimmy, is that woman who raised you still praying for you?" When Jimmy nodded, he said, "My folks believe in God. Go to church regular. I know Mom prays for me. I was always rebellious but maybe there's something in this God thing."

Robby Lee went into Gina's and Jimmy went home to cook meth. He had to laugh. He had gotten Robby Lee contemplating God and yet he knew what Jimmy was doing. Sometimes life is weird. Jimmy started praying as he worked. This affair was getting stranger and stranger.

❀ ❀ ❀
Chapter 16: Who's Your Father?

Gramps told Jimmy that Sally wanted him to spend less time playing deputy and more time cooking meth but Gramps had insisted Jimmy needed to keep up appearances. They knew the other deputies and anyone else who had thought about it, assumed Jimmy was going to eventually take over from Gramps when he retired. They discussed it. Jimmy decided it wouldn't hurt if Gramps thought he might be considering it. Gramps told Jimmy he had a knack for law enforcement. He said, "Look how you dodged Bo John and Robby Lee's traps both. Staying alive is a big part of the job. You got natural ability."

It was only a couple of days later when Robby Lee called and asked if he could come out to talk to Jimmy. He set up a time and when Jimmy got home, Robby was waiting for him on his front porch. Jimmy knew whoever was at the office was listening. Mama Cat and two of her kittens were asleep in the other rocker. Robby Lee said, "What happened to that other cat you had, the one that was a bloomin' nuisance?"

Jimmy looked at him and considered. Then, he shrugged and told him, "Bo John killed him that night he tried to burn down my cabin."

"What'd he do? Kick him?"

"No," Jimmy said, "broke both his back legs and cut his belly open so that his intestines fell out. It was awful. When I found him the next morning, he was still alive."

Robby Lee looked sick and expressed his opinion with a curse. Then, he said, "What I came out here about was Bo John. I need to talk to you."

"What else has Bo John done?" Jimmy asked.

Robby Lee shifted uneasily and then said, "Jimmy, you's pretty good at keeping quiet about stuff. This is something I want kept quiet."

Jimmy shrugged. "Okay," he said.

"The other day after my ma saw you, I knew she was really upset. Yesterday, her and Dad had a talk with me." He stopped and squirmed around again and Jimmy had a thought about what he might be going to say. "My folks, they're good people." Robby Lee said. "Dad runs that lawn mower plant fair and honest and really tries to provide some decent jobs for people here. They've tried their best to raise me decent. All my shenanigans are my fault." Robby Lee looked Jimmy in the eye and said, "I found out why you and me look so much alike." He stopped and Jimmy waited, suspecting what was coming. Robby Lee sighed and finally said, "Bo John is my father."

Robby Lee looked upset and unhappy. Jimmy knew the feeling. He said, "Yeah, that day I went by your house, I figured that's probably how it was. The sight of me upset your mom so bad and I saw those family pictures."

Robby Lee shook his head. "My folks said they had debated telling me ever since Bo John was back. Dad did most of the talking. He said my mom was only 16 and Bo John was her cousin. He said her folks was encouraging her to go after Bo John. His mother's family had money and they thought it'd be a good match. But he'd already got your mother pregnant. Your mother's father was the principal out at the high school. Her family kicked up a big fuss and Bo John's parents made him marry her. By the time my mom knew she was pregnant, Bo John was married to your mother. She was scared to tell her parents. Then, she met my father and he had no idea she was so young and he asked her out. They went out a couple of times before he found out she was only 16 and he said she was too young for him. She started crying and eventually she told him about Bo John. She thought he might know how she could get an abortion." Robby Lee shook his head. "Instead, he married her." He looked up at me. "He's not my biological father but if he hadn't married my mom, I might not be here. He's really tried his best to be a good father."

Jimmy looked at Robby Lee's troubled face and said, "Bo John sure has caused a lot of grief."

Robby Lee nodded. "I reckon so. Mom says she's glad she never married Bo John. She says he was mean to your mother and your mother's father had a couple of serious talks with him about it. Then, your mother's parents and brother were killed in that car accident. Nobody was too surprised when your mother took you and left. Mom says that ever since Bo John's came back, she's wanted to tell me the truth but her and Dad thought it would just encourage me to go wild."

"Does it?" Jimmy asked.

"It might have before I found out so much about him, but now all it does is make me want to prove it ain't hereditary." Robby Lee smiled at Jimmy. "Bro, you may cook meth but you'd never murder anybody or torture a dumb animal."

"Or blow someone's cabin up and maybe them too?" Jimmy asked.

Robby Lee shook his head. "I's really bein' stupid when I did that. Fact is, I normally don't drink much anymore. Bad for my fiddle playing. I's half drunk when I got the idea of coming out here. I admit I've scared a few people and I've beat up a few guys over Rose but I never broke that Luke Walberg's leg back in high school. It was an accident but when the other kids started talking, I let them think I did it. And when Grandpa wanted me to provide distractions while he was moving stuff, I thought it was fun."

"And that deputy of Gramps who broke his neck falling off a ladder? You didn't have anything to do with that?" Jimmy asked.

"No," Robby Lee said. "I've wondered if it was Sally but I don't really know. It might have been like Luke with his broken leg. It may have just been an accident but was a good chance to scare anyone else with ideas."

"Do you know of anyone besides Hank that Sally might have arranged something for?" Jimmy asked.

Robby Lee nodded. "Back before she married, she had a boyfriend from out of the area. She got him a job at the plant. Then, he died in a car accident and I heard he was a narc. I've always suspected that Sally found out and arranged it, but I don't know for sure."

"Lisa Marie says she always gets what she wants," Jimmy said.

Robby Lee nodded. "Sally was also the one who started the meth making business. Uncle Johnny spent a lot of money trying to get Bo John off for killing your mother. To be fair, Bo John told his father that she had a gun on her when it happened and the lawyer kept telling Uncle Johnny he was going to get Bo John off with manslaughter. Uncle Johnny did not go out for the trial because the lawyer said it would look better if he stayed away. Uncle Johnny was way in debt and meth meant money. That was why he got in on it. But Sally is a real snake in the grass and I don't trust her."

After a few moments of silence, Jimmy asked, "How many other halves do you think Bo John fathered?"

"That's a thought," Robby Lee said. "Back when I's a teenager Mom caught me one night with a woman. She told me whatever I did with a girl, at least make sure the girl was willing. She said not to get her drunk or give her anything. Yesterday, that came back to me. I don't want to ask Mom but I wondered if Bo John had anything to do with what she told me. But I have stuck to what she said. I've had more woman than most but I don't get them drunk or give them dope. A willing woman is a lot of fun but I don't see the fun in trying to force one. And I never lie and tell them I'm going to marry them or any bullshit like that."

Jimmy laughed. "Maybe that's why they like you, Robby Lee. You're honest and don't try to force them."

Robby Lee grinned and said, "But even that don't work with Rose. Maybe some women is only for marrying. Do you reckon she'd marry me?"

Jimmy laughed. "Probably not," he said.

Robby Lee said, "I wondered about Felicity. You're about three months older than me. Felicity is about 8 years younger. If Bo John got to her mother while he was out on bail right before his trial, the time would be right."

"Gramps told me her dad has always said she wasn't his," Jimmy told Robby Lee. "But he says her mother is always at that church that handles snakes. Do you think they allow adultery?"

Robby Lee grinned. "No," he said. "I heard there's some weird church that lets a man have more than one wife but I never heard of any church that allowed adultery."

Jimmy said, "You know what's going to happen now. We're both going to keep looking around to see who else could be a half."

"Yeah," Robby Lee nodded his head, "and I'm thinking I better be careful who I hook up with. I wouldn't want to do it with my sister."

After Robby Lee was gone, Jimmy talked to his team. He and Evangeline discussed the convoluted Jones family. Jimmy had a long prayer session. He was more than ready for this operation to be over.

The next morning when Jimmy went on duty, it was Lisa Marie instead of Myrna. When Jimmy asked if Myrna was sick or something, Lisa Marie said, "Or something. You know last night when Robby Lee went out to your place, we listened in. We were just making sure you were okay. I was really shocked and Myrna and I talked about it some before we went to bed. This morning Myrna woke me up to take her shift. She's been drinking. Dad was out at the ranch last night. I don't want to tell him. He just makes her worse. She actually rarely goes on a bender like this. I don't know what to do."

"Do you think it would do any good for me to talk to her?" Jimmy asked.

"I don't know," Lisa Marie said. "She does like you. It wouldn't hurt to try."

Everything was quiet, so Jimmy went over to their house. He didn't knock. He just went in.

Myrna was setting in a chair in the living room with her feet up and a bottle of bourbon beside her. The curtains were pulled and the room was dark. She looked up at Jimmy but didn't say anything. Jimmy went in and sat down in the matching chair. She took another swig out of the bottle and said, "You want some."

"I'd rather have coffee," Jimmy said. "You want some."

"Why not?" she said, so he went to fix it.

He knew how she liked it and when he come back, she took it. Jimmy sipped on his. After a while, he said, "Do you want to talk about it?"

She shook her head. "I wish someone would have said that when I was 12."

Jimmy just waited.

After a while she said, "Mom and Dad were gone to a party. Bo John said beer was fun and we should try it. He got me drunk and raped me." She started crying.

Jimmy reached over and took her hand and she gripped it. "I was only 12 and I was his little sister. He raped me. I was so innocent, I didn't even know what he'd done to me but it hurt and there was some blood. He told me if I told Mom, he tell her about me drinking the beer. So I didn't tell her."

Jimmy felt his anger surging. No wonder Myrna was moody and unhappy and was seeing a psychiatrist. Myrna went on, "Then, one night when Mom and Dad were gone, I was asleep and he came in my room and did it again. I tried to fight him off but he was two years older than me and big for his age. He told me if I told Mom, he'd tell her about me getting drunk." The tears were running down Myrna's face and she looked tragic. "He kept on doing it and I tried not to get left home alone with him. But he stalked me. It went on for more than a year. He said if I told, that he'd make Mom have some kind of accident and die and then he could get me every night. Once he caught me down at the stable. I think that was when I got pregnant. By then, I was 13. I was five months along before Mom noticed. How's that for good parenting?"

Jimmy passed Myrna his handkerchief. She wiped her face and

blew her nose. "Mom took me to a doctor but it was too late for an abortion. She was so angry at me. She told Dad she wanted Bo John punished but Bo John told them I seduced him. He said we were both drunk the first time and I seduced him. Dad believed him and blamed me for it happening. He said I was a girl so I should have known better. I was 12. I didn't know anything."

Myrna was silent for a couple of minutes and then said, "After I had the baby, Mom put me in a boarding school run by nuns. I went to her parents for holidays. After she died, I never came here, not until after Bo John went to prison." She stopped again, and then took a deep breath. "Once I asked Dad about Mom drowning and I figured out Bo John could have done it. Dad never suspected. How could Dad be so stupid?"

Jimmy could not think what to say. It was too tragic and too awful. Some things were beyond words. She cried for a while but then drank her coffee and didn't drink any more of the bourbon. When Jimmy asked if she wanted more coffee, she handed him the bourbon bottle and said, "Get rid of this. I know it doesn't help. I just needed to dull the pain. Last night, listening to Robby Lee brought it all back. I'll sleep it off now. I'll go see my psychiatrist tomorrow."

Jimmy went back to the office. He told Lisa Marie that Myrna had gone to sleep it off and said she would go see her psychiatrist tomorrow. Jimmy had counted up. Lisa Marie was the right age but he wasn't going to ask Myrna. Maybe some secrets really did need to stay buried.

That night, he spent a long time talking to Harry, Grandma, and Evangeline. Later he thought how much better he felt just having people with whom he could talk to about the terrible tragedies of life. Poor Myrna wishing someone had asked her to talk when she was 12 was heart-wrenching. One of the things he had discussed was his reluctance to see someone so wounded sent to prison.

❦ ❦ ❦
Chapter 17: The Dog Show

Grand County was preparing for a dog show. It was a big event and Sally was one of the moving forces behind it. She said she always sold all the dogs she had available and so did other people in the area who bred dogs. The show was called the Working Dog Show. Many of the categories were hunting dogs but there were also sheep dogs, cattle herding dogs, guard dogs, guide dogs for the blind, and this year for the first time, dogs trained to assist with other handicaps. She said they would have entries coming from all over the United States and even from Canada.

Jimmy realized with all those dogs coming and going, other things could also be coming and going. It was late fall and the last of the marijuana patches had been cut and dried. It would be a good opportunity for all the small scattered *farmers*.

The show itself took three days. Gramps said the night before it started, there was always a welcome party sponsored by the Society for the Prevention of Cruelty to Animals. He said the third day ended with a big formal dinner where all the trophies were presented. That would be followed with dancing. It was held at the Grand County Fairgrounds. The fairgrounds had originally been some kind of military base way back when they had horses. When the regiment of cavalry which used it was disbanded, the buildings had eventually gone to the county who had maintained them and used them for the county fair, rodeos, and other events. They included a huge building which had once been an indoor training area for the horses and was ideal for holding indoor events in cold weather. There were other buildings for exhibits and vendors, dinners and dances. Every year during the week of the 4th of July, they had a bluegrass music festival. The Working Dog Show was held every other year the first weekend of November and alternated with a horse show event.

Gramps said he never brought in outside law enforcement. He said they did that once years ago and the outsiders caused more trouble than they fixed. But he did have some men he deputized and used for routine things during the show. He told me I would not be cooking during the show and that all us regular deputies would be on duty the entire time. He told me to plan on not going home at all during the show. I could bunk on a cot at the sheriff's office or on the sofa at his house in town or at the Lilac Bush or the Starlight if I wanted to pay for it but they were both always full up with dog show people.

Sally had set up a service to help out-of-towners find accommodation. Local people could rent rooms to dog show people. Vacant houses were rented out and some people even moved in with relatives and rented their own houses. They set up a campground on part of the fairgrounds for campers not needing electric and water hookups. Just out of town on the river was an RV park which loved the dog show. They had full hook-up sites but they also made some temporary arrangements for more campers. A few farmers even rented their barns. Sally's arrangements for finding accommodations for people were efficient and one reason why the dog show had grown so big.

Jimmy learned that the entry fees for the dogs and the attendees barely covered the cost of putting on the show. It was the rents paid by the vendors which was the money maker. Jimmy was told the money taken in for this dog show would pay the upkeep for the fairgrounds for a year. It was as big a money maker as the bluegrass music festival and the county fair and a bigger money maker than the annual rodeo. The money earned by the various events at the fairgrounds funded a lot of the county expenses.

Gramps' security measures were interesting and Jimmy thought a lot of event managers could have taken lessons. His traffic cameras were already catching the license plates and drivers of all vehicles entering and leaving the county. The fairgrounds had two gates and he had surveillance cameras on both which recorded everything passing through in both directions. He knew which places tended to get crowded and he set up surveillance aimed at catching pickpockets. He said, "The first year we did this, we caught 13 pickpockets. Last year was only 1. I think they pass the word. But we'll keep 'em on their toes."

He also had surveillance aimed at catching shoplifters. He said thievery discouraged vendors from returning in the future so he really tried to keep it to a minimum. He had a security booth where someone was watching the screens all the time. He had two people on duty there and a phone number for vendors to call if they noticed something missing. The security people could check for it immediately. They had a setup for running the surveillance footage back and looking. The cameras did not catch every incident but enough to discourage the thieves. Gramps said every time they held the dog show, their surveillance improved and the amount of thieving went down. He said, "These days, professionals know about surveillance and some of them are tricky but we catch enough that I think word goes around. They look for easier pickings. Also, the vendors pass the word and other vendors are happy to come here. We never have empty space."

Jimmy saw Gramps at his politicking best. He knew everybody in the county and chatted with people about their dogs, their businesses, and their families. He remembered names of non-locals who had been here in the past. Jimmy saw that Gramps loved it. When Jimmy commented on it, Gramps said, "If people like you, they assume you're honest and doing a good job."

At the welcoming party, Gramps told Jimmy to stick by him. Myrna was at the sheriff's office but had sent Lisa Marie so Jimmy acted as her escort. Gramps introduced them over and over as "My grandson, Jimmy Joe, and my daughter, Lisa Marie." A lot of men eyed Lisa Marie with interest and Jimmy found he was expected to talk to a lot of women. He couldn't believe how many times he was asked if he was married. He always said, "Engaged," with a wide smile.

It seemed the SPCA had a lot of supporters. The evening started off with a short speech followed by square dancing and Jimmy saw Robby Lee in the band playing a fiddle. Jimmy played the fiddle along with a good number of other instruments. The summer he went home with Grandma, they caught him plinking out a melody on the church piano. Grandma had been impressed and arranged for him to have music lessons. Musical ability is largely inherited and none of the Wilkersons had it but Grandma was a teacher and knew the joy of watching a child develop a talent. Jimmy had brought no instruments with him to Tennessee and intentionally kept quiet about his musical ability but he could see that Robby Lee was a good player and was enjoying himself. After the square dancing, they had a few singers, a group of clog dancers, and to his surprise, Felicity played the spoons. He then got another surprise when Lisa Marie appeared with a dulcimer and sang a very old ballad called "Barbara Allen." Jimmy was enthralled. She was good, very good. After that, was country music suitable for dancing and a lot of couples took the floor. He was asked to dance several times but excused himself, saying he was on-duty.

As the evening progressed and the alcohol intake rose, things got stickier. Jimmy found himself bypassing veiled invitations with bland innocence and less veiled invitations with jokes. Gramps was totally engaged by a sophisticated looking woman and Jimmy was wishing he could leave when Lisa Marie came dashing up and said, "Jimmy, help me. He's drunk and putting his hands all over me." The lush caught up with her and was like an octopus wrapping his arms around her, calling her *Princess*.

Jimmy peeled him off and said quietly, "Mister, go chase someone else."

The man said, "Who the hell are you?"

Jimmy smiled, "Right now, I'm Sir Galahad. Go find another princess to carry off to your castle."

The man stared at him blankly and said, "Princess?" He looked around and said, "Where'd she go?"

But Lisa Marie had escaped to the ladies' room. When the man was gone, Jimmy told Gramps he was taking Lisa Marie home. He asked a woman to take a message for Lisa Marie into the Ladies'.

On the way home, Lisa Marie said, "I've not had to hide in the can since high school. I still can't believe that man. He just came up to me, put his arms around me and said, 'You're my princess.' I never even got his name. I should carry pepper spray."

The next day, the show got underway. The weather was co-operating and Jimmy saw happy smiles everywhere. The dogs were great. These dogs were not pets but working animals, well-trained, well-behaved, and amazingly intelligent.

Jimmy was drifting around, watching the people and making himself seen, as ordered. Gramps said visible uniforms deterred nonsense. He saw local people whom he knew and frequently found himself chatting. It surprised him how many people he had gotten to know.

Jimmy saw Bo John sulking around. When he mentioned it to Gramps, Gramps said, "He's on parole as long as he behaves himself. I warned him that if he caused a problem publicly, I could not keep him from losing his parole." Jimmy saw him once talking to Sally and felt uneasy. Their body language said they were not wanting to be overheard. How long had they been in cahoots? And over what?

The evening events had even more people and Jimmy saw Robby Lee's mother with his dad and younger brother and sister. They were clearly having a good time but when Robby Lee's mother caught sight of him, she looked scared. He just nodded and focused on her husband and said to him, "The dogs are really amazing, aren't they?"

Robby Lee's little sister said, "They're fantastic. I told Mom and Dad I want a dog but they say a puppy takes a lot of attention and training."

Jimmy smiled at the girl and said, "You might get an older dog that is already trained."

"But the puppies are so cute," she said.

Her mother had rallied. "I told her it's like getting a baby. They take so much attention and you can't just take a day off."

Jimmy smiled at the woman and said to her daughter, "Why not get a couple of kittens? They don't need near as much training and two of them will keep each other company."

"Do you think so?" the girl said earnestly.

"I work too much to have a dog. My cats are great pets but they don't mind me being gone all day," Jimmy told her. "They also have gotten rid of my mice," he added.

As the family moved on, Jimmy saw Robby Lee's mother turn and look back at him. He pretended he didn't notice. She was another one of Bo John's victims but a good man had helped her put her life together again and Jimmy was happy for her.

On the final night, the dinner was a massive barbecue with baked potatoes, salad, and pies all made by local women. After dinner, there was music and dancing. Robby Lee was again in the middle of it. Jimmy saw Bo John lurking around but Gramps had told him he had better not make a problem or he'd lock him up himself.

It was late when Myrna called him on his smart phone. "Bo John is taking Felicity out to the ranch. She doesn't know it but he's actually her father. He . . . "

But Jimmy interrupted her. "I'm on my way," he said.

He looked around and spotted Robby Lee on the dance floor with a cute little blonde. He signaled him and they met with dancers moving around them. "Bo John has talked Felicity into going home with him and Myrna just told me that what we suspected is right."

"Damnation!" Robby Lee said, "Doesn't he know?"

"Come on," Jimmy said. "It may not matter if he does."

When they got outside, the cute little blonde was on their heels. Robby Lee said to her, "Sorry, honey. Family emergency."

Jimmy commandeered one of the ATV's they were using inside the fairgrounds and circled behind the buildings to save time. His truck did not have police lights but there wasn't much traffic and he pushed it.

Jimmy had Robby Lee use his phone to call Myrna and assure her they were on their way out to the ranch. Myrna said, "Hurry."

Robby Lee said, "Why doesn't Myrna call Bo John and tell him? Surely he wouldn't do his own daughter?"

Jimmy said, "I think he would."

They caught up with Bo John at the gate into the ranch. The gate had one of those electronic devices where you had to punch in the code to open it. Bo John was having trouble operating it. Jimmy jumped out of his truck and pulled a taser off his belt which they'd acquired since their last problem with Bo John. He ran up to the open window of Bo John's truck and said, "If you move, I'll use this!"

Robby Lee had gone to the other side of the truck. He opened the door and said, "Felicity, you get out of there!"

Instead, she said, "Robby Lee, what are you doing? I can go with anybody I want. You told me no so I found someone else."

Robby Lee reached in and pulled her out. "You silly twit," he said. "He's your father!"

Jimmy was looking at Bo John's face when Robby Lee said it. Jimmy said to Bo John, "You knew she's your daughter."

Bo John just shrugged. "Who cares? She's a bitch in heat. Stick around. She'd probably give you a turn."

Robby Lee had shoved Felicity into Jimmy's truck and she had not heard Bo John's allegation. Jimmy wanted to use the taser on Bo John someplace really painful but knew it was more important to get Felicity out of here. When he climbed back into his truck, Felicity was saying, "Are you sure?"

She turned to Jimmy, she said, "Robby says that Bo John is actually my father!" As Jimmy restarted the truck and put it in reverse, he said, "Ask your mother."

"Dad always said I wasn't his but I thought it was just him and Mom fighting." She sounded bewildered.

Robby Lee said, "No. Jimmy and I figured it out. You're our sister."

Felicity looked back and forth at the two men. Finally she said,

"You two are brothers."

"Of course," Robby Lee was impatient with her slow thought process. "We all three had the same father."

She shook her head and said, "Bo John gave me a beer on the way out here. I think it must have been extra strong or something. I hadn't had any tonight at the dance."

"Dope," Jimmy said. "He was doping you in case you changed your mind and decided you didn't want to have sex with him."

"I hadn't told him I would," Felicity said. "We were going to watch some old movie he said was great."

Robby said, "Felicity, I can't believe you were that stupid."

"Well," she said, "I thought he'd be fun and surely he wouldn't actually rape me, would he?"

"Yes," Jimmy said, "he would." The grim certainty in his voice induced silence in the truck.

They took Felicity to the First Aide Office where they paged one of the doctors. Jimmy told the lady doctor, "We think she may have been given a date-rape drug. Can you do some kind of test?"

They took a blood sample and then the doctor told Jimmy, "She should not be left alone."

Robby Lee said, "I'll take her home and make sure she stays there."

The lady doctor said, "Robby Lee, that's like asking an alcoholic to take charge of the liquor."

Robby Lee shook his head. "Not this one, Doc. Too close kin even for a Jones."

The doctor said, "Oh, sorry. Wait, she's too old to be your . . . " She stopped.

Robby Lee suddenly realized he had said too much. "Uh, Doc," he said, "can you keep it quiet?"

The doctor looked from Robby Lee to Felicity to Jimmy and back to Robby Lee with the wheels in her brain going round and round. "I don't think I want to know," she concluded.

Jimmy went back to the dance. Gramps was still escorting the sophisticated looking lady but when she went to freshen up, Gramps signaled Jimmy and asked, "Where were you? Some little blonde said you and Robby Lee went tearing out of here and told her it was a family emergency. What happened?"

"Bo John was taking Felicity home with him," Jimmy said. Gramps looked horrified. "We caught them at the gate and brought her back."

Gramps looked relieved. "Good," he said.

Jimmy shook his head. "I think he gave her a date-rape drug. The doctor is doing a blood test."

"Crap," Gramps said.

"Yeah," Jimmy said. "We didn't tell the doctor who gave it to her and Robby Lee is taking her home."

Gramps looked concerned again. "Robby Lee is not a reliable person to take charge of a willing woman."

Jimmy grinned. "Robby Lee knows she's his sister. He'll look after her."

"He knows." Gramps shook his head. "I wasn't sure but as she got older, I wondered. After you and Robby Lee had that talk, I asked Bo John. He laughed and said her mother had too much one night at the Robber's Roost and asked him to take her home." Gramps looked disgusted.

"Myrna must have been listening," Jimmy said.

"Yeah," Gramps looked old and tired. "Bo John knew she was his daughter and he gave her a date-rape drug. Hell, boy, what am I going to do?"

Jimmy shook his head and said, "I don't know. I keep thinking sooner or later he's going to do something we can't keep hid and lose his parole."

That night, Jimmy slipped away and phoned Evangeline. He had to talk to someone. He prayed. He wanted this operation over with.

❈ ❈ ❈
Chapter 18: Behind the Scenes

The next day after the dog show ended, Jimmy watched a lot of traffic leaving the area. Last night, he had stopped by the office to talk to Myrna. He had known she would have heard what was said by all of them. They discussed Felicity and the date-rape drug.

Myrna told him there was a local woman who called Bo John and told him all the gossip. Myrna said, "She's married and she never meets him anywhere but she clearly finds Bo John fascinating. Violence turns her on and Bo John likes it. It's sick and I never listen. "

Jimmy told her, "If you ever need help with Bo John and I'm not available, you can ask Robby Lee. He may be a womanizer but he likes his women willing and he was shocked that Bo John would go after Felicity knowing she was his daughter. Robby Lee's a charmer really and I can see why he has no trouble at all getting women into bed." Then he added, knowing it would amuse Myrna, "Well, except for Rose. He got off on the wrong foot with her and she won't let him get close enough to try."

He had checked back in with Myrna again this morning. She told him, "Jimmy, I'm okay. I'm not on a toot. I'm seeing my psychiatrist this afternoon. She thinks me being able to talk to you is helpful."

Gramps kept the regular deputies on duty all day but about 8, told Jimmy he could go home. He dropped by the office and found Lisa Marie on duty. She said, "Myrna told me about Felicity. Bo John really is terrible, isn't he? Myrna had told me not to ever let myself get alone with him. I know Felicity gave him a come-on but do you think he'd do anything to me?"

"Yes," Jimmy said.

When he didn't say more, Lisa Marie sighed. "I think I'm ready to move south."

Jimmy went home wondering if Lisa Marie would ever figure it out. Maybe not. Maybe that was better.

His cats were happy to see him and Jimmy found the place peaceful. He ate and then went up the path to make phone calls.

He started with Harry who told him, "I've got news. I have been doing some careful checking about what law enforcement agencies have jurisdiction over what. Apparently, that isn't always clear and sometimes they bump heads over it. I got passed to an high-ranking Missouri State Trooper who talked to me privately, off the record. He says Pendegrass is not operating by the book. He made it clear that he is not saying what Pendegrass is doing is illegal but he is saying it is not standard operating procedure. He contacted me again yesterday and he suggested that I talk to a man in Nashville. He's made an appointment for me."

Jimmy then called Grandma. She was happy as always to hear from him and he talked to her a while. He told her briefly about Felicity. He told her again how happy he was that she had taken him and raised him. She said, "I think it was God. I thought so then and I think so even more now. Jimmy, I'm beginning to think God is in you being there in Tennessee. Myrna and Felicity have both needed you."

He called Evangeline. He told her in detail about Felicity. She said, "Grandma and I talked about Myrna. We think God put you there to help her. Maybe you're there to help Felicity, too."

"That's what Grandma said when I talked to her just now. I'm ready for this operation to be over but I really don't want Myrna and Lisa Marie scooped up in it. They neither one are bad people. But Bo John needs to go back to jail and Sally Allen needs to join him."

"And what about your grandfather? Should he go to jail, too?"

"Yes, but I think he's suffering. He's asked me twice now what is he going to do with Bo John? Bo John's a monster and Gramps knows it."

Evangeline asked, "How did he get like that?"

Jimmy said, "I've thought about that. I talked to Myrna. Of course, she's bitter and she hates her father. She blames him for how Bo John is. She said when they were growing up, her father gave Bo John everything he wanted. She said she has talked to her psychiatrist about it. Gramps grew up really poor and then he married her mother partly because her family had money. He wanted his son to have everything he had not had when he was growing up. It sounds like he spoiled him rotten. Whatever Bo John wanted, Gramps got for him. So Bo John developed the idea that he was entitled to anything he wanted. Then he started using drugs and that made him worse. Prison didn't help."

"That's sad," Evangeline said.

"Yes," Jimmy said, "but I don't blame it all on Gramps. At some point, Bo John made his own choices."

"That's true," Evangeline said. "He lied to his father about Myrna and about your mother, too. His lies show that he knew it was wrong."

"Yes," Jimmy agreed. "I've also gotten the idea that Bo John and Myrna's mother may have been rather distant. Lisa Marie was 8 when she died and barely remembers her. Myrna told me she was five months pregnant before her mother noticed."

"If she was not happy with her marriage," Evangeline said, "she may have spent a lot time doing things that took her out of it."

Jimmy said again, "I am so thankful that Grandma grabbed me that day in Bakersfield and run with me. It's the best possible thing that could have happened to me."

"Mom says she remembers when Grandma came back from Bakersfield with you and she says she knew something had scared the living daylights out of you. That's why when you started school, she told Harry to watch out for you."

"Did she?" Jimmy said. "And then, when you started the next year, Harry said we should watch out for you. I still remember that first day of school. You wore a pink dress with pink leggings under it and your hair was up in pigtails and tied with pink ribbons. I thought you were the cutest girl in the whole kindergarten."

"Was I? I've tried to figure out why Carolyn is so jealous of me. I think even back in kindergarten, she envied me because I had you and Harry to look after me."

Jimmy said, "Family. They can be wonderful or they can be awful."

"Yes," Evangeline agreed. "I can understand why you feel for Myrna. She needed a big brother to look after her and what she got instead was a perverted beast. When this drug operation is coming apart, can you warn her to run?"

"I don't know," said Jimmy.

That night in bed, Jimmy thought about it all and fell asleep praying for Myrna.

Jimmy was spending a peaceful day cooking meth. Mid-afternoon, Sally called. "I'm out at the gate coming in. Thought I'd let you know."

"Thanks," Jimmy said. "I'm out in the barn."

She was bringing him supplies. She usually met him somewhere and passed them over so Jimmy knew she was actually checking his operation. Making meth is a precise chemical process and he was at a critical stage so he worked while she unloaded and stacked supplies. She had brought an unusually large lot.

Sally watched him work. She finally said, "Jimmy, you're good at this. You're precise, you're careful, and you're efficient. We really would like for you to spend more time at it." Jimmy noticed the use of the royal 'we.' It was Sally who wanted this, not anyone else.

Jimmy said, "Sally, this isn't the time or place to discuss it. If I'm going to take over as sheriff when Gramps retires, then I need to keep up appearances."

"We can find someone else for sheriff. We need you as a cook."

Jimmy said, "We can talk about it when I'm not busy," and stepped around her to get something he needed.

She left but Jimmy thought about the fact that she left a bad taste behind. He remembered being told, 'Sally always gets what she wants.'

Jimmy felt like a juggler with a lot of balls in the air. It was time to end this act before he dropped something.

After he shut down that night, he called Harry to find out what happened at his meeting in Nashville. Harry said, "Jimmy, I liked this guy a lot better than Pendegrass. We met at a restaurant and he started by giving me information. He says they know marijuana is coming out of Grand County but in the overall picture of things, it's nothing compared to what's coming out of Mexico. He says if they catch someone, good, but it isn't worth sending in an undercover and it certainly isn't worth anyone risking their life.

"He said the meth is more serious. He said it's been going on for years but it's never been a huge amount. Jimmy, I hope you won't be mad at me but I ended up telling him about the whole operation. I started by telling him how Pendegrass recruited you. I could tell he didn't like it but what he said was the he couldn't control what federal law enforcement did, but it wasn't standard procedure. I've decided the the phrase *it isn't standard procedure* is a euphemism for *that's not how it's supposed to be done*.

"Anyway, I told him you went in and you know a lot and want to finish it, but we no longer trust Pendegrass not to get you killed. I gave him a rundown of all the stupid things Pendegrass has done. He never said anything, just shook his head.

"What he did say is that if you would let us know a strategic time and place, he'd have men available to do what you thought would work. He said the best thing would be to catch a meth lab in operation. He said either that or have them intercept a large shipment which could be proved to have come from certain people.

"I told him you knew who the other cook was but not where she worked." Harry paused, and then said, "Jimmy, I liked this man. He said you were the one on the ground. You were the one in danger. You should be the one to say when and where and how they moved in."

Jimmy told Harry, "Set up a communication line with him for you and Evangeline and Grandma. Let me do a little thinking. Add a couple of things to our code list. 'My cat has been chasing a mouse around' means get ready to move. 'My cat has a mouse cornered' means I've located where and when. After that, I'll have to find a way to call with exact place and time."

When they were getting off the phone, Harry said, "Jimmy, we're praying for you."

❀❀❀
Chapter 19: Rising Pressure

When Jimmy reported in for duty, it was Myrna in the office, as usual. She said, "Things are quiet. Everyone is still resting up from the dog show."

Jimmy told her, "Sally paid me a visit. She wants me to spend more time cooking."

Myrna said, "Yeah, she told Dad that and he said you were going to take over as sheriff when he retired so you needed to keep up your deputy job. I found out Dad never told her you were doing this to get money to buy some land up in Missouri. I don't think we better tell her. She wants you here cooking meth."

Jimmy had thought of a ploy. He said, "Tell her I got a cousin from Missouri I can trust. Tell her he's my best friend and my girl's brother. Tell her I'm working on getting him down here to help me cook."

"Are you?" Myrna asked.

Jimmy smiled at her. "Right now it's just an idea but it'll keep Sally off my back for a while. And who knows? If I set up in Missouri later, he can help me."

Myrna grinned. "Jimmy, you do come up with ideas."

Gramps was getting ready to go on a hunting trip to Colorado with his brother, Bobby Ray. Myrna said they went every year Thanksgiving week. She said they might need him in the office some while Gramps was gone.

Jimmy and Robby Lee had a long talk. Robby confessed that truck driving was getting old and maybe he needed to do something else. He said, "Dad took me on at the plant when I finished high school but I hated it. Too boring."

"Do you hunt?" Jimmy had asked.

"No," Robby said. "Dad doesn't hunt. Grandpa talks about it but the only hunting he really does any more is that trip he takes every year to Colorado. That's coming up soon. He flies out with your grandpa. He hasn't ever offered to take me and I'm not sure I'd like it. The idea of shooting some poor defenseless animal doesn't really appeal to me."

Jimmy had said, "I grew up hunting but Grandpa had a rule: if you killed it, you ate it. Hunting for food was fine but doing it just for sport was a violation of the natural order of life and Grandpa considered it a sin."

Robby Lee nodded. "If I needed the meat, I expect I could do it but all that bragging about how big the buck was and so on is childish. It's like bragging about how many women you've had." He paused and then said, "I've learned if you want to keep a woman sweet, don't mention her name." Robby Lee grinned. "When I had my first one, I was only 14 and she's long gone but she was a school teacher and she taught me how a woman likes it done." He paused and then said, "Getting arrested over at Batesville made me stop and think. The judge had set my bail so high, I told me family I'd just set it out. I was there two months waiting for my court hearing. Lots of women like a tickle and I can tell when they're thinking about it. But they aren't trophies to be hunted down and those fights I was getting in were all over women. I thought it was fun to winkle a girl away from some other man. I needed to change my ways." He sighed. "I've tried being a little more grown up about it."

Jimmy said, "Rose told me she felt like a target."

Robby Lee shook his head. "I need to quit chasing that girl. I started on it in high school and somehow I've never been able to forget her. She was not only a looker but a top student. Every boy in school wanted her. But I need to quit chasing her."

The next Sunday after their talk, Jimmy was surprised to see Robby Lee in church sitting with an older couple. He made no attempt to talk to Rose.

Jimmy asked Gramps if he had ever thought about using Robby Lee as a deputy. Gramps said, "That trouble-maker? He plays those gigs in bars and gets into fights. He's been in bed with more women than you can shake a stick at. Bobby Ray uses him to help move product but he's not reliable."

"How long since he got into a bar fight?" Jimmy asked.

"Well, now I'm not sure. A couple of years maybe."

"How about since he was in jail over that girl from Batesville? He had just turned 21 so it was three years ago."

"Well, now that I think about it, that's right."

Jimmy said, "I think I could work with him. We're more alike than I thought at first. Other than his chasing women, he isn't bad and I think part of his trouble is being bored. If he was busier, he'd do better. Think about it. I'm going out on patrol."

Jimmy had been right about the local farmers using the dog show traffic for cover to move their product. A couple of them had a room rigged with Grow Lights to produce stuff through the winter but that was mostly for local consumption.

Jimmy learned his Uncle Bobby Ray grew some weed in the winter in his green houses. They hid the plants in the center of large groups of tomato plants. Robby Lee told him that Bobby Ray was looking into moving to Colorado and was planning to look at a few pieces of land while he was out there hunting this time.

Sally called and arranged to meet him at Gina's. She didn't beat around the bush. "Who's this cousin you are talking about bringing down here?"

Jimmy said, "At this point, it's just an idea I had. I wouldn't move on something like that without talking to everyone down here first. He's my girl's brother and my best friend. Good jobs are just as scarce up there as here. He'd never betray me and he's smart enough to do this job well. He and I could both work out at the cabin where I am now. If no one knew he was here, he could work every day. One of the questions I had though, was how much of this stuff can you all move? I don't know anything about how you get it out of here or how you find customers so I don't know how much of it you can sell."

Sally said, "I've got customers. I can move however much we can make. I just need to get the supplies in to do it and I know how to do that. How soon can you get him here?"

Jimmy said, "I'd need to sound him out. I am sure he would never betray me but the first thing I'd need to do is tell him what I'm really doing down here. I think by talking to him about it, I can tell if he's open to joining me or not."

"What's his name?" Sally demanded.

Jimmy smiled at her and said calmly, "I'm not telling you until I talk to him. You don't need to check his background. I've known him since I was five and I know a lot more about him than you could ever find out. I'll have my first conversation with him and let you know how he responds. If it gets to the point that I know he's interested, then I'll give you his name."

"I'll expect to hear from you tomorrow," Sally said.

"It might take a day or two," Jimmy said. "I don't want to talk to him about it when he's around other people. He lives with his parents so I might need a little time."

"Arrange it," Sally said and got up and left. Jimmy paid their tab and thought about how little he liked Sally – and how little he trusted her.

That night, Jimmy talked for a long time with his team. If Harry were down here when he called in the law, it would give him more protection. But Harry taught school and coached the school's basketball teams. In small town Ellsinore, basketball was bigger than football. It would be very difficult for Harry to get away right now. The only way he could really do it would be to say he had some awful contagious disease and had to go to Phoenix or somewhere for treatment and was allowed no visitors. Everyone would want to know what hospital he was in so they could send cards and call him on the phone. Somebody would probably have a local cousin who would show up at the hospital to try to get a glimpse of him and confirm that he was in good hands. His parents would have to be in on it. It would be complicated. And put Harry in danger. They concluded it just wasn't feasible. But Harry said, "If you know ahead of time when it's coming down, call me. I can always arrange a couple of days."

That evening, Gramps told him, "I been thinking about Robby Lee. I asked around and it does seem like that stay in jail over at Batesville did teach him something. Sheriff over there told me it was rough and Robby Lee was real lucky it wasn't a whole lot worse. He says that underage girl Robby Lee had hooked up with had lied to Robby Lee about her age, even said so in court, but her family are big wigs and they were foaming at the mouth about it. And Robby Lee had been in several fights over there already. Sheriff told me the night Robby Lee was arrested, he wasn't there and the jailer put him in a cell with a couple of real son-n-so's who he knew were known for raping cellmates. The sheriff said it was a good thing Robby Lee is big, knows how to fight, and wasn't really drunk. He said Robby Lee gave those two rapists a good beating. Sheriff said the next morning when he found out, he fired the jailer. He said he put the fear of God into the deputies who were there when Robby Lee was put in that cell. He said when they found out Robby Lee's uncle was sheriff over here, they were scared. When I asked around, people told me ever since that jail time, Robby Lee has behaved himself a lot better. He hasn't been in any fights and no one has seen him really drunk. I asked about his womanizing and no one knew of any woman who ever claimed he forced her or took advantage of her."

Gramps shook his head and said, "I even talked to a woman I know Robby Lee's been with and she laughed. She said Robby Lee is sweet, which is sure not how I thought anyone would describe him. She said he makes it clear its a one night arrangement with no strings attached. He brings his own protection and he likes his women willing and not too drunk. She said Robby Lee's a lot of fun."

So Gramps and Jimmy discussed Robby Lee for a while. Gramps

admitted that since he had seen Jimmy, he had wondered if Bo John fathered Robby Lee. He had asked Bo John and he admitted it. Jimmy was curious and hesitated, but then asked, "Gramps, Bo John followed Mom and I all the way to California to get me. If he knew Robby Lee was his son, why did he not try to get him?"

Gramps looked old and tired. "I asked Bo John that too. He said my brother, Bobby Ray, had figured it out way back when you's both little. He said Bobby Ray had held a shotgun on him and told him if he ever so much as even talked to Robby Lee's mother about it or approached Robby Lee, he was going to shoot his balls off. Bo John knew he meant it."

Jimmy asked, "What about Felicity?"

"Well, her father always said she wasn't his and as she got older, I wondered about her but it would have had to have happened while Bo John was out on bail. I couldn't really picture her mother hooking up with Bo John. I figured some evangelist they had out at that snake church was more likely." Gramps shook his head. "Now, I know different."

Gramps was still cautious about Robby Lee but he had Jimmy call him and have him come by the office. Gramps told Robby Lee that sometimes they needed another deputy and they wondered if he was interested at all. Robby Lee looked at the two of them and said, "Isn't that a bit like asking the wolf to guard the sheep?"

Jimmy couldn't keep from grinning. "Isn't that what is going on now?"

Robby Lee laughed. "I guess so," he said.

Gramps told him they would let him ride around with Jimmy for a few days and see what it was like. Then, they'd talk about it again.

As Robby Lee was leaving, he told Jimmy, "Drop in at the Robber's Roost tonight. We're doing a gig there."

That night, Jimmy found that the band Robby Lee was playing with was called the Rockin' Roosters. Among the roosters, Jimmy saw one hen – Felicity. She was playing a guitar. They had her do the spoons and the men in the crowd obviously thought she was great. When the band took a break, Jimmy pulled Robby Lee aside and asked, "What's Felicity doing here?"

Robby Lee said, "I've got her where I can keep an eye on her and I been talking to her about the stupidity of some of the things she's been doing."

Jimmy said, "You've not been a good example for her to follow."

Robby Lee shifted and said, "No, and that's bothering me." A waitress handed him a mug and Robby Lee said, "Bring Jimmy one, too." When Jimmy started to say something, Robby Lee said, "It's root beer. Beer ain't good for fiddle playing."

When Jimmy had his mug, Robby Lee told him, "Felicity's father has always said Felicity was not his because he was gone on a construction job at what he figured was the right time. Her mother has always said Felicity was born premature but she weighed more than nine pounds so it doesn't seem likely. Felicity had a serious talk with her mother. When she told her mother she had gone home with Bo John, she says her mother about come unglued. Felicity finally got her mother to admit that Bo John was her father. She says her mother said when her husband was gone, she started hanging out at a bar because she was lonely. She said one night she drank too much and didn't think she should drive herself home. So when Bo John offered to take her, she thought he was just being nice. He took her home alright and raped her. She didn't tell anyone because she was ashamed of getting drunk and she didn't think anyone would believe it was really rape."

Jimmy shook his head and said, "How many more of us do you think might be out there?"

Robby Lee took a big swig of his root beer and said, "I decided I ain't doing the tickle with any redheads."

Jimmy laughed. "What's the deal with Felicity and the band?"

"Part of her trouble is she's bored," Robby Lee said. "I remember what I was like at her age. My younger brother and sister at home are so different from me. They're smart but they seem to enjoy doing what they're supposed to do. Me? I's always kicking over the traces. I made a deal with Felicity. If she'll go to school and keep her grades up, I'll let her play gigs with us and I'll let her run around with me." Robby Lee shook his head. "I quit my truck driving job and have got busy setting up a lot of gigs for the band."

"A big brother looking after you can be a good thing," Jimmy commented.

"Yeah," Robby Lee said, "I told the guys hands-off and if I catch anybody giving her alcohol, I'll turn 'em in myself."

Sally called Jimmy. He told her he had arranged to talk to his friend the next day and he would get back to her. She was irritated because he was too slow. "Sally," he told her, "above everything else, we need to be careful about security. I'm not risking talking to him about this at a time when he might be overheard or interrupted. Patience. I'll let you know."

Jimmy thought about it. He wondered how much Sally knew about the surveillance. From what Lisa Marie had said about her, Jimmy did not think they would have told her everything. If Sally knew about the phones and bugs, she might ask Myrna or Lisa Marie about his phone calls. Jimmy could ask Myrna and Lisa Marie not to tell her if she asked but he decided that would make them curious and they would check. He decided it was better not to say anything.

He picked up Robby Lee mid-morning the next day and took him around with him. He quickly learned that Robby Lee knew a lot about the lack of official paperwork on how things were often dealt with in the county. Myrna called for Jimmy to shadow one strange car but it went straight to the lawn mower plant and Myrna called back saying it was someone sent from the corporation which owned the plant. He'd had an appointment and was expected.

Robby Lee asked how Myrna knew about the car. When Jimmy explained about the traffic cameras, Robby Lee was highly amused. "We all know about those cameras and make sure we're not speeding when we pass them. I never thought about the fact that they could be used to see who comes and goes." He was quiet for a minute and then said, "That's real useful, ain't it?"

Jimmy grinned. "If outside law enforcement comes into the county, we know it."

Robby Lee was tantalized. "This deputy deal might be fun."

That night, Jimmy checked in with his team. Harry had heard from the man he talked to in Nashville. The man had made it clear that it was an unofficial conversation. He said that several years back, Pendegrass had sent an undercover agent into Grand County who died in a car accident which probably was not an accident. Pendegrass had been seriously reprimanded for it. His career had stalled. What he was doing now with Jimmy was probably an attempt to redeem his reputation within his own agency.

Jimmy reflected on how complicated things were getting, too complicated. Sooner or later something was going to slip.

Chapter 20: Off to Colorado

Jimmy gave it a couple of more days and then called Sally. She was busy and said she'd call back. When she did, he told her his talk with his friend had gone well but his friend wanted to think about it. Sally immediately bristled, "He's either in or out. He can't know about us and not be part of the operation."

"Relax," Jimmy told her, "I didn't tell him anything except that I was cooking meth and making money at it. I didn't tell him anything else. He'll not get me in trouble. He's a real steady kind of guy, like me, reliable. He needs time to think things over. If he decides he's in, we can trust him. If he decides not to do it, he'll forget what I told him."

Jimmy had Sunday lunch with Myrna and Lisa Marie. Gramps was not around and things were a lot more relaxed. Jimmy told Myrna and Lisa Marie about Robby Lee and Felicity. They both said they couldn't believe it. Jimmy said, "Sometimes secrets cause more trouble than they solve. Robby Lee and Felicity are both better off knowing that Bo John is their biological father. Robby Lee understands Felicity and suddenly he's a big brother concerned about his little sister. The responsibility is good for him and she's enjoying it."

Lisa Marie shook her head and said, "And you all joked about making Robby Lee marry her."

Jimmy grinned. "Robby Lee told me he's swearing off redheads. He doesn't fancy the idea of doing his sister."

Lisa Marie was laughing but Myrna wasn't. Jimmy tried to read her expression but the conflicting emotions were leaving her face blank.

Jimmy changed the subject by asking when Gramps would be

leaving for Colorado. Lisa Marie said, "It was supposed to be next Sunday but for some reason, Uncle Bobby Ray wants to go earlier, on Thursday."

"Robby Lee says Uncle Bobby Ray is thinking about moving to Colorado and having a legal marijuana farm. He's wanting to look at some land while he's out there."

Myrna said, "Dad has grumbled about that some but I didn't know Uncle Bobby Ray was actually going to look at land."

Jimmy shrugged, "Robby Lee was not asked to keep it a secret but maybe Uncle Bobby Ray never thought about him talking to any of us about it."

Lisa Marie said, "Yeah, you and Robby Lee becoming buddies has been a surprise to all of us. I heard that Robby Lee was seen at church with his aunt and uncle and he was behaving himself and made no attempt to bother Rose. Jimmy, maybe you're a good influence."

Jimmy shook his head. "I don't think so."

On Monday, Jimmy asked Gramps about his upcoming trip to Colorado. He said, "Bobby Ray wants to go early. He's got some idea about maybe setting up a business out there. I told him it was not totally straightforward. He would need to apply for a license, there would be state inspectors, and so on. Dealing with the government is always a nuisance."

Robby Lee was sent out with Marvin Jones for orientation, just as Jimmy had been. Jimmy spent Tuesday and Wednesday cooking so he would go back on duty Thursday when Gramps left for Colorado. Jimmy went into the office early so he would see Gramps before he left. "Dang it," Gramps told him, "Bobby Ray is taking Jeanna. He didn't tell me before because he knew I'd object. The woman is a party-pooper, a total wet blanket."

Jimmy smiled and said, "Why don't you take someone with you, too? I'm sure you know someone who'd make the excursion a little more fun."

Gramps looked at him with the wheels in his head turning. "Boy, you do come up with good ideas."

Jimmy laughed and left him in his office. Myrna said, "Jimmy, you make things a lot easier around here. He's been fuming ever since he found out Jeanna was going." Jimmy noticed she was no longer even trying to hide the fact that she listened in on everything said in her Dad's office. Later, Myrna told him her Dad had called that sophisticated looking woman he had spent so much time with during the dog show and she was going to meet them in Colorado.

Jimmy circulated around and chatted with people. He dropped into the Dollar General and Rose invited him back to the staff break room. She told him, "Robby Lee has been coming to church with an aunt and uncle. He hasn't made any attempt to talk to me. His sister came in here early this morning for something and I asked her what the deal was. She says he told his family he was going to quit chasing me, that he needed to grow up and act like an adult. What's going on with him?"

Jimmy smiled. "He told me he knew he needed to quit bothering you. He says he started chasing you in high school and somehow he just kept on. He says Luke Walberg breaking his leg was really an accident but he did beat up a few guys and make some threats."

Rose said, "I heard he's being taken on as a sheriff's deputy. Surely not!"

"Well, yes," Jimmy said. "I expect you won't understand but it was my idea. I've gotten to know him better and he gets bored easily. We're just trying him out but it might work."

Rose shook her head. She said, "Mom says it's no accident that you and Robby Lee look so much alike but when I asked her what she meant, all she did was tell me again to never hook up with any of the Jones men."

"That's good advice," Jimmy said.

Rose regarded him in silence and then finally said, "You know a whole lot that you aren't telling."

Jimmy smiled and said, "All families have a few secrets but I think the Jones family has more than most."

That afternoon, Jimmy saw Sally's car parked at the dog kennels located at the animal clinic and made a casual stop. She was giving brisk orders to the girls who actually trained her dogs for her. Jimmy admired the dogs and Sally walked him back to his sheriff's car. "What's the news with your friend?" she asked.

"He has a temporary job which will be over in a couple of weeks. He'll decide by then," Jimmy told her.

"Why can't he come now?" Sally demanded.

"Sally, he's a reliable worker," Jimmy told her. "If he took off before this job is done, people would wonder what was going on." He went on to say, "I spent the last two days out at the cabin. I go off duty at 10. Is the Robber's Roost okay? Robby Lee's playing there tonight." He normally met Sally somewhere busy to pass on the meth he had ready to go. Robby Lee had asked Jimmy if he'd pick up Felicity and see her home. She had school tomorrow.

"You and Robby Lee have gotten really chummy all of a sudden. Is he a possible cook?" Sally asked.

"No," Jimmy said. "He bores too easily. But we're trying him out as a deputy."

Sally nodded and said, "That might be a help."

When Jimmy went back to the office before going off duty, Lisa Marie said, "Jimmy, just so you're prepared, the next time I go down to Florida, Myrna's going with me. Not much goes on here in the winter and with you here to run the office, we can both go."

Jimmy looked at her and after a brief silence, he said, "And maybe the two of you will just decide not to come back."

Lisa Marie smiled. "Maybe," she said.

Jimmy drove his truck to the Robber's Roost and passed his stuff to Sally. She stowed it in the back of her station wagon. She had a dog in a carrier which she placed behind the boxes.

Felicity was complaining about being sent home. She cussed and carried on until Jimmy said, "Girl, you're throwing a temper tantrum like a two year old. You want to be treated like an adult, act like one."

Out in his truck, she was sulky. They traveled in silence for a while and then Felicity said, "Robby Lee has done all kinds of stuff. Why is he kicking up such a fuss about what I do?"

"Because experience has taught him how stupid it was and he's trying to help you not have to learn the hard way."

"Why?" she demanded belligerently.

"Because he cares about you," Jimmy said. Felicity was silent the rest of the ride.

At home that night, Jimmy went up the path and called Evangeline. He talked to her about Felicity. Evangeline wished he could be home for Thanksgiving. Jimmy remembered past holidays and also wished he could be there. Jimmy told her about Lisa Marie's warning. Jimmy said, "That'll be in the first part of January. If I could wait that long to call in the troops, they'd be out of it, but I don't think I can wait that long. I've got this uneasy feeling that something is going to explode."

Evangeline said, "Jimmy, whatever happens, don't get yourself killed. It's not worth it. Dump the whole investigation if you need to. Come home."

"I will," Jimmy promised.

❀ ❀ ❀
Chapter 21: Explosion

Sunday morning during church, Jimmy felt his smart phone vibrating. It had never happened before. He slipped out of the sanctuary and looked at his phone. There was a text saying, "MRGNC CALL LM"

Lisa Marie said, "You've got to get out to the ranch as soon as possible. Your truck or get a patrol car. Whatever's fastest. Run."

She disconnected and he found Robby Lee at his elbow. "What's up?" he asked.

"Come on," Jimmy said and he ran for his truck. On Sunday morning, the roads would be pretty empty. Only when they were out on the road and running 85 on a narrow two-lane road with potholes, did Robby Lee say anything else. "I take it there's a fire somewhere."

Jimmy passed Robby Lee his smart phone and said, "If it rings, answer it. I'll keep both hands on the wheel and both eyes on the road. Lisa Marie texted me that there was an emergency. When I called, she said to hightail it out to the ranch ASAP. That's all she said and hung up so I think she was on her way out there herself."

"Bo John!" Robby Lee said. "What the hell has that polecat done now?"

Jimmy was in his sheriff's deputy uniform but not wearing his gun. He told Robby Lee it was under the seat and Robby got it out. Jimmy told him, "There's a shot gun behind the seat. When we arrive, you get it out."

At the gate to the ranch, Jimmy punched in the code. After their trip out here to retrieve Felicity, he had asked what it was and memorized it.

As they approached the house, Jimmy saw Myrna's car and behind it, the truck that Bo John used. Behind both of them was a patrol car with its roof lights still on and its door open.

Jimmy jumped out of his truck and buckled on his gun holster. He took out his pistol and checked that Robby Lee had the shotgun. "Caution," he said to Robby Lee as they moved toward the nearest door into the house, which also stood open.

Jimmy took the safety off his gun but held it pointed up in the air while he peeked around the door frame. He was looking into a casual garden room with wicker furniture and plants, most of which appeared neglected and unhappy. There was an open door on the opposite side of the room and from in there he heard Lisa Marie's voice. He headed that way and heard Robby Lee following him.

It was a living room and Lisa Marie was bent over Myrna who was in a large chair. She was saying, "Myrna, Myrna, can you hear me?"

Jimmy moved to Lisa Marie's side and felt himself go cold with shock and then hot with anger as he looked at Myrna. Her blouse had been ripped off and one bra strap broken. Her slacks were open, unzipped. She had clearly been beaten. She had been hit in the face and her nose and mouth were both bleeding.

He knew immediately that Bo John had done it. Lisa Marie had a wet cloth she was using on Myrna. "Where's Bo John?" he demanded. Lisa Marie gestured and Jimmy went through a door into a study which showed obvious signs of a fight. Bo John was lying on the floor. He had been shot at least twice, including once in the face. Jimmy forced himself to check closely. He was dead, definitely beyond help.

He turned away and managed not to vomit. Robby Lee was standing in the doorway to the room and Jimmy said, "Don't look."

Robby Lee looked at Jimmy's green face and didn't go look.

Myrna was moaning and Jimmy found a sofa comforter to put around her. He said, "Myrna, it's okay. We'll help you." She turned her face toward him and he knew she heard him. "It'll be okay. We'll look after you." He saw the gun lying on an end table by the chair. He took out his handkerchief and scooped it up.

He went to the kitchen and made coffee. He brought Myrna a cup, weak with lots of sugar which she normally didn't take. He'd put it in a mug with a straw. He told her, "Drink this if you can. It'll help with shock." She managed.

Lisa Marie checked her and said, "I think she needs a doctor. She says some of her teeth are a little loose."

Robby Lee said, "I've had that happen. Mine were okay after about a week but the dentist told me to be real easy on them and give them time to heal. He said to eat mush for a week."

Robby Lee moved in and checked Myrna. He had been in lots of fights and clearly knew more than Lisa Marie about injuries. He concluded, "I don't think anything is broken. I checked her ribs and they're okay. She's gonna have some bruises." He sent Lisa Marie to make an ice pack for Myrna's nose.

Jimmy was thinking. Bo John was dead. It was going to cause a big flap. What else would be uncovered? He really didn't want Myrna to go to jail. He knew Bo John had it coming but he appeared to have been unarmed so would a jury see it that way?

Myrna revived a little and insisted on getting to her feet. Jimmy went looking for her blouse. He had seen it in the study. He also found one of her shoes. He looked around the room. No other weapon. The fight had left a lot in disarray. The safe was standing open. He saw some envelopes and papers on a nearby desk and scattered on the floor. Inside the safe was a lot of money with some of it also out on the floor. What had been going on here when the fight started?

Jimmy and Robby Lee went to the kitchen to get coffee while Lisa Marie helped Myrna put her clothes back together. They heard Myrna telling Lisa Marie where to find some pins. In the kitchen, Robby Lee asked quietly, "What the hell happened here?"

Jimmy said, "I think Myrna came here for something and she and Bo John got into a fight. She killed him."

Robby Lee shook his head. "Can we call it justifiable homicide?"

"Knowing Bo John, definitely, but I haven't found another weapon so others might not see it that way," Jimmy said. "And if there's a big investigation, what else is going to come to light? And Myrna will be arrested while they investigate."

Lisa Marie ducked into the kitchen to get a plastic bag for the gloves Myrna had been wearing. Jimmy asked, "What happened?"

"Bo John took off and we thought he was going after drugs. He's always gone several hours and often overnight. Myrna said she wanted something out of the safe here and now while Dad was gone was a good time to get it. She gathered up an assortment of envelopes and papers and when I asked why, she said she wanted to make it look like what she was going to take was still there in the safe. I was listening in on the surveillance we have out here to keep track of Bo John. She was in the study and Bo John came home. For some crazy reason, he was only gone an hour. I could hear what they were saying." She paused and then said, "Bo John was going to rape her. From what they were saying, he's done it before. Myrna started trying to fight him off." Lisa Marie looked at Jimmy. "I started to call you but then realized you were in church so I sent a text and then jumped in a patrol car and started out here."

Lisa Marie took Myrna more coffee and Robby Lee said, "You knew about the rape. That's why you were so sure Bo John would do it to Felicity, isn't it?"

Jimmy nodded and Robby Lee called Bo John a few choice epitaphs and then asked, "Can we make it look like suicide?"

"No," Jimmy said, "but I'm thinking. Could we make it look like a burglary gone wrong? In a way it was. Myrna was wearing gloves because she didn't want to leave prints."

They talked to Myrna. She insisted on going back into the study. On the desk was a large manila envelope which she had opened. She stuffed the papers back into the envelope and said, "Can you make another envelope that looks like this one?"

Jimmy asked, "Myrna, what are we going to say happened?"

She stopped and said, "Oh, God. I can't face it. I can't face the questions, the pointing fingers, the insinuations that it was my fault. I can't face it."

Jimmy said, "Let's think about it."

They discussed making it look like a burglary gone wrong. Lisa Marie said, "All the surveillance recordings and phone calls would need to be erased. I can do that but if a real burglary took place here, it would all be on the surveillance."

Jimmy said, "We don't need to fool Gramps. He's going to know. But could we fool outsiders?"

Gramps was gone for another week. There no reason why they had to call anyone right now. They had time to set things up.

Lisa Marie said, "I can fix all the surveillance out here. I'll remove all the bugs, even the one in the phone. I can remove the surveillance camera at the gate. Outsiders would never know they had been here."

Robby Lee said, "Those gates with a key pad will keep honest people out but thieves know how to play with them until they figure out the code."

Lisa Marie said, "They could on this one. It's old and not very complicated."

Myrna had worn gloves but all the rest of them had left prints everywhere. And none of them normally came out here. Jimmy hadn't been here since he was 5 years old, Robby Lee hadn't been here since before Bo John came home, and even Lisa Marie had not been out here in months.

Jimmy said, "We can wipe down for prints. Thieves normally would."

As they had talked, Myrna had visibly drooped. She had been beaten. She had sustained a terrible shock. Lisa Marie wanted to take her home but she needed to fix the surveillance. None of the rest of them knew how. Robby Lee offered to take Myrna home. He said, "I've been in a few fights. I know what it's like."

Privately, Robby Lee told Jimmy, "I won't leave her. She might really need a doctor. Do you think there's any chance she'd suicide?"

Jimmy said, "I hadn't thought of that. Take her home. Stay with her."

Jimmy helped Lisa Marie disassemble all the bugs and other equipment in the house and the camera at the gate. Before they started, they both put on latex gloves out of the stock in the trunk of the patrol car. They wiped down every surface they thought any of them might possibly have touched. Jimmy told Lisa Marie, "I'd like to cover up the body but burglars wouldn't do that."

Jimmy handed Lisa Marie tools and steadied the ladder. When they were done, they both walked around checking that nothing had been overlooked.

Lisa Marie said, "I heard more of what Bo John and Myrna said to each other than I mentioned."

Jimmy waited. She went on, "Bo John was a total monster and my mind is reeling." She sighed. "I'm thinking that Myrna and I should just run. We're actually ready. We don't have to wait for my friend to take us on the sailboat. You can even fly to Grand Cayman."

Jimmy said, "I don't think Myrna could stand up to being questioned but if you two run now, it will draw suspicion."

"I'm so rattled, I'm not sure I could hold up to being questioned," Lisa Marie said. "I don't know why I didn't figure it out. When I found out that Bo John was Robby Lee and Felicity's father, I still never suspected." She was silent and then said, "You knew, didn't you?"

"Yes," Jimmy said.

"Myrna was 14 when I was born. Her own brother raped her and got her pregnant."

"Yes," Jimmy said.

"She came out here to get the copies of the DNA tests done after I was born. They were in the safe," Lisa Marie said.

"Yes," Jimmy said. "I saw them. They're in that envelope Myrna took with her."

"Why the hell didn't someone lock him up then?" Lisa Marie said vehemently. She had tears running down her face.

Jimmy shook his head. "Now, you know why Myrna hated Bo John."

"I need to take her away from this, don't I?" Lisa Marie said.

"Yes," Jimmy said. "Robby Lee's worried she may try suicide."

"She did when Bo John was coming home. Used her sleeping pills. I found her in time. I'll take her and go. I can check on the internet. Some places don't extradite to the States," Lisa Marie said.

Jimmy said, "I was thinking we might make it simpler. I'll be here. We need a story about why you two have gone. How about saying you or Myrna suddenly decided to marry someone you met at the dog show?"

Lisa Marie said, "We could make it me and say I was pregnant so it was urgent. That would give all the gossips something to talk about."

Jimmy had another idea. He turned the heat off and the air conditioner on. He'd stop by later and turn that off too. They were not expecting it to freeze so he would leave the heat off all week. It was late November and the cold would help preserve the body.

They checked the house one more time. Lisa Marie suddenly said, "How could we be so stupid? We need to take the money. No thief would leave the money behind!"

So they packed it into a Walmart bag and put it in the trunk of the patrol car along with the gun. Lisa Marie said, "Myrna asked me to find out the combination for the safe. Dad nev . . . I guess he really isn't my dad, is he? Grandfather on both sides. It's sick."

"Yes," Jimmy agreed.

When he didn't say anything else, she said, "Jimmy, you've been a breath of fresh air blowing through this family and we needed it. I think I've known for a long time that something was screwy. But all this with the drug business was distracting. I think because of that, I didn't see what else was totally off."

Jimmy asked, "How soon can you pack and be gone? I think the quicker you get out of here, the better."

After one more look around, they drove back into town. Instead of going to her house, Lisa Marie went to the office. Once they were inside, Lisa Marie said, "I need to fix the surveillance here." Jimmy nodded.

As Lisa Marie worked, she gave him a rundown on what was what and what it did. As Jimmy had suspected, everything said in the office was recorded. So were conversations from the ranch, from his cabin, and from the jail.

Lisa Marie was going to erase the recordings from the ranch but asked if Jimmy wanted to listen to what Bo John and Myrna had said so that if it ever went to court, he could testify. He told her to make him a copy and he'd keep it until he was sure it wasn't needed.

With steel in her voice, Lisa Marie said, "If Dad kicks up a fuss, play it for him."

As she worked, Lisa Marie also told him something else. She said, "I was going to tell you but all this made me forget. I was going back through recordings made during the dog show from Bo John's phone. I actually was checking to see what he and Felicity said to each other and Felicity was telling the truth. However, I caught something else. It was Bo John and Sally. Sally told Bo John that she and her husband were having trouble and she was worried he was going to divorce her. She asked if Bo John would be willing to help her fix the problem if she needed it."

Jimmy asked, "Fix it how?"

"It wasn't exactly said but Bo John said why couldn't she do it herself and she said because of Hank, she thought she might be under suspicion. Bo John asked if she had fixed Hank and she said some things were better not said. I'll give you that recording, too. I'm thinking we need to warn her husband."

Lisa Marie erased what had been recorded from his cabin. When she asked if he knew where the equipment at his place was located, he said yes.

Lisa Marie commented, "One of the things I have found so

refreshing about you, Jimmy, is that you weren't keeping secrets. You didn't care that someone was spying on you."

Jimmy nearly laughed. Then he said, "Lisa Marie, before you're gone, there is one thing I want to ask. Where does Sally make meth?"

Lisa Marie said, "The old jail." She looked at him and when he still looked puzzled, she said, "The old jail was on the top floor of the courthouse. The prisoners used to think it was funny to stop up the plumbing and flood the floors below them. They moved the jail. That area is used now for storage. Sally's father is the custodian. She has keys. No one else ever goes into the part she uses. Meth makes a smell but from four floors up, even a small breeze is enough and no one notices. She mostly works on weekends when no one's in the courthouse but even during the week, no one really notices. She uses all those trips out of town buying and selling dogs and attending dog shows to cover up when she's actually making meth."

Lisa Marie focused on her work for a few minutes and then turned to the computers. "I'm erasing some files and then cleaning out the delete files. A really hot computer expert could retrieve stuff but I don't know of any reason anyone would look."

As she worked, she said, "I told you I suspected that Sally did Hank in. I had asked Dad about putting surveillance on Hank. We should have."

When she was ready to go, they moved everything from the patrol car and went to her house in Jimmy's truck. On the way, Lisa Marie said, "Jimmy, that was the first time I remember you asking anything about the drug operation. I concluded a long time ago I don't like meth, I don't like the business, and I don't like Sally. She was the the one who started all this with the meth and she's the main operator. If I could have turned her in without getting myself and Myrna in trouble, I would have."

Robby Lee was waiting. Myrna was in bed. Lisa Marie checked and she was asleep. Robby Lee said, "She had some sleeping pills so I asked her about suicide. She said she was thinking about it and I said I'd let her take one pill and get a good sleep. I told her she might feel different about it tomorrow. I said you all were working on making it look like Bo John was killed by burglars and if she committed suicide with all those bruises on her, it would raise questions. She said she could always change her mind later and took one pill and went to bed."

Robby Lee hesitated and then said, "She also talked some about why she wanted to kill herself."

He was looking at Lisa Marie and she said, "Yeah, I overheard her fight with Bo John. I had no idea." She was shaking her head. She looked at the two men and said, "We really had an abomination from Hell for a father, didn't we?" Then, she added, "I'm glad Myrna killed him. If she hadn't, I think I would've had a try at it."

Robby Lee snorted. "I think Jimmy Joe and I would have volunteered to help you. We sure don't mind covering up for Myrna. Definitely justified homicide."

Jimmy asked Lisa Marie, "How long will it take you to pack?"

Lisa Marie said, "A couple of hours. But can Myrna travel?"

Jimmy said, "You can drive. Myrna can sleep. Get yourself out of the country as soon as possible just in case someone starts looking for you."

Lisa Marie packed up her computer system. She packed clothes for her and for Myrna. Jimmy and Robby Lee loaded her car while she got Myrna up and got her dressed. Myrna was drowsy and when they put her in the back seat with pillows and blankets, she promptly went back to sleep. Lisa Marie made another run through their rooms to be sure she hadn't left anything behind. Outside by the car, she looked at Jimmy and said, "I been thinking about the wedding story. Last time I went down to the Caribbean, I met a man in Georgetown called Andre Dubois. He was from some island called St. Lucia. We danced all night together and then ran around together for a couple of days. He even asked me to marry him but his family's creole, you know, mixed blood. But I was thinking to look him up again. That was in October, which is the right timing for a rushed wedding. Even my friends in Florida would believe it."

"Andre Dubois. St. Lucia. But I'll tell everyone it's a secret for a while. Give you some time to really get away."

"Jimmy, I'm sorry we're leaving you holding the bag but I'm glad to be out of here."

Jimmy looked at her and grinned. "It's okay. I won't be holding it for long. You remember you all thinking that Fed was here because he had sent in an undercover agent." He paused and Lisa Marie looked puzzled. Jimmy went on, "He had. Me."

As Lisa Marie absorbed what he had said, she looked stunned. "No," she said, "you can't be. You're not the type at all!"

"Yeah," Jimmy said, "I know. I didn't want to do it. I haven't enjoyed it at all. But that Fed put pressure on me and the only way out was to come do it. I've actually gotten attached to you and Myrna. Get on the road and get out of here and don't get stopped by the police and don't get caught. I'm going to try to set Sally up and she'll probably betray you all."

Lisa Marie suddenly reached out and hugged him. "Jimmy, I'm going to miss you. You're a good brother."

When they were gone, Jimmy turned around and found Robby Lee standing like a statue staring at him. Jimmy said, "You heard."

Robby Lee said, "I'll be a danged ring-tailed possum. I can't believe it. You're a narc!" And suddenly he started laughing.

Jimmy looked at him puzzled. "What is so funny about it?"

"All these precautions they was taking to not get caught. Sally thinking you're the best thing that ever come her way! And there you were in the middle of it all and no one ever suspecting. It's funny." Robby Lee was still laughing.

Jimmy grinned. "I guess it does have it's funny side."

"Well," Robby asked, "are you turning everyone in?"

"No," Jimmy said. "Only Sally. I want to set it up for her to get caught cooking meth."

"What about all that marijuana?" Robby asked.

"Nobody really cares all that much," Jimmy said. "I was told that it was nothing compared to what's coming in from Mexico." You heard Lisa Marie and she's right. Sally is the one who needs to be nailed. Gramps is probably going to be caught in it, too, if she talks but I'm not pointing the finger at him." He turned toward his truck and said, "Come on. Let's go pick up your truck."

In the parking lot of Love and Truth Worship Center, they sat and talked for a long time. Jimmy needed Robby Lee to help him during the next few days and in the end Robby Lee was willing.

Before Jimmy went to his cabin, he went back out to the ranch and checked one more time that they had not forgotten anything. He picked up a coffee mug that had been overlooked. The house was down to 60 degrees and he left the heat off. It was going to be a week before Gramps came home. He stood over Bo John's body and prayed. He wasn't Bo John's judge and wasn't altogether sure about this praying for the souls of the dead but he decided it wouldn't hurt. God knows the hearts of all men and His judgment is just.

❀ ❀ ❀
Chapter 22: Covering Tracks

Jimmy's cats welcomed him home and he apologized for being gone so much but they were still uninterested in the bowl of dry cat food he put out. He had forgotten to buy food for himself so he ate tomato soup and cheese and crackers. In all the hoopla, he had not eaten since breakfast.

Out of habit, Jimmy went up the path, left his official phones on the rock and used his secret Tracfone. He called Evangeline first. He said, "This is going to be finished in a week or so." They talked for an hour but he didn't tell her about Myrna killing Bo John. Knowing about it and not telling was a prosecutable offense. He told her Myrna and Lisa Marie had decided to take off. He was sure Sally would be cooking meth over the Thanksgiving holiday and he was going to try to arrange for her to get caught.

Evangeline said, "You warned Myrna and Lisa Marie to run."

"Maybe," Jimmy said, "but you don't know anything about it. Tell Pendegrass that Gramps is out of town all this week on his annual hunting trip to Colorado so nothing will be happening until after he gets back." Then he told her, "Pass the news to Grandma and Harry. I've still got things I need to do tonight and I have to be at the office in the morning."

Jimmy disassembled all the bugs and other equipment in the cabin and barn. He opened the office at 8. Clarence arrived and he sent him out on patrol without telling him anything. He had ran the office before and Clarence didn't ask about Myrna. Jimmy called Gramps phone number and left a message for him to call when he got time.

At nine, Jimmy called Sally and said when she had time, to call him back or drop by. She dropped by in only about 20 minutes. Jimmy made a brief phone call to Robby Lee and then said to Sally, "We've got a small glitch but it's not serious. Lisa Marie is getting married this coming weekend. She and Myrna have left already. Myrna will be back next Monday but this week I'm going to have to run the office."

Sally said, "Getting married! Couldn't she wait! What do you mean you have to run the office!"

Jimmy said, "Sally, relax. It's only a week."

Sally frowned. "Someone else can answer the phones for a week!"

"Yes, but no one else is trained to use the systems here. We do need to know when outside law enforcement comes into the county," Jimmy said.

"Don't the other deputies know how to do it?" Sally demanded.

"No," Jimmy said. "It's a complicated system. You need someone with more brains than average and then it takes time to train them. Gramps doesn't even really know how to do it. Myrna will be back next week and we'll find someone and train them. But it needs to be someone we can trust completely."

"Crap," Sally said. "What's with that friend of yours?"

"He's not decided completely but I'm pretty sure he's going to do it," Jimmy reported.

Sally grumbled some more but finally left. Jimmy noted that Sally had not asked who Lisa Marie was marrying, or when or where. Sally was totally self-centered. The only part of the situation which had her attention was the part that interfered with her meth business. Jimmy wondered what kind of a mother she was.

Gramps called and Jimmy said, "Gramps, you need to sit down."

"I'm sitting. What happened?" he demanded.

"Lisa Marie is getting married."

"What! Who's she marrying?"

Jimmy paused and then said, "In October when Lisa Marie was out sailing with her friends, she met a man named Andre Dubois from some island in the Caribbean."

"And she's decided to marry him," Gramps said. "I'll have him checked out. Have they set a date?"

Jimmy said, "As soon as possible. She's left already."

"What!" Gramps said. "Why?"

"She's pregnant," Jimmy said.

There was dead silence on the phone and then Gramps said, "How can she be pregnant? Everyone knows how not to get pregnant these days. She's not that dumb."

Jimmy said, "Well, apparently the preventative failed at the critical moment."

Gramps said, "And now-a-days a girl can get unpregnant about as easy as she can get pregnant."

"If she wants to," Jimmy said. "But Lisa Marie doesn't really want to and she said the man had asked her to marry him back in October. Now, when she called him, he is enthusiastic and wants to get married immediately so that no one will know they jumped the gun."

Gramps laughed. "Sounds old-fashioned. I'll call Lisa Marie. What's Myrna think about it?"

"She's gone with her. Asked me to hold down the fort for a week. She'll be back next Monday."

"Well, okay," Gramps said. "You can handle it."

After they got off, Jimmy wondered how soon Gramps would start to worry. Lisa Marie had left her and Myrna's phones behind. Jimmy planned to drop them in a river somewhere along with the gun. The Mississippi would do nicely.

Jimmy next called each of the other three deputies and told them he would be doing the office all this week. When they asked why, he said Lisa Marie was getting married and Myrna had gone with her for the wedding. Myrna would be back on Monday.

As Jimmy anticipated, it was only 15 minutes before one of the Jones women called for the details. Jimmy said, "Look, there's a reason why it's so quick." He knew by tonight it would be all over the county about Lisa Marie getting herself in the family way and getting married.

Sure enough, he got two more phone calls that afternoon seeking confirmation of the rumor.

Then, Aunt Lilac stopped by the office. She said, "Is it true that Robby Lee is being taken on as a deputy?"

"Yes," Jimmy said, "and it's also true that he's promised to leave Rose alone. I think he means it."

"He's been coming to church some with his Aunt Ceily and he hasn't made any attempt to talk to Rose. If he does, I'll let you know. Now, what's this story that's going around about Lisa Marie?"

"She's getting married," Jimmy said.

"Who to?"

"Well, someone she met the last time she went to Florida but I was asked not to give details. Myrna's gone with her for the wedding. She'll be back on Monday."

"I also heard we can expect a Sears and Roebucker but that may just be an embellishment," Aunt Lilac said.

Jimmy was puzzled. "What's a Sears and Roebucker?"

Aunt Lilac explained. "You get them faster. Now-a-days they probably say ordered it over the internet or something." Jimmy still looked puzzled. Aunt Lilac laughed. "Jimmy, some babies don't take nine months. You get them sooner."

Jimmy's face cleared and he laughed. "Yeah, that's what all the rush is about. It seems the man involved cares about reputation."

Aunt Lilac said, "Well, maybe this time she's picked a good one."

When she left, Jimmy reflected on the gossip dynamics of a small town. Aunt Lilac wasn't a gossip. She was more like a source of reliable information. Others would consult her for confirmation of rumors. Jimmy knew by the time Bo John's death came to light, Lisa Marie's eloping to get married because she was pregnant would be an established fact in the minds of all of Grand County.

That night, Jimmy forwarded the sheriff's office phone to his smart phone and went over to the Robber's Roost. Robby Lee was meeting him there in the parking lot. Robby's band was playing Friday and

Saturday nights at the Robber's Roost. He had originally scheduled a gig on Thursday, Thanksgiving Day, somewhere out of town but had managed to cancel it, saying his band had objected to being away from their families. On Wednesday, school in Ellsinore was out early and Harry and Evangeline would be arriving sometime Wednesday night. Jimmy had given them careful directions on how to enter the county unseen via gravel roads.

It was Jimmy's guess that Sally would take advantage of the courthouse being closed over the Thanksgiving holiday to cook meth. Robby Lee told Jimmy, "I got the bugs in Sally's house and set up the recording machine. I just went by and changed the card. Here's today's take. I looked for Sally's keys but didn't find any. I thought I might hang around at the courthouse tomorrow and see if I could get a chance at her Dad's keys. I could talk to him saying I was looking for work and wondered about being a janitor."

Jimmy called Harry who told him their man in Nashville said, "Officially, I won't know anything until Wednesday. You come through Nashville and I'll send someone in with you."

Jimmy slept on the cot in the sheriff's office. Keeping up with all this was leaving his sleeping time short and he needed to be alert with his mind in gear.

Tuesday morning, Marvin said, "Is it true about Lisa Marie? She got herself knocked up and is getting married."

Jimmy said, "Well, I guess that's the short version."

Marvin wanted more details but Jimmy said he'd been asked not to talk until it was official and Myrna would be back on Monday. Marvin said, "Getting gossip out of Myrna is like trying to get blood out of a turnip. The sheriff'll tell us more when he gets back."

Marvin had asked about his schedule over the holiday. Jimmy hadn't even thought of it and asked what they usually did. Marvin said law enforcement duties would be light until Thursday about mid-afternoon. Then they could expect a domestic, usually two, but sometimes more. Marvin said, "Always one or two who drink one too many and get into it with the wife or the in-laws." He said it would be quiet otherwise but they could expect a few drunk drivers. He said they always had a higher than usual number of drunk drivers the whole weekend. So with Marvin's help, Jimmy worked out a schedule for over the holiday. With him in the office, they were really a man short and Marvin commented it was too bad Robby Lee wasn't ready to solo.

Because Jimmy had Robby Lee busy doing other things this weekend, he told Marvin, "When we started training Robby Lee, he had already scheduled gigs over the holiday but when he's available, I'll send him out to ride with you for more training."

When Marvin left the office, Jimmy tried to think of what else he had forgotten to do because his mind was so busy with other things. He prayed.

❀ ❀ ❀
Chapter 23: Getting Ready

Jimmy listened to the take from the bugs in Sally's house. He figured Sally probably did her meth business calls on her cell phone and not on their land line at home. She could use her cell phone anywhere so Jimmy didn't expect to really get much from the bugs in her house. Their main purpose was to know when she wasn't home. Jimmy had hoped she might give her husband some excuse for being gone so much.

On Monday, she made one phone call which was interesting. It started with her saying, "Mac?"

The voice on the other end was not audible.

"I've set up a delivery for next Monday at the pet store as usual. It'll be Lilac in the brown and tan station wagon. Look, it won't be as much product as I hoped. One of my cooks is having to do something else most of the week."

A brief silence was followed by, "I know. It's a nuisance but his aunt is getting married. There's nothing I can do about it."

After another brief pause, Sally said, "No, we couldn't plan ahead. It's a quickie wedding. She got herself pregnant."

There was another pause and she said, "Look, I'll do the best I can and it looks like in a few weeks I may have another cook so we can produce at least twice what were turning out now."

She paused and said, "Okay. Monday the usual time."

Jimmy liked it. He was sure Sally would be doing some cooking over the long weekend. They would get Sally's phone records but if her buyer was smart, it would an untraceable phone.

Robby Lee got a look at the courthouse keys on Tuesday but Sally's dad kept them on his belt so he couldn't borrow them, even for a few minutes. But he said it helped to know what they looked like. He'd see if he could get another look in Sally's house. The courthouse elevator went up to the fourth floor, as did the stairs, but all the doors up there were locked. Robby had planted bugs in the courthouse, one by the basement door which Sally's dad used, one in the elevator, and one on the fourth floor. The problem was where to put the recording machine. Now in the daytime, it was in a vehicle in the parking lot. Robby Lee said, "We can leave the vehicle there in the evening because after the courthouse closes, patrons of that bar across the street use the courthouse parking lot but we can't leave the vehicle there after the bar closes. Someone would investigate. But I thought of using one of those plastic storage tubs. The courthouse has a big dumpster but no one would think anything about a plastic tub in the dumpster except Sally's dad if he noticed it. He works from 2 in the afternoon until 10. He cleans the offices and everything after everyone goes home. As long as I get the container out before he comes to work and return it after he gets off and before the bar closes, we're fine. If anybody asks what I'm doing looking in the dumpster, I'll say I'm looking for cardboard boxes to use for storage. If they see me with the plastic tub, they'll think I found it in the dumpster."

Sally's house was located near the animal clinic and they typically didn't lock their doors. Her two small children were in daycare every day. The animal clinic was at the edge of the downtown area on the site of what had once been a livery stable. It was within easy walking distance of the courthouse. Sally's father lived only two blocks away. Her mother had taken off with someone years ago but her father had a live-in who often babysat Sally's children.

Jimmy passed the news about the Monday delivery to Harry. He said, "Tell those Nashville people that Lilac Jones has no idea about the meth. I know her. If we can keep Sally from warning her buyer, we might can get him, too."

Tuesday's recording from Sally's house included a discussion with her husband about Thanksgiving Day. They were having Thanksgiving dinner with his parents.

Robby Lee told Jimmy the Allen family were one of the farmers in the county who didn't grow any marijuana. He said as far was he knew, they didn't even know about it. They had bought land in the area when their son was in veterinarian's school, mostly because they could also buy the old livery stable property where his animal clinic was now located. He was their only child. He had married a girl while he was in school but she had Multiple Sclerosis and had eventually committed suicide. He had married Sally after that. Robby Lee said, "One of the problems about knowing that Sally did Hank in, is nnow it has made me wonder if she helped her husband's first wife out of this world, too."

Sally told her husband she would be taking off Thursday afternoon for Batesville where she planned to meet a girlfriend and do the Black Friday sales. She thought she might stay over until Sunday and do a lot of Christmas shopping. So Jimmy was sure she would be cooking meth.

Robby Lee reported Tuesday about noon before her dad came to work at 2, Sally had taken some things up to the fourth floor of the courthouse. One of the bugs was in the elevator and someone had helpfully spoken to Sally. Robby played the relevant part for Jimmy. They heard noises which sounded like the elevator being loaded with boxes. Then, it had stopped on another floor and a woman's voice said, "Can I squeeze in?" Then she said, "You're Everett's daughter, aren't you?"

"Yes," Sally said. "I brought these supplies for dad. He stores them up on the fourth floor."

"Your dad is always so obliging. Somebody vomited in the ladies' room on the second floor the other day and he insisted on cleaning it up. If we ask him to do some small thing extra for us, he's so nice about it. My sister works as a secretary out at the grade school and she says their custodian will do things if they ask but he let's them know he feels like they're taking advantage of him."

The doors opened and Sally said, "Yes, Dad's always so helpful."

The doors closed. On the fourth floor, we heard the boxes being unloaded.

By Wednesday morning, Jimmy was exhausted. He got the day started and planned to nap when Gramps called. He said, "Jimmy, have you talked to Myrna or Lisa Marie? I've called several times and left messages but neither one of them has called back."

"Try texting," Jimmy said. "I haven't talked to them but Lisa Marie did answer a text."

Gramps grumbled about hating texting but Jimmy suspected he might not know how to do it. He said, "Get a kid to do it for you. They think it's fun."

"How are things going there?" Gramps asked.

"Quiet," Jimmy said. "Everyone's getting ready for Thanksgiving."

"Huh," Gramps said, "other years I've usually had a half a dozen calls by now."

"Nothing unusual has happened," Jimmy said, and felt uneasy about how readily he lied. "Will you be home Sunday?" Jimmy had tried really hard not to think about what shape Bo John's body was going to be in after a week.

Jimmy stretched out on the cot in the office coffee room with the door open so if the phone rang, hopefully he would hear it. He knew he should be watching the traffic cameras but he needed sleep so bad, he was nodding off and no one had let him know they were moving anything today. In fact, everyone knew Gramps would we gone that week and they had not planned any movements. He slept a solid three hours and woke to find things still quiet.

He checked and Gramps had sent texts to both Myrna and Lisa Marie. On Lisa Marie's phone he typed, "Wedding is going to be lovely. Will send pix. LM"

That night, he listened to the day's take from Sally's house. There was really nothing except that Sally was a poor mother. She yelled and cussed at her kids and then shut them in a bedroom with a TV going. When her husband came home, he went to the children and was upset with his wife when he discovered one of them had peed on himself because he said his mom said he wasn't to come out of the room. The other one had an overflowing diaper.

Sally said, "I'm sorry, Honey. I have a headache and they were screaming and running everywhere."

Jimmy listened as the man sent his wife to bed and dealt with the kids himself. Jimmy thought it might be interesting to give this recording to him after his wife was arrested. The kids had not been screaming and running everywhere. The younger one had wanted to be held and the older one had said he was hungry.

Robby Lee reported no luck with finding the keys. One of the things Jimmy had listened for on the recordings was the sound of a large bunch of keys but hadn't heard any.

Wednesday night Jimmy went out to the cabin after listening to the recordings. He called Evangeline and she said she and Harry were in Nashville picking up the man who was coming with them. Jimmy went to bed on the sofa. He had put clean sheets on the bed for Evangeline to use. He had borrowed two cots from the sheriff's office. Evangeline would bring more blankets. He had warned her the cabin was cold. At some point in the past, someone had bricked up the fireplace and replaced it with a stove. The current version was a gas affair with a metal pipe going into the chimney. It gobbled propane but did a poor job of heating the cabin so Jimmy used it as little as possible.

The gate buzzer woke Jimmy up. He looked at the time and knew it was Harry and Evangeline. When he heard the vehicle, he got up, put on his coat, and went out to meet them. Evangeline was the first out of the vehicle and he was surprised when she hugged him. Then, she introduced the man they had brought with them saying, "This is Clint."

The man shook hands and said, "Clint Jones."

When Jimmy said, "Jones?" the man laughed and said, "Yeah, I think somebody thought it was funny."

They carried in blankets, bags, and other things. Evangeline had brought Thanksgiving dinner. While they were doing this, Robby Lee arrived. Jimmy watched the faces. Evangeline said, "It really is incredible."

Robby Lee laughed over Clint being a Jones. They put Robby Lee's truck and Harry's SUV in the barn. Jimmy had set it up so he would not be into the office until noon Thursday. Phone calls to the sheriff's office would come in on his smart phone and the deputies were all oriented.

To Jimmy's surprise, Mama Cat investigated the newcomers and accepted them, even Clint Jones. Her kittens followed her lead.

They held a conference. Jimmy made coffee and Evangeline produced sandwiches.

Clint asked questions and Jimmy talked and talked. Clint was attentive and remembered what he was told. He had studied maps of Grand County and of Big Creek. When Jimmy talked about their inability to get the courthouse keys, Clint said, "I can pick locks but it will slow things down."

When Jimmy finally wound down, Clint said, "I've never seen or heard of an operation like this one. These people are rank amateurs, not professional criminals, but they've set up the most sophisticated surveillance system I have ever seen. Who set all this up?"

Jimmy had not mentioned Myrna or Lisa Marie. Now he sighed and said, "This Jones family has got some problems. Gramps, Sheriff Johnny Jones, had his two daughters running the office. The two of them set up the surveillance. Gramps probably come up with the traffic cameras to begin with but it grew from there. Neither of the women like the meth business and they have been planning to jump ship for a long time. The sheriff being gone was a good opportunity. They left last Sunday."

Clint said, "You tipped them off."

Jimmy shook his head. He said, "I knew they planned to go in January. I suggested now might be a better time."

Clint smiled. He said, "Part of what bothers me about this drug business is the people who get hurt. Often the really guilty get away, or turn co-operative and get light sentences. The less guilty are often the ones who end up with the most jail time."

Clint made a phone call and set it up for four more men to come in Thursday evening. He said, "By our usual standards, this operation is not dangerous at all. This Sally may have a pistol or a shotgun but I doubt if she has an assault rifle, and she won't have a squad of bodyguards protecting her. If we're quiet, we might can take her out without the rest of the town even knowing anything happened. If we can, then it might give us a chance at getting her buyer on Monday."

Jimmy asked, "What kind of vehicle will those guys coming in drive?"

Clint asked, "Does it matter?"

"If you don't want to be noticed, it does," Jimmy said. "That one time Pendegrass came in, he used a rental but it still was a modal that screamed *Fed*. Tell them to drive an older pickup truck – preferably red and dirty. Fed vehicles are always clean. Some dings or a dent would be even better."

Clint made another phone call. He settled it with, "Our man here on the ground knows what he's talking about."

Robby Lee had said almost nothing. Privately, aside from the others, he told Jimmy, "This is very interesting. All this you knew and never said a word. Even now, I notice there's things you aren't talking about. And no one suspected you at all." Robby Lee shook his head.

Finally Clint said, "I think we're ready to start planning." Evangeline asked Clint if he minded if they started with prayer and he smiled. They prayed and then got underway.

❀ ❀ ❀
Chapter 24: Going Trapping

Jimmy was at the office before noon. They had eaten the Thanksgiving dinner Evangeline had brought and gotten a few hours sleep. Gramps had called and Jimmy had assured him that everything was going well. He told him he had gotten Lisa Marie on the phone and she sounded happy. The wedding was this evening.

Evangeline, Harry, and Clint went with Jimmy to the office. They would hide in Gramps office when anyone came in. Marvin dropped by at 1 to take over from Clarence as scheduled. Joey checked in by phone. They knew they were all on call if needed.

Jimmy wondered if Sally would leave the county at all. She might, because her car being around would give her away. Evangeline would help watch the traffic cameras. Outside law enforcement might follow a suspected drunk driver into the county.

As Jimmy showed Evangeline how the cameras worked, they were close and inevitably made contact at times. She smelled nice and Jimmy knew he really wanted to kiss her. He tried to keep his mind on business.

Last night, Robby Lee had asked if they could put a camera on the court house. It was a great idea and Jimmy didn't know why they hadn't thought of it before. But they didn't know that much about how to set it up. Clint did. They could put it in a vehicle and park it in the right place. They could watch it from the office. Sally's father always came and went from the basement door located by the trash dumpster. He suspected Sally would use the same door.

Robby Lee had also made another suggestion. "That bar by the courthouse is not very busy usually and Thanksgiving night will be dead. If we could create more traffic in that area, it would help hide our activity. I could call the bar owner and ask if he'd like some entertainment. I know Felicity would be on for it."

The bar owner had been ecstatic. Robby Lee reported, "He can have it announced on the local radio station and will make phone calls to pass the word. He wants to call it a family night and offer cheap soft drinks."

Robby Lee came by the office to pick up the camera and Clint to help him do set up. Robby Lee said, "My cousin, Jason, and Felicity are both on for doing a small gig tonight. Jason's real good on the banjo. I can sing and so can Felicity but Jason's voice is better."

Jimmy asked, "What if we have some real trouble and need you?"

"I'll have my phone on me," Robby Lee said. "I'll be handy. There'll be a reason for my truck to be parked in a good place. Jason and Felicity can hold it down if I need to duck out. And if you need eyes somewhere else for a few minutes, I can provide a distraction."

Jimmy had to laugh. It was good. It was great.

They borrowed Jimmy's truck and set up the camera in Robby Lee's truck. Robby Lee dropped Clint back to the office and left in Jimmy's truck to go organize his gig. Harry and Clint decided on naps.

Sally did leave the county about 3 o'clock in the Batesville direction. Then, a hour later a small motorcycle came in from that direction. It looked like one of the girls who worked for Sally but why would she be coming from out of the county? Because Marvin was handy, Jimmy had him shadow the bike. Marvin said it looked like Amy Lancaster who worked for Sally Allen and when the bike went to the dog kennels, Jimmy sent Marvin on his way.

They got a domestic call just after that and Jimmy called Joey to go help Marvin. By the time they got to the house, the relatives had mostly dealt with it, but one man had left. The family described him as very drunk so the deputies went looking for him. They found his truck on its side in a ditch with him asleep inside, basically unhurt, and took him to jail. The jailer was bored and it gave him something to do. They called the family to go retrieve the man's truck. Jimmy knew they would keep the man overnight, charge him an unofficial fine to cover lodging at the jail, and let him go in the morning with a stiff warning and probably a thumping headache.

In the middle of this while Jimmy was on the phone, Evangeline said, "Someone's at the courthouse." Jimmy tried to look while talking to Joey. It was a blonde female, hair in a pony-tail like Amy Lancaster wore hers but this woman looked taller. When she produced keys and unlocked the basement door, Jimmy said, "It's Sally."

Jimmy called Robby Lee and said, "That raccoon that's been such a nuisance has just gone into the barn."

Clint's colleagues were not arriving until about 7:30. Robby Lee was not starting his entertainment until 7. Jimmy let Clint and Harry sleep.

Then just after 6, Robby Lee called, "Bro, we's here at da Water Hole sittin' up 'n' Sally's dad 'n' his woman 'as showed up. Said dey hear'd we's here 'n' dey wants a good seat." Robby Lee was in full hill-talk mode. "I'm a thinkin' dat he ain't haulin' dat whoppin' hunk a keys on 'im."

Jimmy woke up Harry and Clint. They talked it over. Clint said it might not be best from a legal standpoint for him to actually go in the house and get the keys. They decided to send him and Evangeline on foot. She would not watch him pick the lock but would go in and look for the keys. They came back in about 20 minutes laughing. The back door of the house that Sally's dad normally used to come and go had not even been locked. Just inside the door was a row of hooks for jackets and coats. Thinking that he might have left his keys in his coat pocket, Evangeline checked. They weren't in a pocket. They were hanging on one of the hooks under a jacket. They were even very helpfully labeled.

Clint shook his head and said, "Rank amateurs," but he was smiling.

Just before 7, Jimmy forwarded the sheriff's office phone to his smart phone but set it on vibrate. He wanted a look at the scene. He used a patrol car and parked in the street outside the bar. If Sally was watching out a window, she'd see him go in the Water Hole. Jimmy scanned the place and nodded to people he knew. A pretty good bunch had already arrived and a popcorn machine was putting out an enticing aroma. Some of Robby Lee's relatives were there with Coop, the cousin with epilepsy.

Robby Lee started with a fast traditional bluegrass tune. Robby Lee was on his fiddle, Jason on a banjo, and Felicity on a guitar. It got the crowd quiet. Then, Robby Lee picked up a mike and said, "Well, folks, we's a welcomin' ya'uns ta da Water Hole. Dis here's a fam'ly night so Clyde tole me ta keep it clean." He proceeded to tell a joke about a hillbilly taking his annual bath. It really was funny.

They did a song and Jimmy listened with appreciation. They were good. After that number, Robby said, "Clyde here's a sellin' soft drinks tanight fer a buck a bottle so get jours. Dey's draft beer fer ya older folks but if ye's under 40, Clyde wants ta see yer ID. 'N' John Bob, I knows all 'bout dat fake ID ya got so keep it in yer pocket." The crowd laughed. Robby Lee had them in his pocket.

Jimmy drifted out and his phone vibrated. He pulled it out, hoping it was not a sheriff's office call. He had sent Joey home and Marvin was on patrol in a certain area where one family was known for their holiday brawls. It was Clint. His people were nearly here. Jimmy took the patrol car back to the office and had the men come there. They parked their older model red extended cab pickup next to his pickup in the parking lot. Jimmy smiled. It wasn't actually dented but it was dinged, not too clean, and had a big tool box in the back. Grand County had at least a dozen identical vehicles.

Inside the sheriff's office, they gathered in the room with table, chairs, folded cots, and a coffee machine. It had no windows. Two of the four *men* were actually women. One of the men and one of the women were in uniform but had plain dark jackets. The two non-uniforms were forensics but also had training for regular police work.

The woman said, "I understand we're mopping up a meth lab."

Evangeline watched the cameras. If Sally took a break, they wanted to know it. She had carried in a small backpack. Being an experienced cook himself, Jimmy figured it was food. A continuous operation was the most efficient.

Harry had offered to watch and let Evangeline sit in on the conference but she said, "I'm actually the least useful so you join them and I'll watch."

Jimmy let Clint fill in the team. At some points, they laughed and others just shook their heads. At the end, one of the women said, "We were told this might not be a very standard operation. If nobody gets shot, it'll make a great 'Can you believe it?' story."

No one got shot. The newcomers shared bullet proof vests all around and passed out tasers. They went in the two pickup trucks which looked right at home with the collection already in the courthouse parking lot. One of the men had told Jimmy that they had borrowed their *appropriate vehicle* from his father. Jimmy unlocked the door and they all slipped in. They mounted the stairs silently and Jimmy unlocked the door into where the jail used to be located. The door was well oiled and opened silently. They slipped in one by one.

The area was much larger than the new jail. The old reception area was populated by a lot of discarded furniture and boxes of cleaning supplies. Jimmy quietly checked a door at the back. One by one, he signaled the team and they slipped in and hid in the shadowy space containing various things brought up for storage over the years since the new jail had been built. Last of all, he walked in himself and stopped a dozen feet behind Sally's turned back.

"Sally," Jimmy said. She turned, picking up a pistol. She was wearing a protective mask. "Very clever," he went on, looking around. "I have wondered for a long time where you worked. This is ideal."

She said, "Jimmy, you about gave me a heart attack." Her words were muffled by the mask. She lowered the pistol. "What are you doing here?"

"Somebody called the sheriff's office and said they saw someone entering the basement door of the courthouse. I came to check it out."

"How did you get in?" she asked and laid her pistol down and turned to check what she was working on.

Jimmy moved and Clint and the two uniforms joined him. They had her cuffed before she knew what was happening. She had lost her mask and as they moved her to the door, she said, "Jimmy, what the hell's going on?"

Jimmy turned to the meth operation, donned a mask, as did the two forensics people, and they began safely shutting down the operation. As soon as they had it in hand, Jimmy left the forensics people to their job and went back out to the former reception area. They had given Sally an old chair to sit on. "She's had her Miranda," Clint said.

Sally focused on Jimmy and her face got hard. "You snot-nosed brat, you're working with them!"

"Yes," Jimmy told her, "federal law enforcement sent me in as an undercover."

She came out with a string of imprecations that proved she was not a lady. When she paused for breath, Jimmy said, "Sally, as another Jones, I'll see that you get a good lawyer. I also strongly advise you not to say another word until you've consulted with him."

Jimmy sent a text to Robby Lee saying, "Let me know." It was their signal that they needed a distraction. In a few minutes, he got a text back saying, "Go."

The two uniforms loaded Sally up with no one watching, which was good, as she tried to run, and then screamed and yelled for help, trying to attract attention. They left Clint Jones with the forensics people and returned to the sheriff's office. Jimmy sent Harry with Evangeline to return Sally's dad's keys. The forensics people had Sally's. By the time they got back, the two uniforms had taken Sally away to Nashville.

Jimmy, Harry, and Evangeline looked at each other. Jimmy grinned. "The Three Musketeers," he said, and they all laughed.

Jimmy said, "We all feel so relieved but it isn't over yet."

"Yes," Evangeline said, "but you're not going to get shot finishing up."

Chapter 25: Wrapping Up

Jimmy got a phone call from Marvin. The Fowler family were at it again. Jimmy sent Clarence and Joey both and told them to call if they needed more help. The Fowler family had no blood ties to the Jones family, or if they did, the Jones family had kept it well hidden. Most of the Fowlers were slow minded and several children had been removed from the family. In a county full of rednecks and poor whites, they were considered the epitome of poor white trash. Jimmy got another call and dispensed the paramedics and their ambulance which were part of the fire department. He called the doctors and warned them what was coming. Three people had been shot and Clarence said one of them might not survive it.

Jimmy told Marvin to do the paperwork, knowing that Marvin's wife would actually do it. Marvin was the best of the three other deputies. He was intelligent and had good common sense but he was only semi-literate. Sure enough, when they brought the paperwork in, Marvin's wife was with them.

It looked like all of the perforated Fowlers were going to live but the serious one was being passed on to a hospital over in Batesville. The three deputies, the wife, and Jimmy moved into the now empty room with the coffee pot to discuss the family brawl. Evangeline and Harry were hiding in Gramps office.

Clarence commented, "This paperwork is mostly a waste of time. When it comes down to it, none of them will testify in court and they'll all claim it was gun accidents. Too bad we can't just accident'ly shoot a few of 'em. Save us all a lot of work in the future."

Joey said, "I heard they made the mother of that last kid they took away get her tubes tied. Can they do that?"

Marvin's wife said, "I don't think so. If they could, I'm sure they'd do that whole Fowler family." They all laughed and left, Joey on patrol and the others home to bed. Jimmy told them, "I'm sleeping here. No point in going home now. Clarence, can you go back on at 8?"

The forensics people worked most of the night and in the early morning hours, Harry parked his SUV by the trash dumpster and they loaded up what they wanted. Robby Lee parked his truck as a screen and he and Felicity stood watch while they loaded, prepared to engage any curious investigators. The forensics people had very cleverly secured the door to the old jail by exchanging the lock with one on a closet down in the basement. No one would be in the courthouse anyway until Monday. What few people were up and moving that time of the morning after Thanksgiving were at the clinic or had gone to Batesville for the Black Friday sales.

Jimmy, Harry, and Evangeline had had time to talk which had produced an idea or two which Jimmy thought might be helpful.

Clint returned to the Sheriff's office and he and Jimmy discussed the situation. They wanted to try and get Sally's buyer. Clint had arranged for Sally to be denied a phone call until he okayed it.

They had no idea if Sally's people expected any more phone calls. Jimmy was going to talk to Aunt Lilac and send her anyway unless something let them know the whole thing was definitely off. Clint had Sally's phone. He'd check it for messages and text Sally's husband that she was staying over to shop. If he still didn't know she had been arrested on Sunday, they would text him saying she had real bad diarrhea and would not be home that day. They hoped to stall her husband knowing she was arrested until after the Monday delivery.

Clint said not letting Sally make a phone call was a tricky legal maneuver so they needed to have her a lawyer immediately. She was entitled to one phone call but his people were concerned she would call her drug buyer and on those grounds, they were going to try and stall her phone call. But it would look a lot better if she had a lawyer immediately.

Robby Lee said the lawyer he had used three years ago over in Batesville was pretty good so Jimmy called him and insisted he see him right away before he saw his client. It seemed some lawyers thought predawn calls on holiday weekends were normal.

Jimmy's talk with Harry and Evangeline had prepared him on what to say and he had time to run over it in his mind as he drove to Batesville. He was short on time and blunt with the lawyer. "I was sent into Grand County as an undercover but I'm actually a Jones myself. Sally's being charged with making and distributing meth. She was arrested actually making it so I don't think there's any way she can plead innocent. Your job is to get her as light a sentence as possible. She's got a good husband and two small children so there's sob stuff. However, Sally herself is something else altogether. I'm quite sure she has murdered a couple of people, maybe more." Jimmy admired the bland face of the lawyer as he heard this. "One of them was an undercover. It couldn't be proved. The last one was a guy who was cooking meth for her named Hank Henderson. He was related to Sally and the Jones family. Sally has been blackmailing Sheriff Johnny Jones for years into looking the other way about the meth. The blackmail point involves a very old family scandal that I have no intention of telling you about but it would have political repercussions. Out of spite, and in hopes of getting a lighter sentence, Sally may try to take Sheriff Jones down with her. We want that prevented. You tell Sally that if she tries to take the sheriff down with her, we can produce proof that she killed Hank."

Jimmy stopped. The lawyer said, "Can you?"

"Yes," Jimmy said, "tell her we have surveillance recordings."

"Why are you covering it up?" he asked.

"In order to blackmail Sally into keeping quiet. The sheriff is my grandfather. He's old and has suffered enough."

"But if my client is paying my fees, she should get the best I can give her," the lawyer said.

Jimmy said, "We will be paying your fees. If you get anything out of Sally on top of that, good. And Sally is a whole lot better off if Hank's murder does not come out so you are doing what's best for your client." Jimmy paused and then went on, "Tell her, too, that trying to have me silenced won't work. I've already told my story and put the proof with someone I can rely on to use it if anything happens to me."

Jimmy went on, "Another point is that we are after her buyer. We don't want her making any phone calls so we want you to see her immediately. You tell her you'll make any phone calls she needs done but you actually will wait until Monday afternoon to do it. You can even tell the court later that Sally helped get her buyer if you want. I will go tell her husband myself on Monday afternoon."

Jimmy paid the man 5,000 dollars, got a receipt, left phone numbers for contact, and scooted back to Big Creek as quickly as possible. He had found it interesting that the lawyer had not made any fuss about him as an undercover agent withholding evidence of a murder.

Harry had hauled the forensics people and their evidence to the next county in his silver-gray Ford Escape where they were met by onward transport. Harry said, "It was one of those black SUV's that just screams unmarked law enforcement vehicle."

Robby Lee, Clint, Harry, and Evangeline had taken over the coffee room at the sheriff's office. Clint said, "These people have been entertaining me with the tale of how you got to be Jimmy Wilkerson instead of Jimmy Jones."

Jimmy smiled. "I was not kidnapped. Grandma was just helping me hide. Once we evaluated the situation, we adopted each other."

Clint laughed while shaking his head. "A good lawyer could argue Stockholm Syndrome."

Jimmy shook his head. "If I was Stochholmed, then I'm glad it happened."

They double checked that all of them had their plans clear. Clint would handle Sally's phone calls. He would answer messages to do with the meth business with texts, citing the possibility of being overheard. He would text her husband if necessary. Clint would arrange things at the pet shop. Jimmy would handle Aunt Lilac. Jimmy would find out what was was normal and let Clint know but he didn't want to talk to Aunt Lilac until Monday just before her trip. She would worry and the stress would not be good for her. Aunt Lilac was not an actress and Rose might notice and wonder what was up. Robby Lee was going to escort her as had he had done in the past with marijuana shipments. Of course, Aunt Lilac would not really be carrying meth but they did want to make sure nothing happened to her.

Clint finally sighed and said, "This only has about a fifty percent chance of working but we'll try. It sometimes amazes me how information gets out. In this case, the fact that almost everyone involved is not a professional criminal with lots of nefarious contacts gives it much more of a chance."

Jimmy told them what he had told the lawyer. Clint asked, "Does this proof exist?"

Jimmy looked at Robby Lee and he said, "Sally tried to get me to do it."

Jimmy said, "We also have a recording of a conversation Sally had with someone which alludes to it. Lisa Marie said they had considered setting up surveillance on Hank and she wished later they had because they suspected Sally killed him. The recording isn't conclusive and the person she was talking to is someone who won't confirm it but because Sally is definitely guilty, she'll believe we have proof."

"And what was she blackmailing the sheriff over?" Clint asked.

Jimmy and Robby Lee exchanged looks. Jimmy sighed and looked at Clint. "Robby and I are supposed to be cousins but you can see we look like twins and that's no accident. There's more and if it all came out, it might topple Gramps out of his job as sheriff even though it's all water under the bridge a long time ago."

Robby Lee ran Clint Jones over to Batesville where he arranged onward transport back to Nashville. They all had phone numbers and with no one listening in, could call any time.

Jimmy reluctantly sent Harry and Evangeline home on Saturday. They took Mama Cat and her kittens with them. Evangeline hugged him goodbye and said, "Monday it will all be over."

After they were gone, Robby Lee said, "So that's your girl. You're lucky. She ain't got eyes for anyone but you, Bro. Treat her right and she'll stick."

Jimmy looked at Robby Lee in surprise. He and Evangeline had not bothered to keep up the romance act during this operation.

Robby Lee went on, "Don't look so surprised, Jimmy Joe. I know about women. I can tell when they got their eyes on a man. She's not looking around. She's focused on you." Robby Lee was grinning at him. "Got you hooked, too," he added as he left.

Jimmy had not told Harry and Evangeline about Bo John. Gramps would be back tomorrow and he was not looking forward to dealing with that. Gramps had called on Friday and said, "Them blame girls ain't talking to me. Have you talked to either of them?"

"Yes," Jimmy said. He had known Gramps would call. "I talked to Myrna. Lisa Marie is off on her honeymoon and left her phone behind. Myrna said the wedding was lovely and some widower who was at the wedding is taking her on some kind of an excursion."

"That ain't like Myrna to go off with some man," Gramps said.

"The man's daughter and her fiancé are also going and the man want's Myrna along to chaperone his daughter who's only 18," Jimmy said.

"Oh," Gramps said with understanding in his voice. "How's things going otherwise?"

They discussed drunk drivers and the Fowler family. Jimmy made Gramps laugh telling him what the deputies and Marvin's wife had said.

Jimmy had told Uncle Bobby Ray's son, Billy Ray, to call him when the plane was landing. He said, "There's been one small thing come up that I want to discuss with Gramps but I didn't want to do it over the phone. It could wait and Gramps would have just fumed about something he couldn't do anything about from Colorado."

Sunday afternoon, Gramps called. Billy Ray, who wasn't the brightest mind in the Jones family, had told Gramps why he was supposed to call Jimmy rather than actually doing it. Jimmy thought to himself that Uncle Bobby Ray probably should move to Colorado before Billy Ray got them arrested.

Gramps said, "What in blazes happened that you didn't tell me? You should have told me everything!"

Jimmy said, "It's not a big deal and there was nothing you could do from there. It's okay. You can come by the office and discuss it before you go home if you like."

"Okay, dang it," Gramps said. "I'll be there in 15 minutes."

Jimmy prayed the whole 15 minutes. This was going to be ugly.

❀ ❀ ❀
Chapter 26: Dealing with the Fallout

Gramps almost skidded when he stopped out in the parking lot next to Jimmy's truck. He stalked into the office and said, "Now I want it all. Don't leave nothing out!"

Jimmy said, "Gramps, I know you're on blood pressure meds. Did you remember to take them this morning?"

Gramps looked at him and said with a lot less belligerence, "Boy, is it that bad?"

"Yes," Jimmy said, "it's that bad."

"What happened?" Gramps asked.

Jimmy Joe decided on the bombshell first. "Bo John is dead."

"Did you kill him?" Gramps asked with a return of some of the earlier aggression.

"No," Jimmy said. "He was shot during a burglary that went wrong."

"How come you didn't tell me?" Gramps asked. "You must know who did it. We had surveillance and bugs out there."

Jimmy said quietly, "Because it was Myrna."

"Myrna!" Gramps said. "She never went out there when Bo John was home. Not even when I was there."

"Did you know that Myrna was going to go with Lisa Marie in January to Florida?" Jimmy saw that he hadn't. "They didn't plan to come back."

Gramps just shook his head. Jimmy went on, "There was something in your safe that Myrna wanted, something in an envelope. When Bo John left to go buy drugs, she went out there to get it and was going to replace it with a look-alike so you wouldn't notice. For some reason, Bo John came home after only about an hour. He caught Myrna there and was going to rape her."

Gramps didn't say anything. He just sat there with a look on his face of complete devastation. After a long silence, he looked up at Jimmy with tears in his eyes and said, "Hell, boy, what am I gonna do?"

Jimmy said quietly, "Lisa Marie took Myrna and they're somewhere in the Caribbean. The marriage story was a cover and we'll keep it up. We'll say she married some rich man she met the last time she was down there. We'll stay with the pregnancy. It's all over the county and no one will question it."

Gramps said, "But you called in the State people and they're good. They'll know when he died and their story won't cover them."

"I didn't call in the State people. Lisa Marie and I removed all the surveillance out there. Then, we wiped our prints and made it look like a break-in that went wrong. I turned the heat off to preserve his body and this morning, I dropped by and turned it back to normal. The State people will think it was there the whole time. With Bo John's drug use, they'll think it was some of his drug contacts."

Gramps sat in complete silence for a while, thinking it over. Then, he opened a drawer in his desk and produced a bottle. He took one big swig and put it back. He shook his head and said, "Boy, I don't know where you got your brains. Must have been your mother because it sure wasn't from Bo John."

Jimmy smiled. Gramps was rallying. He said, "Gramps, right now you need to go on out to the ranch, find Bo John's body, and call me. I'll call in the State people and then come out there. Remember, Lisa Marie is pregnant and went off to get married. Myrna went with her."

Gramps said, "Why do you need to come out there?"

"Gramps, you're not young and you've had a terrible shock. I'll come hold your hand and if the State people get too pushy, I'll tell then to back off. You can even collapse and leave me to talk to them if you want to. I've had a week to get my story straight."

"Why don't you act like you're the one who found him?" Gramps asked.

"Because everyone knows how I feel about Bo John," Jimmy said. "I'd be their number one suspect."

Gramps took a pill and drank some water and left.

When Jimmy got the call, he called the State people, forwarded the phones, let Marvin know the sheriff was back, and that he was going to be out at the ranch but would be answering the phones.

Gramps was sitting in one of the wicker chairs in the garden room. A female officer was standing over him. He looked terrible. Jimmy went up to him and said, "Gramps, are you okay? Do you need any of your pills?"

"Yeah," he said. He took out a pill bottle. The officer went to get him water.

Jimmy said, "Take a pill and act like you're going to sleep. I'll winkle you out of here and take you to the doctor."

Instead of letting Jimmy take him, they send Gramps with the female officer. They parked Jimmy in the garden room and said for him to stay there.

Later, an officer came and wanted to talk to Jimmy. He asked if Jimmy minded if he recorded the interview. Jimmy said, "No."

The man said, "First of all, what's your name?"

Jimmy thought, *here goes,* and sent up a silent prayer. "I'm known as Jimmy Wilkerson," he said. "I was . . . adopted. The sheriff is actually my grandfather and Bo John was my father."

"Was. You knew he was dead."

"Not till Gramps called. Gramps said he was dead. I asked if he was absolutely sure and he said yes, several days dead, so I called you all."

"When were you out here last?" the officer asked.

Jimmy said, "When I was five years old."

"Five years old!" the man said.

"When I was five years old, Bo John killed my mother over custody of me," Jimmy explained. "A woman who saw it happen, grabbed me and run. I decided to stay with her. I adopted her or we adopted each other. Anyway, I only came back here in August. I don't like my father. He should have still been in prison. He was using drugs. I never came out here. Not even once."

"Hell," the officer said, and then, "sorry but that's the weirdest adoption story I ever got told. So why did you come back here at all?" he asked.

"It came to light, about me running off with Grandma and staying with her and we never told anyone," Jimmy said. "I'm grown now so maybe they can't do anything but Bo John was threatening to file kidnapping charges.

"This woman was your grandmother?"

"Not really," Jimmy said. "She had lost a grandson only a few months older than me so we just used his papers and I became Jimmy Wilkerson instead of Jimmy Joe Jones."

"So Jimmy Joe Wilkerson-Jones, you haven't been out here since you were five years old," the man said. "Who did live out here?"

The officer went on with questions for more than an hour. Some things he repeated. He wanted Grandma's name and contact information. Someone came and fingerprinted Jimmy. Then, the officer asked Jimmy to ID the body. Jimmy said, "I thought Gramps did that.'

"He's an old man. The body is not in the best of shape. We just want to be sure." Jimmy knew the man wanted to watch his face as he viewed the body.

Jimmy prayed and said, "I've actually only seen Bo John briefly since I've been back."

"You said you hadn't been out here," the officer pounced.

"I haven't," Jimmy said. "One of those times I saw him, I was eating at Gina's Cafe in town. Bo John came in and wanted to eat with me. I left the cafe and he followed me out. I laid him out in the parking lot. The whole county was talking about it so it shouldn't be too hard to find witnesses."

The man gave Jimmy a piercing look and said, "We'll have a look anyway."

Jimmy looked. There were flies and Jimmy did not want to think about why. Bo John actually didn't look as bad as Jimmy had imagined. But he was starting to smell and Jimmy saw maggots in the wound on his face. Jimmy turned green and ran through the garden room and outside where he barfed up his socks.

As Jimmy leaned weakly against a state vehicle, the officer said, "Sorry, that one was worse than usual. Was it Bo John?" Jimmy nodded.

The officer left Jimmy outside with a younger officer who commented, "I lost my lunch, too. And your grandfather threw up all over in there."

Eventually, the older officer returned and sent the younger one back inside. "You didn't tell me everything," he said and Jimmy's heart thumped. He motioned and they moved down to some chairs on a deck by a pond.

The officer said, "This is not being recorded." He looked at Jimmy again like he was trying to read his mind. "Clint Jones," he said.

The relief was so dramatic, Jimmy felt dizzy. He looked over the pond and after a minute asked, "How high up are you in State law enforcement?"

"In this area, I'm tops," he said. "The death of a law officer or one of his family rates top priority."

"What did Clint Jones tell you?" Jimmy asked.

The man shook his head. "Let's see if your story matches Clint Jones' story?"

"It's not over," Jimmy said. "We are trying to catch Sally Allen's buyer tomorrow. Her courier is Aunt Lilac who's a sweet old lady and has no idea what's going on. If someone jiggles our elbow, she may end up getting hurt."

"And how does Bo John's death tie in?" he asked.

"It doesn't," Jimmy said, shaking his head. "In fact, it's beyond inconvenient. It may trigger the deal tomorrow coming up empty."

"You told me you all knew Bo John was using. Is that how you found your meth maker?" the man asked.

"No," Jimmy said. "I was staying strictly away from that. Gramps was trying to find out where Bo John was getting his stuff but it was over in the next county. He wanted to get his supplier without getting Bo John arrested. He had some idea he could shut off the source. I was not really after a pusher. I was after a meth maker."

"And got her." The officer was smiling. "Clint said her lab was in the old jail on the top floor of the courthouse."

"What are we going to say about Bo John that won't scare off our buyer?" Jimmy asked.

"Accident," the officer said. "Clint Jones and I discussed it. We'll announce the death and say it appears to be an accident but our investigation is incomplete. We need an autopsy anyway before stating an official cause of death. Those thieves probably knew the sheriff was out of town. They could have been some of Bo John's drug contacts. He may have even let them in. They probably forced Bo John to open the safe thinking there would be money. Your grandfather said there wasn't, only papers but also a handgun, possibly the one he was killed with. He may have tried to use it. It's not uncommon for criminals to take a gun away from a householder and use it on them."

Jimmy nodded, "Could be." He was silently thanking God for Clint Jones.

Jimmy asked, "Do you mind if I get some water out of my truck?"

The officer said, "You can go. If I need to ask you more questions, I know where you are."

Jimmy started back into town. He found himself wanting to talk to his team about it all but couldn't. He would tell them about Bo John getting killed but not that Myrna did it. He prayed that he and Lisa Marie and Robby Lee had not slipped up anywhere.

❀ ❀ ❀
Chapter 27: Disengaging

Jimmy went to the clinic where he found Gramps in bed with tubes and wires. "How you feeling?" Jimmy asked.

Gramps said, "I ain't gonna die yet. These fool doctors want to send me somewhere for surgery. My dad lived to be 98 and he never went to a doctor."

Gramps had been the youngest of two sets of kids and his father had outlived both wives. Jimmy said, "Yes, but he was not overweight and probably didn't have time to sit down."

"I ain't letting them cut me open," Gramps said.

Jimmy asked the doctor how bad it was. She said, "He needs heart by-pass surgery but he won't even consider it. You summed it up. He's overweight, smokes, sets on his duff most of the day, and eats at Gina's – bacon, ham, and pork chops." She shook her head. "Stubborn old coot. We can't force him to have surgery."

Jimmy had a quiet talk with Gramps. "That State cop said they are releasing the news that Bo John is dead but saying it looks like an accident. I think they got some idea they might can catch the culprits."

"Yeah, they're tricky like that," Gramps said.

"It was clever you saying there was no money in the safe."

Gramps nodded. "I didn't want to have to explain why I had so much money there or where it came from." He sighed. "Those girls probably needed some cash anyway."

"They didn't actually take it," Jimmy said. "Most of it's in your office."

Gramps shook his head. "I'm gonna miss them girls." He paused and said, "Laying here all wired up and unable to move has forced me to think. I been stupid. Years ago when Myrna turned up pregnant, I was blind, wasn't I." He sighed, "You and Robby Lee both look like Bo John. He was such a fine looking boy and I just couldn't believe he did what Myrna said he did. I was blind and stupid. Will you tell Myrna I said she did the right thing and I hope she don't get caught? Tell her if she ever needs anything, to let me know."

Jimmy went to the office and Marvin turned up. He asked, "What's going on? I thought you never went out to the ranch. Then, someone told me they saw State cars out in that area. I thought about calling you but didn't."

"Why not?"

Marvin grimaced and said, "I figured Bo John did something I didn't want to know about."

"Gramps came home and found Bo John dead," Jimmy said.

"Drug overdose?" Marvin asked.

"No," Jimmy said. "They are saying it looks like an accident but they want to wait on the autopsy before they officially say."

"Had anybody been out there?" Marvin said. "They've got that surveillance camera out there."

Jimmy had thought up a story. "That camera quit on Saturday. Lisa Marie is the one who knows how it works and she went out there. Someone had sabotaged it and we figured it was Bo John. She brought it into the office for repair but she was getting ready to take off for her wedding and she said if she fixed it before her dad got back, Bo John would probably just break it again."

Marvin shook his head. "What about your grandpa? What's he saying?"

Jimmy said, "You know he has some health problems. He's over in the clinic. They want him to go for heart by-pass surgery and he refuses."

"Stubborn as a mule," Marvin said,

"I guess law enforcement around here is back to us," Jimmy said. "What do you think about Robby Lee."

"Been surprised," Marvin said. "He's done worlds better than I expected. I thought he'd be cocky but he isn't. He listens but he's not ready to solo yet."

"Can I pair him with you this week?" Jimmy asked.

"Sure," Marvin said.

When the news was announced Sunday evening, people started calling to confirm Bo John's death.

Lisa Marie called on the sheriff's office number. She said, "Jimmy, it was a lovely wedding. We had it in a little church called Chapel on the Sea. The Dubois family is wonderful. I'm so happy. Andre's mother is the sweetest thing. She asked me to call her *mom* and we have our own little house on the estate. It's a darling house. Anyway, things are perfect. I'm really calling you about Myrna. She's staying a little longer. The Dubois's have a neighbor and he's interested in Myrna. She wants some time to check him out. He's older, a widower. He's wealthy and has lovely manners. So she's not coming home right away." Jimmy was startled at how similar her story on Myrna was to his own invention. Lisa Marie added, "Oh, I'm sending pictures via e-mail."

"Okay," Jimmy said. "Let us know when Myrna's coming home."

"Okay," Lisa Marie said. "Gotta run."

Jimmy laughed. Lisa Marie had given a stellar performance and it was recorded. Then, she sent pictures. He didn't know how she arranged them but there she was, marrying a handsome man with hazel eyes but skin a shade or so too dark to be Caucasian. Myrna was her maid of honor but there was another bridesmaid, the same color as her groom but with blonde kinky hair and huge brown eyes. There was a pleasant looking older couple, parents of the groom. The woman was very fair and the man was handsome but darker than the son. There were pictures of the reception, cutting the cake, dancing, the whole nine yards. Jimmy shook his head. Lisa Marie was clever. The pictures alone would explain why Lisa Marie had the wedding there and why she would not be bringing her husband to visit. Jimmy printed several pictures and took them over to the clinic to show Gramps.

Gramps was astounded, "Boy, how did she do this?"

Jimmy shrugged. "Paid actors? Said it was big joke on her family? Who knows? Lisa Marie is smart."

Gramps laughed. "The whole danged county will be talking about it. You can see the man's colored. These pictures will cause more talk than her being pregnant."

Jimmy said, "I checked and there really is an Andre Dubois on St. Lucia. The Dubois family is wealthy. And yes, their ancestry is somewhat mixed. There are some photos on the internet and they match these people. The mother is Dutch." Jimmy was thinking Lisa Marie must have done some wizardry on a computer.

Gramps shook his head. "Leave it to Lisa Marie to get the details right."

That night, Jimmy's cabin was lonely. Even the cats were gone. He called his team. He knew Bo John's death would be on the evening news. He told them that at this point, they were going to say it looked like an accident but actually it looked like Bo John was killed in the course of a burglary. He talked about Gramps and his health.

Evangeline asked the relevant question, "Are they really convinced it was a burglary? Is there any way they could think you did it?"

"The man in charge talked to Clint Jones," Jimmy said. "After that, he didn't appear to suspect me."

"We're praying for you," Evangeline said.

Monday morning early, Jimmy talked to Clint Jones and it looked like they were still on for the delivery. Jimmy called Aunt Lilac and asked her to drop by the sheriff's office before she went to Sally's dog kennels. She popped in and said, "Jimmy, I didn't even ask why you wanted me to stop."

He took her back into the coffee room and said, "Aunt Lilac, this is probably going to be a shock for you but Sally has been using you to carry drugs to Nashville."

It was a shock and they discussed it. Jimmy needed to know what was the standard procedure. Sally had not returned and Aunt Lilac said she had always been there to load the car and send her off. She said, "Now that I think about it, Sally is always ordering everyone around. It was odd that she always loaded my car herself."

Jimmy told her it might not work but they were going to try to get Sally's buyer. Aunt Lilac left but called him after she was on the road. She said, "I went over to the kennels and Amy Lancaster said Sally was sick. She had gone over to Batesville for the Black Friday sales and gotten sick. She had sent directions to her husband to just send the dog and the usual load of dog food. Amy asked me how much food to send. Anyway, I'm on the road and everything looks normal. I feel like I'm Mrs. Polifax."

Jimmy laughed. "You can always take karate lessons."

The operation went smoothly and they snagged two people, her buyer and the pet store owner who was in on it. They thought the pet store owner was going to give them the man who supplied Sally with the ingredients for making the meth.

Jimmy set the office phones on forward and went over to talk to Sally's husband. He was busy but Jimmy told his receptionist that it was urgent.

Jimmy told him, "I'm sorry but I came to tell you that your wife has been arrested."

"Arrested!" the man said.

"We caught her making meth."

"Meth!"

Jimmy felt sorry for the man. He clearly had had no idea and was totally shocked. Jimmy told his receptionist to call his parents.

Jimmy had told the doctors to keep Gramps until Monday. He went by the clinic and warned them, "I'm about to give Gramps some shocking news so be on standby."

When he told Gramps that he had been sent in as an undercover agent by federal drug enforcement, Gramps was incredulous and said, "No."

Jimmy said, "I'm sorry, Gramps. We arrested Sally last Thursday night and this morning we got her buyer."

Gramps said, "And now you're here to arrest me."

"No," Jimmy said. "And I think I've blackmailed Sally into keeping you out of it."

"How could you do that?"

"I said we knew she had killed Hank, that we had proof."

"The Feds'll figure it out," Gramps said.

"I told them Sally was blackmailing you into covering for her," Jimmy said.

"Blackmailing me! Over what?!"

"I said there was an old family scandal that would have had political repercussions for you if it came out. I didn't give any details but if anyone insists on knowing, you can tell them whatever you want. Sally will probably keep quiet. When Lisa Marie checked back through the recordings from Bo John's phone made during the dog show, she found something interesting." Jimmy told Gramps exactly what she had found.

"I'm not surprised," Gramps said. "You're using it to cover for me."

"Yes," Jimmy said, "but the meth making operation is over and if there's any of those farmers who you don't want picked up, you better warn them. To get arrested, they need to find them with marijuana so if you pass the word, I expect most of them will listen."

"That ain't really doing your job as an undercover agent," Gramps said.

"Well, isn't putting a stop to it the whole point?" Jimmy asked.

Gramps said, "I can't believe it. Here I was sure you could be trusted. You's the best cook we ever found. How could you turn out to be an undercover agent?"

Jimmy shook his head. "Gramps, most criminals are dumb. If you're smart, you can figure out a legal way to make a living."

"Yeah," Gramps said, "I've been pretty stupid about some things."

Jimmy left him to contemplate that.

Jimmy called all three deputies and asked them to come to the office immediately. Clarence, who had been on patrol, arrived first. "What's up?" he asked.

"Sally Allen has been arrested," Jimmy said.

"How did that happen?" Clarence asked.

Jimmy said, "When the others get here, we'll talk about it."

Marvin and Joey arrived together. "What's the deal?" they asked.

Clarence told them, "Sally's been arrested."

"What!" Marvin said. "How could that happen?"

Jimmy said, "Everyone take a seat."

As they sat, someone said, "We're all in trouble."

Jimmy looked at them and then dropped the bomb. "I was sent in here as an undercover agent by federal drug enforcement."

All three deputies looked appalled.

Jimmy smiled. "Before someone shoots me, I want to say that if we play this right, there will not be any more arrests."

"What do you mean, play it right?"

"Just that," Jimmy said. "Sally was the main mover in this and she was arrested Thursday night. She was caught actually cooking meth." Jimmy paused and said, "I was maneuvered into doing this job. I didn't want to do it and I haven't liked it. I've tried to set it up so that no one else gets arrested."

"Does the sheriff know?"

"I just told him today," Jimmy said. "I think he's going to warn all those farmers that the game is over. If they quit, they won't get arrested."

"Sally will talk. She'll cut a deal with them for a lighter sentence and she'll talk."

Jimmy said, "Maybe not. She killed Hank and I told her lawyer to tell her if she kept quiet, we'd not tell anyone."

"She killed Hank! Are you sure?"

"She tried to get Robby Lee to do it," Jimmy said. "We have a recording of her talking to Bo John about it. She told Bo John she was having trouble with her marriage and asked him to help her fix her husband if she needed it. I'm telling you three so you can keep your eyes open. Her husband probably will divorce her and you need to make sure she doesn't hire someone to kill him."

"So you think she will keep quiet?"

"Probably," Jimmy said.

They talked a while and Jimmy assured them that if everyone laid low, he thought it would all blow over.

As they left, Marvin said, "I still can't believe it. This whole time you been here, you were a narc."

Aunt Lilac came home with an empty car and stopped at the sheriff's office. Aunt Lilac had reached the indignant stage. "I can't believe Sally was using innocent old ladies like me to shuttle her drugs around!" But she also said, "I'm actually not totally surprised that Sally was selling drugs."

The doctors released Gramps and he came by the office. He said, "Jimmy, boy, I still can't believe it. You never showed any curiosity or asked any questions. I don't understand why you did it."

Jimmy explained about Pendegrass and Clarke, his supervisor. Gramps nodded. He told Gramps, "I never wanted to do this job and I hope Sally is the only one who goes down."

Gramps looked at him and said, "Boy, will you stay and be sheriff when I'm gone?"

"No," Jimmy said. "I have a job with the National Park Service and I like it. You've got Robby Lee. I think he might make a good sheriff someday."

"Robby Lee?" Gramps said.

"Sure," Jimmy said. "He's smart and not really a criminal. He's good with people. I've discovered he can even read and write."

Gramps shook his head and said, "Maybe."

"We do have a more immediate problem," Jimmy pointed out. "You need office help."

"Myrna ain't coming back, is she?" Gramps said.

"No," Jimmy said. "Do you have any ideas?"

"No," Gramps said. "You need somebody who doesn't gossip and most of these hens spend most of their day talking about everybody else in town."

Jimmy said, "How about Aunt Lilac and Rose? That job Rose has is just minimum wage and the Bed & Breakfast is not a steady income. But they would only be willing if you went totally honest. They would not condone even weed."

Gramps said doubtfully, "Maybe, but I should be able to find someone else."

"Having them run the office would convince everyone that you were basically honest and really intend to put a stop to the drug and marijuana operation," Jimmy said. "Think about it."

Jimmy told Gramps he would be leaving on Sunday. Gramps said, "I wish you'd stay."

Word went around about Sally's arrest and everyone was talking. Jimmy discovered that his own dislike of Sally had been pretty universal. He heard 'self-centered,' 'inconsiderate,' 'bossy,' 'conniving,' and 'bitch.' But people were sympathetic towards her husband.

The local newspaper printed some of Lisa Marie's wedding pictures and did a whole write up on her wedding. They were lavish with their descriptions of the Dubois family's wealth and size of their estates and said nothing in print about their mixed ancestry. The pictures said it all. It got more attention than Sally's arrest and definitely more than Bo John's death.

Bo John's death was ruled a homicide at the hands of person or persons unknown in the process of a burglary. Everyone had known he was using drugs and they all thought it was his drug contacts. The lab people had put his death at probably Monday, so Myrna and Lisa Marie were out of it.

Jimmy e-mailed Lisa Marie, giving her the official ruling on Bo

John's death.

She sent back, "Sad for Gramps."

He then sent her the official story on Sally.

She sent back, "Wow."

Gramps had had Bo John cremated. They had a small private gathering at the cemetery and his ashes were interred with a simple stone giving only his name and the years he was born and died. There was no inscription.

On Sunday morning, Jimmy loaded his truck and left. He had said goodbye to everyone the day before. He had gotten attached to some of these people but they were not family like Grandma and Grandpa.

❀ ❀ ❀
Chapter 28: The End?

When Jimmy arrived home, Harry and Evangeline were waiting. Grandma had made a special meal and they celebrated. Jimmy saw how elated they all were to have him back and his heart was touched.

He told them frankly that if he had known what he was getting into, he would have taken the flack from his supervisor and never have gone. Nevertheless, he did think God had been in it.

Harry entertained them with what Pendegrass said about how they wrapped up the operation. He added, "I talked again to that man in Nashville. He asked for those recordings you had us make. He says Pendegrass will probably be forced into retirement."

Monday morning, Jimmy called his supervisor out at Sequoia who said he would arrange the official end for Jimmy's leave of absence. Jimmy asked for a favor. They discussed it. On Friday morning Jimmy received word. He was being transferred to Ozark National Scenic Riverways.

Jimmy called Evangeline with the news. She said, "We should celebrate."

Jimmy said, "I need to check in at the office in Van Buren. Let's go out to eat this evening."

"Fine. Shall I call Harry?"

"Would you consider just the two of us?" Jimmy asked.

After a brief pause, Evangeline said, "Yes."

He took her to dinner at the Float Stream in Van Buren. When they came out, Jimmy said, "It's a nice town. It's a lovely park. I'm going to enjoy working here."

"We'll like having you back," Evangeline said.

"Is that a royal *we,* as in *I* will like having you back?" Jimmy asked.

"Well, we all will, but me too, of course."

"Evangeline, do you think . . . " Jimmy hesitated and then started again, "Do you think you and I might be more than friends?"

Evangeline said, "Maybe. Will you kiss me and then I might know for sure?"

He kissed her – a polite, controlled kiss. She said, "Jimmy, I need an all-out kiss."

He pulled her close and kissed her and then when she snuggled closer, he kissed her again, thoroughly. His hormones were zinging. "Wow!" he said, "this is dangerous."

Evangeline said, "Yes, I know. I asked Mom how to pick out a husband and she said to choose a man with good character, a man I respected. Then, she said to kiss him and if he stirred my blood, then marry him."

Jimmy was quiet, thinking about what she said. "Eva," he asked, "do I stir your blood?"

"Yes," she answered.

"Will you marry me?"

"Yes," she said.

"Really!" he said, with excitement in his voice. "When?" he asked.

"A week from tomorrow," she answered.

"Can we arrange a wedding that soon?" Jimmy asked.

"Mom has been planning it ever since we went over to the Highway 21 Drive-In Theater together."

"That long?" Jimmy asked. "Well, I guess we better do it then," and kissed her again.

❀ ❀ ❀
Postscript

Evangeline's mother did have it planned but she wanted two weeks which would be the starting of Christmas break and Evangeline would have time off for a honeymoon. The ceremony was in the old country church which the Wilkerson family had helped found back in 1839. They had built the new building in 1878. Because of limited seating, invitations were restricted to family, close friends, and a few people representing the Jones family.

Robby Lee came without his beard and brought Gramps and Felicity. Lisa Marie arrived in an impressive gleaming silver Rolls-Royce driven by an equally impressive, elaborately uniformed chauffeur, a tall blue-eyed Sikh complete with a red turban. The car and driver got as much attention as Jimmy's look-alike brother, Robby Lee.

Wanda Wilkerson had told Robby Lee, "Jimmy warned me how much the two of you look alike but it really is incredible. I can tell you're not Jimmy but I expect a lot people couldn't."

Robby Lee said, "Well, maybe for a few minutes but probably not for long." He gave her a mischievous grin and said, "I'm not nearly as well-behaved as Jimmy."

Lisa Marie was traveling with Andre Dubois and his sister, Saskia. She told Jimmy, "I liked Andre when I first met him but I love his mother. She saw right away that Myrna needed help and we've arranged it. I've ended up telling Andre pretty well everything and he still wants to marry me. I'm seriously considering it but we decided to give it a little time."

Gramps greeted Lisa Marie with actual tears. He asked her to tell Myrna he was sorry. He asked, "Do you think she'll ever forgive me?"

Lisa Marie shook her head and said, "I don't know. She's lived with the hurt for so many years, I think it'll be hard."

"I know it doesn't make up for what happened but if she ever needs anything, let me know," Gramps told her.

The reception was held at the Ellsinore High School and most of the town was present. There was the traditional wedding cake with punch and finger food in the cafeteria. Jimmy's band provided music for dancing in the school gym. Jimmy laughed over Robby Lee's reaction to finding out about his musical ability. His friends quickly absorbed Robby Lee and Felicity into the band.

People moved back and forth between the food and the dancing all evening and it was late when Wanda Wilkerson found Sheriff Jones sitting on the bleachers in the gym watching the dancers. She sat down by Gramps and said, "Are you mad at me for taking Jimmy away?"

Gramps said, "I was but I'm over it now."

"He's a fine boy," she said. "I had no trouble at all loving him and I was never sorry I took him." She shook her head, "But he sure did take a lot of energy and prayers." She stopped and looked at Gramps. "Do you believe in God?" she asked.

When he nodded, she went on. "I felt like I failed with my daughter. I didn't manage to teach her what she needed to know to live a happy, secure life. I felt like Jimmy was given to me as a sacred trust and I prayed every day. I prayed for Jimmy and I prayed for myself and my father, for wisdom to be good parents to him."

Gramps shifted and then looked at her and said, "Ma'am, you're a fine lady and you did a whole lot better job of raising Jimmy than I would have done." He paused and then sighed. "As a parent, I've haven't been much of a success."

Wanda Wilkerson smiled at him and said, "You've got grandchildren and they will be producing children soon."

The band started a waltz and Robby Lee looked over the dancers. Harry Wilkerson was dancing with Saskia Dubois. Her exotic beauty had tempted Robby Lee to pick up the challenge in her protective brother's eye but they had left Lilac and Rose Jones running the office. If he wanted Rose, he was going to have to resist temptation. Lisa Marie was dancing with Andre and then he saw Gramps lead Wanda Wilkerson onto the floor.

Robby Lee smiled.

Points to Ponder

1. Is it permissible for a Christian to accept a job that requires lying? (undercover police, spy, etc.)
2. Is it permissible for a Christian to go to a country that forbids missionary work with the intention of doing that? If the Christian goes to such a country, is the Christian allowed to lie to officials about it?
3. Is it ever alright for a Christian to lie to protect someone as Jimmy did to protect Myrna?
4. Is it ever alright for a Christian to not report something illegal like Jimmy knowing that Sally killed Hank?
5. Is it ever alright to use blackmail to protect someone like Jimmy protected his grandfather?
6. What about divorce? Was Lisa Marie justified in divorcing her husband? Is it okay for her to remarry? Do you think she might have had grounds for an annulment? (Annulments are given if fraud was committed. Is it possible that Lisa Marie's husband married her with no intention of adhering to his vows? Would this be grounds for an annulment?)
7. Do you think first cousin marriages are wrong? How about a Christian marrying a non-Christian? And marrying across racial lines?
8. Do you think Wanda Wilkerson was justified in taking little Jimmy Joe home and keeping him?

OHP
Ozark Heritage Publishing
723 North Ninth Street
Poplar Bluff, Missouri
63901

< ozarkheritagepublishing@gmail.com >

Ozark Heritage Publishing specializes in stories set
in the Ozarks that reflect Christian values.
Our Points to Ponder series are stories
that raise thought provoking ethical questions.
Our Bigfoot Tales series are stories
born out of the legends of the Ozarks and
incorporate elements of fantasy.

Printed by CreateSpace, an Amazon.com company.

Made in the USA
Columbia, SC
24 May 2021